Family Likeness

Caitlin Davies was born in north London in 1964. She studied American Studies in England, at the University of Sussex, and English at Clark University in Massachusetts. In 1989 she trained as a secondary school teacher and moved to Botswana, later becoming a journalist and working for the country's first tabloid newspaper *The Voice*. She then became editor of the *Okavango Observer*, was arrested for 'causing fear and alarm' and received a Journalist of the Year award. Many of her books are set in the Okavango Delta, where she lived for twelve years, including a memoir *Place of Reeds*. After returning to London she wrote education and careers features for the *Independent*, and she still works as a freelance journalist and teacher. In 2013 she was selected as a Royal Literary Fund Fellow in London. Read more about Caitlin Davies and her work at: www.caitlindavies.co.uk or follow her on Twitter @CaitlinDavies2.

ALSO BY CAITLIN DAVIES

FICTION

NON-FICTION

Family Likeness

CAITLIN DAVIES

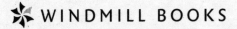WINDMILL BOOKS

Published by Windmill Books 2014

2 4 6 8 10 9 7 5 3 1

First published in Great Britain in 2013 by Hutchinson

Windmill Books
The Random House Group Limited
20 Vauxhall Bridge Road, London SW1V 2SA

Addresses for companies within The Random House Group Limited can
be found at: www.randomhouse.co.uk/offices.htm

The Random House Group Limited Reg. No. 954009

www.randomhouse.co.uk

A CIP catalogue record for this book
is available from the British Library

ISBN 9780099558682

The Random House Group Limited supports the Forest Stewardship
Council® (FSC®), the leading international forest-certification
organisation. Our books carrying the FSC label are printed on
FSC®-certified paper. FSC is the only forest-certification scheme supported
by the leading environmental organisations, including Greenpeace.
Our paper procurement policy can be found at:
www.randomhouse.co.uk/environment

Typeset in Sabon LT Std by Palimpsest Book Production Ltd,
Falkirk, Stirlingshire
Printed and bound by CPI Group (UK) Ltd, Croydon, CR0 4YY

In memory of Shirley McGlade and Pamela Winfield,
who fought tirelessly for the right of children
to know their fathers.

CHAPTER ONE

I've never kept a diary before, because it seems to me that the point of a diary is to record intimate things, and I don't find it easy, or necessary most of the time, to go into detail about intimate things. And if you do keep a diary then there's always the question of who you're keeping it for, as well as the possibility of who might find it; who you secretly *hope* will find it and who you most fear will find it. But I've started now.

Tomorrow is Mother's Day. The sky is low and heavy like a swollen stomach. Outside my kitchen window the trees are covered in sticky yellow buds and I don't know why I'm so surprised by this, when it's inevitable that spring will come and the buds will grow. Nature, I think, becomes more interesting in middle age. There's far more chance that when the sticky buds come next year, or the year after, you won't be around to see them.

I haven't chosen anything special for my diary, just a simple discounted book from the newsagent's, and I've written only one entry so far and that's because this morning I saw him. After months of wondering and weeks of watching and waiting, today is the day we first spoke. I'd just stopped at the bus shelter to escape the drizzling rain, and I was standing there with a handful of other people on a typically miserable English spring day, the sort of day when everyone appears tired and depressed, when no one looks like they've heard any good news in a very long time. Then a bus pulled up, splattering us all with dirty water, the doors opened and there he was, Jonas Murrey. He stepped out backwards on to the pavement, neatly lifting out a child's buggy, so that all I saw of him at first was the hunch of his wide shoulders and the back of his thick, expensive-looking green jacket. He set the buggy down and fiddled with something, the brake perhaps. It was a large, new buggy covered in a plastic rain sheet so thick it was impossible to see who was inside. It could have been a baby; it could have been a child as old as three.

He turned slightly then, and I saw his profile: a strong nose, a clean square jaw, smooth black skin that looked recently shaved and well cared for. His lips were slightly pursed as if in distaste, and there was something about him that suggested he didn't belong here, that he came from somewhere else. Perhaps he didn't often take a bus but normally drove a fancy car, or sat behind tinted windows while a chauffeur drove him.

He waited on the pavement, holding out his hand, and his daughter got off the bus as well. She is eight or nine, or younger and tall for her age, with a lighter complexion than her father, her plaited hair decorated with brightly coloured clips in the shape of tiny butterflies. She stepped off the bus, dragging a silver scooter and hurling it on to the pavement. She wore a fashionable raincoat and shiny flowered wellington boots, and she looked like she'd chosen the outfit herself and was pleased with it.

Jonas Murrey took his daughter by the hand and set off hurriedly across the Holloway Road, ignoring the zebra crossing only a few yards away and beginning instead to dodge furiously between the lines of waiting traffic. I watched him, this tall, well-built man with his baby buggy and his child and her scooter, and I thought, if their mother could see the way he's hurtling across the road, she wouldn't like it at all.

He reached the other side, passing a takeaway chicken shop, its door and windows covered in grey mesh as fine as fish scales. I could see where he was heading, to a doctor's surgery up a steep flight of stone steps. He was such a big, strong man that the buggy seemed to get smaller, more vulnerable, the further up the steps he went. Once, when he hesitated for a moment, it seemed to balance quite precariously, as if it might at any second come rolling down. Then I saw that the girl hadn't followed her father; instead she was still at the bottom of the steps, holding her scooter and stomping her wellington boots in a puddle. Jonas Murrey hadn't noticed; he was trying to get into the doctor's surgery by pushing backwards against the door, and by the time he did realise his daughter wasn't following him, there was little he could do.

I could see, as I stepped away from the bus shelter, that he was shouting for her now. But she clearly had no intention of doing as she was told. Instead she appeared to sense a possibility of freedom; her father was too far away to stop her from doing whatever it was she thought she might do. As I reached the zebra crossing, I saw her step on to her scooter and set off zigzagging along the pavement, one foot pushing expertly away on the ground, paying no attention to the people before her: two men in suits drinking takeaway coffees, a man swaying drunkenly, a group of teenage boys walking slowly in a pack. Then a cyclist appeared from around the corner, head down and pedalling just as fast, pushing a gap between the people. I knew her father wouldn't be able to get down the steps quickly enough to stop his daughter's flight. He couldn't leave the buggy where it was; he could do nothing except watch.

But by then I was there. I stepped out in front of the little girl as she sped towards me and I gripped the handlebars of her scooter, heard the frustrated squeal of the cyclist's wheels behind us, his muttered '*What the fuck?*' I bent down and said very quietly, 'Your father's calling you.' Then I took the girl firmly by the hand, the way it's sometimes necessary to do, and although I could feel her trying to break away, I took her back to the doctor's surgery and up the steps.

'What the *hell* are you playing at?' Jonas Murrey asked, and I thought, yes, he is American, an American who has spent some time in England perhaps, but definitely an American. '*Ella*, didn't you *see* the bike?' He reached for the girl and brought her to the doorway, and I could see she wanted to argue, that she was on the verge of protesting that cyclists shouldn't be on the pavement perhaps, when her father turned to me. Up close I could see that his hair was closely cut, with a faint widow's peak above his forehead that made him look distinguished, even a little self-satisfied. 'Thank you,' he said. 'I don't know what I would have done if you hadn't been there. How did you know she was going to do that?' He laughed then, and his strong-featured face became soft for a moment. 'You seemed to know what she was going to do before she did it!'

I smiled, pleased that he'd noticed. 'I work with kids.'

'Is that right? Ella, just stand there while I talk to the lady.'

I took out one of the cards I'd had made last week and gave it to him, and he read it in the manner of someone who's used to evaluating information quickly. 'And I guess you must be working at the moment?'

'Not at the moment, no.'

'But you're looking for work?'

'Not exactly looking.'

'Daddy!' said the girl, and she put her hands on her hips.

Jonas Murrey nodded. 'Come on, Ella.' He pushed at the door again, and his voice was tender now, and tired. 'Come on, honey.'

I wondered who it was that needed to see the doctor. Was it the child in the buggy? Was he very ill and was that why his father had rushed across the traffic-filled road in such a reckless way? I waited a moment, then I waved at the girl as I walked back down the steps, and she, of course, refused to wave back. Instead she glared at me as if I were in competition for her father's affection, when it was her behaviour that had caused all the fuss. Girls like her present a challenge. In nearly every class I've ever taught, there has been a girl like her, and I've always liked a challenge.

I'd almost reached the zebra crossing when it happened. The same cyclist who'd been on the pavement was on the road beside me now, pedalling in the opposite direction, and it was then that a large blue car swung suddenly left. At first it seemed the cyclist would simply fly over the car as it crossed his path and land on the other side, and I willed for it to be like this, for it all to be over soon. But instead the cyclist hit the bonnet and his body turned in the air and he bounced off the car again and his arms flailed as he came down and hit it one last time. I could sense a wall of fear that was keeping everyone still in their tracks on the pavement, because no one knew what to do, everyone hoped the man would live and no one wanted to go nearer and see. And during all of this there seemed to be no sound, no impact of the bike on the car, no horn or squeal of brakes, no bystander's frightened cry. And it was so slow, like a beautifully choreographed dance, as the man flew over and hit the car and bounced and flew and hit it again.

Because this is how it is when you witness something terrible, when there's no preparation and your mind tries desperately to make sense of what you see. So much can happen in a few moments that time slows down to allow you to take in every tiny detail. And the more memory you have, the longer you think a horrific event has taken.

Then it was over. The cyclist was lying in the road. He twitched once or twice, and his back jerked with a dreadful electrocuted clumsiness. The wall of fear dissolved, people began moving again, to take out a mobile phone and call an ambulance, to reassure a crying child. The driver of the car got out and stood in the road, the skin on his face stretched tight with shock. By the door of the takeaway chicken shop a woman bent to pet her trembling dog. I looked back, to where Jonas Murrey and the buggy and his daughter had stood, and I caught a quick glimpse of them as they disappeared into the doctor's surgery. Then I walked home and bought a diary, because this is a day I need to record, and I know that, finally, this is only the beginning.

CHAPTER TWO

Yesterday I had a phone call from Jonas Murrey. It wasn't entirely unexpected, but it was enough to make me hum afterwards as I boiled the kettle and sliced a fat fresh lemon for my tea. He sounded hurried, even a little anxious. Was this Rosie Grey? Was I busy? Was he ringing at a bad time? He knew it was rather out of the blue, but he couldn't forget the way I'd helped outside the doctor's surgery on Saturday, and he had a sudden vacancy for a nanny. Would I be interested? I thought it an odd word to use, *vacancy*, as if his family were an office or a business, but I agreed to 'discuss the matter further', as he put it, and meet him today at his home.

Pembleton Crescent is one of those genteel London roads you don't know exist until you find it. It's long and rather dark, and because it curves in the middle you can't see the end of the street until you get there. It's a wealthy, stylish-looking road in a designated conservation area, lined with handsome three-storey red-brick buildings with large basements set behind small stone-paved courtyards. The houses are partially enclosed with freshly painted wrought-iron railings, while more decorative railings hug the bottom of the lower windows, between which colourful flowers spill out of wooden boxes, as if all the inhabitants have agreed the street should look as pretty as possible. Even the rubbish bins are neat and in their place, each with a house number in bold white paint. Most of the houses have sombre black doors with shiny silver knockers and gleaming brass letter boxes, and the doorways are surrounded by a band of white stonework, which peaks at the top, giving an almost religious, chapel-like air to the road. Above each door the face of a man is carved in stone. He has a long thick beard and a wide nose, and wears a flat cap cheekily on one side of his head. The face appears both jovial and sinister; the man could as easily be a jester as a gargoyle. It made me think of Amina, because she would like this street. She would know when it was built and what sort of people used to live here and why there was an odd-faced man above the doors, but I haven't spoken to her properly in months.

As I continued along the crescent, blossom from the roadside cherry trees began to fall in sudden showers of pink, and I could hear the soothing sound of doves in the air above me. I looked in through living room windows, at interiors empty but for mahogany dining tables and unoccupied chairs, and I thought, what I would give to live in a place like this.

I glanced behind me then. The sky was clouding over; rain clouds slid quickly across the sun, and as I stopped at number 68, the entire street was thrown into deep purple shadow. I walked up a short flight of black steps and knocked on the door, framed on either side with olive trees planted in large earthenware pots.

The door was opened by an elderly white woman wearing the sort of pinafore my mother wears, small and pink and mostly decorative. 'Yes?' she said, looking around as if it wasn't me who was supposed to be there. Her face was lined but firm, and made me think of a sea captain in a child's picture book, weather-beaten but wise, with bright blue eyeshadow and traces of pale seashell-pink lipstick on her lips.

'I've come to see Jonas.'

'Mr Murrey is working,' she said, as if I'd been far too personal. She had the nozzle of a vacuum cleaner in one hand and she pointed it suddenly at the doormat, giving a loud blast of suction. Then she turned it off. 'Who shall I say is calling?'

'Rosie,' I said. 'Rosie Grey.'

'Wait here then.' She ushered me in and left me standing in a narrow hallway. Its walls were covered with framed antique prints, but it was oddly empty of any signs of children, and I looked ahead, at a long flight of stairs that led up to the next floor, carpeted a soft chestnut brown. 'He will see you now,' the woman announced, returning to take me down the hallway and then flinging open a door on my left. I had a fleeting sensation that this was some sort of game, that surely now she would drop her air, overly deferential to her employer, unnecessarily haughty towards me, but instead she just left me at the doorway.

It was a large room, with clean white walls and thick wooden floorboards as shiny as treacle. Jonas Murrey sat at one end behind a desk, with his back to me, facing two large four-panelled windows that I assumed looked down over a garden. The desk appeared old and valuable, with a row of small drawers on the right and green blotting paper inlaid on the surface. It was the sort of writing desk on which you'd expect to find an inkwell and a feather pen, but instead I could see a small expensive laptop. As I waited for Jonas Murrey to turn, his size struck me again, just as it had when I'd seen him climb the steps to the doctor's surgery with the buggy in his hands. He seemed too large for the chair, the room, even house. I stood there, happy to look around for clues. On the left, above the tiled Victorian fireplace, were some portraits in ornate oval frames, hanging in a row from a picture rail. In one there was a woman alone, in another a crowded family scene and in a third an elderly couple. The room was silent except for the slightly erratic tick of a grandfather clock. I wondered what exactly Jonas Murrey did to live in a place like this. Was it his; had he lived here long, this American in London? And where was Mrs Murrey, the children's mother?

As in the hallway, there were no signs of infant life, no discarded toys or broken pens or forgotten socks. I coughed, without realising it, and Jonas Murrey whipped around in his chair. 'I was miles away,' he laughed, although he must have known I was there. 'Bobby's fine,' he said in an easy fashion, as if we often spoke about Bobby. 'It was just an ear infection. I guess I should have taken him earlier, but the car was at the garage and . . .' He turned and looked briefly at the laptop. 'So,' he crossed his legs, stretching them out, and indicating that I should take a chair just to his left, 'you must be wondering about my call. I'll outline it to you like this,' and he leant forward, resting his chin on one fist. 'What I need is a nanny.'

He had a business trip, he said, and it couldn't be changed. His law firm was sending him to New York for six weeks. The person he usually employed had unexpectedly left London, giving him virtually no notice at all when in seven days he was due to go to the States.

'And there's no one in America,' I asked, 'who could look after the children?'

Jonas Murrey grimaced, and for a moment I thought he was going to say that this was none of my business. 'No, there isn't.'

'And no one here who could help?'

He seemed taken aback at the suggestion. 'I am on my own.'

'Oh,' I said, and the room seemed very quiet and the grandfather clock very loud.

'It can be difficult for the children. I have a sister-in-law, but she can't take my two . . .'

'And have you tried an agency?'

'Yes, I have,' he said, losing patience. 'I tried a very high-profile agency and they sent me a total asshole. So then I thought of you. I mean, this is what you do, isn't it?' There was a slight challenge in his voice now, as if I was in danger of wasting his time. 'As I said, it would be six weeks, you'd have to live in.'

I nodded, a little unnerved. For an outwardly polite man to use the word *asshole*, to someone he'd only just met, seemed aggressive. But I'd got this far and I had to know what would happen next, because after all, this was why I'd left my job, and this was why I was here. 'I'd have to live in?'

'Yes, because you'd be in charge of everything. You'd wash, iron and organise the children's clothes, ensure their toys are tidied away, take them to school and to nursery, arrange the social side of things during the Easter holidays, play dates, outings to . . . Well, you'd generally plan and supervise the daily regime. There'd be no heavy housework or other chores, that's up to Mrs B. You'd have your own bedroom and bathroom, fully furnished, and all food provided. You'd be paid weekly, on a Friday, with additional pay on the Easter bank holidays, and I'd cover the nanny tax and National Insurance. Obviously I'd need to see your qualifications, first aid certificate and criminal record check, contact your referees . . . I mean,' Jonas Murrey took his chin away from his fist, 'should you be interested.'

'Well,' I smiled, 'I haven't really met the children yet.'

He stood up then, and for a moment I thought he was coming to where I sat, but instead he strode to the door and called out, 'Mrs B!' He looked at me. 'Mrs B has been looking after them, if you could call it that.'

There was some commotion out in the hallway and I heard Mrs B saying, 'Put them down, Ella, you shouldn't have that,' and then Ella's voice, sharp and deliberately loud, '*Daddy* lets me.' Then the door opened and in came a child of two or three, with wild uncombed hair, wearing dungarees, a checked shirt and miniature combat boots. He had a beautiful boyish face, with large eyes and a small dent in the middle of his chin, and he was obviously being let loose in a room he wasn't usually allowed in, because he ran over to his father and threw himself like a bullet against his legs.

'So this is Bobby,' said Jonas Murrey. 'And Ella you've already met.'

At this the girl came in, brandishing a pair of children's scissors, small and plastic-coated but with blades sharp enough that they could still inflict some damage. She decided she had to run as well, and a second later she caught her foot on a small fringed rug and slipped. I stood up to remove the scissors from her hands and she shouted out, in annoyance rather than pain, as I closed the open blades and put them on my lap. I looked behind me then, to the doorway, where Mrs B stood, and she made a gesture with the nozzle of her vacuum cleaner which I took to signal agreement with what I'd done.

'So, Rosie,' said Jonas Murrey, who'd watched the whole scene with a strangely detached air. 'Can you drive and is your licence clean? Bobby . . . put it down . . .'

His son had run to a wooden box on the floor, out of which he'd picked something up and was now struggling to hold it. 'This is Guinea!' he said in a voice of great delight, and he thrust the animal, a small messy ball of white and ginger, in my face. I took the creature and cupped it carefully in both hands, feeling the trembling beat of its heart beneath the thick, slightly ragged hair. It began to make a high-pitched squeak and its eyes, solid orbs of black, darted nervously around the room. I couldn't tell if it were afraid or excited.

'Aren't you scared?' asked Ella, striding towards me, the scissor incident apparently forgotten.

'No,' I said, stroking the guinea pig's hair. As I did, it seemed to settle down, and to make a fluttery, rattling, bird-like sound that suggested contentment. 'Why, should I be?'

'She can bite you.'

'She can, but she probably won't.'

'Look!' shouted Ella. 'She's crapping on you. Hey, Daddy! Guinea's taking a crap!'

I held the guinea pig away from me as a dozen firm pellets skated down my arm, fresh and shiny and yet oddly not wet at all.

'They have very weak hearts, guinea pigs,' said Jonas Murrey thoughtfully. 'Put it back in its box, Bobby. We spend the entire time making sure the door's closed so the cat doesn't come in, or it would die of a heart attack. Do you have any pets, Rosie?'

'No.'

'Any children or other dependants?' Jonas Murrey smiled.

'Yes,' I said, thinking of my mother and then immediately feeling guilty because she would hate the idea that I saw her as a dependant.

Jonas Murrey looked a little surprised at my answer. Perhaps he didn't want to see me as a person, with her own life and arrangements; he just wanted someone who would fit into his. But I was used to this attitude, with all the children and parents I'd had to deal with over the years. I was just the teacher; I wasn't supposed to have any problems or dreams of my own.

'I want to go home,' said Bobby, sidling up to Mrs B at the doorway.

'Of course you do, love.' She smiled down at him and patted his head. Confused at this exchange, I looked at Jonas for explanation, but he was busy again on his laptop.

Mrs B removed the children and took them out into the garden, and then returned briefly to hand me a glass of tepid grapefruit juice while Jonas Murrey outlined his terms. He was very businesslike; this was obviously an arrangement he was keen to have settled. He emphasised that the offer would be very competitive, and he'd already drawn up a draft contract. As he printed it out, I took the chance to walk over to the windows and look down over the garden, a long, glorious expanse of lawn, vivid in the sun. At the far end was a wooden shed and two apple trees, while nearer to the house was a paved patio, set with garden chairs and a table, on top of which was a pot of purple flowering lavender. I could see Bobby lying on his back in a blue paddling pool while Ella ran round and round with a hosepipe, spraying him with water. Bobby was hysterical with happiness; every time he tried to stand up on his fat little legs, he slid against the slippery sides of the paddling pool and fell flat on his bottom again. And as I watched them, I felt a jealous tightening in my chest, because this is how a childhood should be, with everything a child could ask for: a lovely house, a lovely garden, and a sibling to play with in the sun.

'There you go,' said Jonas Murrey, handing me the contract. 'Read it over, see what you think, and we'll speak tomorrow.'

By the time I left Pembleton Crescent, it was clear what he wanted: to have his children looked after efficiently, to know they were in experienced hands, but not to be bothered by any updates. He would not want to know about domestic disputes or childish dramas; he was used to delegating and he was delegating them to me. Perhaps this is how it is with people who have more money than sense and virtually no interest in their children, because Jonas Murrey seemed to find nothing unusual in handing them to a total stranger for six weeks. He hadn't really questioned who I was, what I might want, or why I had been at the doctor's surgery just at the right time. He simply assumed that I would want to put my life on hold to work for him, and he obviously couldn't wait to be off. I could have been anyone.

CHAPTER THREE

Name: Muriel Wilson
Age: four
State of health: good
Ever had fits: no
Any other physical defects or maladies: half-caste

Branch home admission report, 5 July 1950

How do you begin the story of your life when it has never been your story to tell? I don't have all the facts or explanations, the reasons or the motivations. I can't answer why or when or how. I know not a thing about my life before the age of four. But here I am in my sixty-sixth year, with my admission report on my kitchen table. And here I am remembering.

I was born in London in 1946. The war was over. The soldiers had mostly come home. But life was tough for the majority of people, including my mam. That was what I called her, I remember that. The day she left me, she was wearing her favourite coat, orange camel hair with a fur trimming. She had gloves to match, and a handbag too. My mam was a well-groomed lady. It was bristly as a rug, that coat, and I could hook my fingers around the big brass buttons and tug on them to get her attention. That's what I remember most, the overbearing physical urge to get my mother's attention.

'Here we are then, pet,' she said as the big black car drove slowly along the road. It was a long trip from London, not like the trips we usually made. Something was happening and no one was going to tell me what. I was nicely dressed, in a clean white dress with red berries and a Peter Pan collar, and I sat very neatly, trying not to crease my clothes. It must have been a Sunday because everywhere was so very quiet and all the shops in town were shut. The grey streets of Widenham were empty but for a man going slowly on a bicycle. There was nothing by the road but advertising hoardings set on metal legs on the edge of bombed-out scrubland. We passed a boarded-up hotel, its windows black as holes, and a derelict row of shops with rippled sheets of corrugated iron around the walls. One house was sliced in the middle like a cake, with nothing but debris where its neighbour used to be.

Then we drove through a large gate and along a gravel path with flower beds on either side. And there was Hoodfield House. It was set back from the road, old and gloomy, with a gabled front and ivy-covered walls the colour of biscuits. A lady standing at the doorway made a vivid impression on me, dressed as she was all in black, her face as hard and shiny as a spoon. Miss Peal, the matron. Above her head hung limp bunting left over from a recent celebration. There was a flag as well, a Union Jack at one of the windows, and by her feet was a broken cardboard crown.

I wouldn't say my memory is good, but you'd be

surprised at the little things you can recall as a four-year-old. The other day I read that each time we think of a memory, we create it from where we are now. I don't believe that. I believe we remember things just as they were. And recently this is all I seem to do: try and remember the past.

Miss Peal walked quickly towards the car. My mam picked me up and I clamped my legs around her like a limpet clings to a rock. 'You'll get my dress all clarty,' she said, and her voice was thick like her throat was full and she couldn't swallow. She put her hand in her pocket. I heard her fingers rustle around in a paper bag. Then she brought out a clutch of currants and popped them into my mouth, one by one, as if to silence me.

We went into the house and waited in the hallway. It was cold and dark and smelt of cough drops. On the wall was a picture of Jesus, and a portrait of a man with thin lips and thick brown sideburns. On a side table was a glass vase with wilting sweet peas. My mam bent to smell their feathery petals. 'Call me Auntie,' said Miss Peal. 'We're like a family here, a proper Christian family.' And then she left. A man came out. Mr Barnet, the superintendent, an ex-serviceman with the jowls of Winston Churchill. He talked to my mam and she said she was going to the ladies' room. I sat on my own for a while, my hands held under my thighs for comfort. Then Mr Barnet told me to go with him. I said I couldn't, I was waiting for my mam. 'You'll see her in a bit,' he said, and I could tell, with the instinct of a child, that he did not like the look of me. She did come back. She touched Mr Barnet on the arm, whispering urgently as he led us up the grand central staircase.

I remember how I grasped the first post, the newel shaped like a fancy table leg. My hand fitted exactly around the narrowest part before it bulged out into a satisfying bulb. I went up a step, trailing my fingers along the handrail, feeling the pitted holes where the worms lived. And when I looked at my hand, I saw a coating of sawdust like fine yellow sand.

Mr Barnet took us to the bedroom, its walls as brown as the jelly in a basin of dripping. There were two rows of iron-framed beds. 'That one's hers,' he said. 'I'd advise the less fuss the better.' Still I waited for my mam to tell me what was going on. 'It's for the best,' she said, as if speaking to herself. She left the room then, followed Mr Barnet out. And I stood there, terrified that my mam had gone. But shortly afterwards she returned. I watched as she arranged my things. Put away my clothes. Told me to change for bed. 'Get yourself some sleep, you've had an awful long day,' said my mam. The bed had wheels and it shifted slightly as I clambered on. The mattress was thin and smelt of damp lettuce. I could feel the coils beneath and hear the slippery sound of the rubber sheet. But I didn't want to complain.

'Away to sleep, Muriel.' My mam sat down on a chair next to the bed.

'But it's still light,' I said, and from outside came the sounds of children and a football hitting a wall.

'Those are the naughty children,' said my mam.

I tried my best to snuggle down and pretend to sleep, safe in the knowledge that I wasn't a naughty child. I was good and did as I was told. 'Will you stay with me?'

'Course I will, pet.' My mam pulled the sheet up to my chin and tucked it in.

'When I wake up, you'll still be here?'

'Course I will, my love.'

'You promise?' I peeked through one eye. She wasn't looking at me.

She cleared her throat. 'Of course I do, pet.'

'Mam,' I said with sudden urgency, 'you promise?'

'Yes.' She closed her eyes. 'I promise.'

I felt the warm weight of her hand as she smoothed down the sheet and stroked my back. But when I woke up, it was pitch dark in the room, and my mother had gone. All that remained on the chair were two squashed currants. Did she tell me anything, before she left me all alone? Had she tried to explain, or had she thought it best not to say a word?

The next day I had my photograph taken, because that was what they did on admission. They took it so they could show foster parents how you looked, what colour you were and whether your hair was straight or fuzzy. Auntie Peal brushed mine just as straight as she could beforehand. I have a photograph of her, on my table next to my admission report. She is holding me in her arms and I don't look happy at all. I'm wearing a heavy dark dress, my legs and feet covered in white tights as thick as bandages. I'm trying to get away from her; you can see that. Because Auntie Peal was a woman you couldn't mess with. She was as brittle as the little glass cats she liked to keep on the windowsill in her sitting room, with long necks and hard blue eyes. She wore the same black dress every day, even in the midst of winter. I don't believe she ever felt the cold, and it was always cold in Hoodfield House. The fireplaces had been removed from the children's bedrooms, and on winter mornings we woke to find patches of ice like frozen mountains on the inside of the windows.

But that was what it was like back then. They did the best they could. They kept us dry and mostly warm. They had us fed and clothed. In many ways, I'm thankful for their care. They told us nothing of who we were, because they believed that children were better off not knowing where they came from. The adults at the branch home had to behave as if we had no past; that was the rule. A child was considered to have settled in well, as long as she never asked about her parents. 'Cheerfulness is the best medicine,' said Auntie Peal, as cheerlessly she stabbed a needle in the cloth of a faded green pullover, chain-stitching my number into all my clothes. 'We are your parents now, Muriel.'

CHAPTER FOUR

It's Thursday, and today I began work; a fine, blue-skied April afternoon, with Pembleton Crescent bathed in a glory of sunshine and blossom. I arrived the way I'd come the day of my interview, only this time I had a suitcase, a small, compact case with a long handle that bumped unevenly on the pavement behind me. I wasn't sure I'd packed enough for six weeks – I couldn't really believe I was going to be away for that long – but I'd cancelled everything I had to cancel, and I hoped I had everything I'd need.

Mrs B appeared a little friendlier when she opened the door this time, the same pink pinafore round her waist, the same vacuum cleaner nozzle in her hands. 'He's gone already,' she said. 'Come in.' I did as I was told, and followed her downstairs. I'd already had a detailed tour of the house when I'd come to sign the contract and spend a morning with the children, and I'd decided the kitchen was my favourite room. It takes up the entire basement area, with marbled worktops and a row of large brass-bottomed pans hanging on the wall, and the air is cooler with a comforting smell of stone. At one end, near the street side of the house, is a wooden table almost medieval in its thickness. I could see the remains of an afternoon snack: slices of carrots and cucumber, a half-eaten banana, butter-smeared crusts of brown bread, a jug of juice. But all this had been cleared to one side to make room for a pad of writing paper, an address book, a couple of pens, and a small pile of padded envelopes. One had been newly addressed and stuck with stamps and was clearly waiting to be posted. Either Jonas Murrey had been doing some administration tasks at the kitchen table before he left, which seemed unlikely when he had his own office, or Mrs B had been taking the opportunity now her employer was away to write letters. I watched as she walked towards the table and collected the paperwork, and as she picked up the padded envelope something fell out. It looked like a handkerchief, small and flimsy and a pretty sea blue. Mrs B held it up and looked at me a little challengingly. 'Nice, aren't they?'

She was holding a pair of knickers; a silken thong with little embroidered flowers around the edge.

'My favourite colour, blue,' said Mrs B, carefully folding the knickers up and putting them back in the envelope.

I watched her without saying a word, and this seemed to unnerve her, because she suddenly burst out, 'It's a chain letter thing. I never would have done it, but I got a letter from an old friend. I'm to send a new pair of knickers to the person whose name is at the top of the list, then I copy the letter to six friends. They put *my* name at the top of the list, and in time I'll get thirty-six pairs of knickers, all for the price of one.'

'That sounds like a bargain.'

Mrs B looked at me with an expression of satisfaction. 'My husband thinks I'm mad. But he often does.'

Then the door to the garden flew open and there was Ella, holding a long-haired grey cat with watery green eyes.

'It's Rosie!' she shouted. 'Daddy's gone and Rosie's here.' She threw down the cat, grabbed me by the arm and pulled me outside to join her brother. I went with her, thinking it odd that her father hadn't waited until I'd arrived, that he'd left without saying a word of welcome.

The afternoon passed easily enough. Ella had decided we were to be friends, and she enjoyed instructing me on how things should be done: how to deflate the paddling pool, who sat where at the table, what plates should be used, which bib Bobby was to wear. Mrs B gave me a typed seven-day rota listing the meals I was to make for the children. But the menu for our first evening together, tuna salad, sounded dull, so I made sausages and mash instead. Ella informed me that Daddy said she could have an ice pop afterwards, and in the spirit of friendship, I said she could. Then, while Bobby played with the last of his mashed potato, and Mrs B busied herself upstairs, we sat and eyed each other, Ella sucking the colour from her strawberry ice pop.

'I think this is going to be fun,' she said, sounding remarkably self-assured for a child whose father had just gone abroad for six weeks, but then perhaps for her that was normal.

'Yes,' I said. 'I'm sure it will.'

'Are your mum and dad dead?'

Surprised at the question, I got up and began to clear away the dinner things. 'My mother's not dead, no.' I waited to see what Ella would say, but she'd already lost interest and was heading back out to the garden. I washed up the plates and bowls, and listed in my head what I would do next. Bobby would have his bath, before Ella. He would have his milk; Ella would choose a story. And by eight, they would both be in bed and with Mrs B gone I could really settle myself in. Tomorrow I would have to be up by six, to give the children breakfast and to get Bobby to his nursery. It was Ella's last day of school before the Easter holidays, and I thought it would be interesting to wait in the playground, not as a teacher for once, but more of a parent.

I lifted Bobby out of his high chair, and as I did, he put his chubby arms around my neck and looked at me with his big brown eyes. 'I want Guinea,' he whispered. 'I love my Guinea so much.'

'Okay, we can go and see Guinea, but she's not to leave your dad's room, is she?'

I put Bobby down and he rushed off towards the stairs, climbing each step slowly and carefully. When he got halfway, he turned and looked at me, proud at how far he'd gone alone. I allowed him to lead the way to his father's office, but the door handle was too high for him to turn, so I let us in and then carefully closed the door, aware of the family cat sitting in the hallway rhythmically licking its paw.

It was very still in Jonas Murrey's office, as if it had been deserted for a while; the curtains were half closed and the air was a little stale, as though someone had been smoking a pipe. Bobby ran across the treacle floorboards to the guinea pig's box and lifted up his pet, while I walked over to the photographs on the wall. As I'd seen on the first day, one picture was of a woman alone, and although the frame was ornate and old-fashioned, the portrait was modern. The woman was in her thirties perhaps, with a pale, fine-featured face and butter-coloured hair. She looked happy, as if she'd turned in surprise when someone had called her name and she was pleased to find whoever it was.

'Who's this?' I asked.

Bobby looked up from where he sat on the floor, the guinea pig purring in his hands. 'That's my mummy.'

'She looks lovely,' I said, wondering why there were no other pictures of her on the wall, no wedding pictures, no images of the happy Murrey couple. Was it because they'd separated? Had Jonas taken down all her photos but this one?

The next picture was a crowded scene, a large group of people having a picnic somewhere in a field on a summer's day. They sat on a chequered red and white blanket, around an expensive-looking wicker hamper, amid several bottles of wine and champagne. It could have been a family day out, a simple summer's picnic, or it could have been a celebration of some kind. I looked at each person in turn, recognised the man sitting on the far left with a glass in his hand as a younger Jonas Murrey, but I couldn't see anyone who looked like Ella and Bobby's mother. Then I came to the last portrait, an elderly black couple sitting very close to each other on a swinging chair set on a wooden-floored porch. There was a low wall behind them, with potted plants, a trowel and a pair of gardening gloves. The porch was brightly lit, the plants were in colourful bloom, and to the right was the corner of a table with what looked like a jug of lemonade. I stared intently at the man on the swinging chair, at the rather arrogant tilt of his chin, the dapper suit and waistcoat, the confident way he had his arm around the woman's shoulder, and I thought, yes, here he is at last; this is Jonas Murrey's grandfather.

In the afternoon, just as Mrs B was preparing to leave, she handed me a pile of letters. 'These came earlier, you'd better have a look at them. You can put everything for Mr Murrey in the tray on his desk and chuck away the rest. He can't stand junk post.'

I began sorting through them, making a pile on the table, an electricity bill, a computing magazine, two letters from a bank, until I came to one addressed to 'The parents or guardians of Ella Murrey'. On the top left-hand corner the envelope was stamped with the name of a school, Fairacres Primary.

'You'd better open that one now,' said Mrs B.

'You think so?' I asked, surprised she wanted me to open something clearly not addressed to me, but I did as she suggested and took out the letter. 'It says they'd like to have a chat with Jonas.'

Mrs B didn't comment; she was busy putting on her jacket.

'What do you think it's about?'

'Well I would imagine it's about Ella.'

'Should I email him?'

Mrs B shrugged, concentrating on doing up her buttons.

I put the letter back in the envelope, unsure why, if there was a problem at school, he hadn't mentioned anything to me. I looked at Mrs B again, but she was in outdoor mode now, her working day over, and was already heading for the stairs. Then she stopped by the double glass doors that led to the garden and looked at Ella outside. 'She can be bad.'

'Bad?' I asked, as I stood up to take Bobby from his high chair. Bad is a harsh word to use about a child. Naughty, maybe, but not bad.

'Ever since her mother . . .' Mrs B stopped as Ella came back into the kitchen. 'Well,' she said, 'I'd best be off.'

I walked her up the stairs, with Bobby on my hip. It was as if I was the hostess now, and when I said goodbye she paused for a second at the doorway as if aware that our roles had shifted slightly and she wasn't sure if she liked it. 'See you tomorrow then,' she said, tucking the envelope containing the silken knickers under her arm, and heading off up the street.

CHAPTER FIVE

Before I went to bed last night, I emailed Jonas Murrey to tell him about the letter from Ella's school. My room is at the top of the house, in a converted attic. I'd much rather be on the same level as Ella and Bobby's bedroom, so that I can get to them quickly if I need to, but otherwise it suits me fine. It's a low-ceilinged room with vertical-striped wallpaper, possibly to create an illusion of height. The furniture is dark: a double bed with a headboard, a dressing table, a chest of drawers and one low shelf on which sits an old printer. On the wall facing the bed is a row of landscape paintings and next to the window a potted palm which looks real but is in fact artificial. It's a guest room but there doesn't seem to have been a guest in here for a very long time. There's a feeling of abandonment, of something missing.

It's the same in the en suite bathroom; there's a claw-footed bath, a sink that is slightly stained where it meets the tiles on the wall, and a small bare cupboard, but there's no sign of who might have been here before me. At the far end of the room there's a window with a rusty latch, which almost came away in my hand. The open window gave a sudden view of the sloping tiled roof; so steep I couldn't even see the guttering.

Jonas hasn't replied to my email. Perhaps he hasn't arrived at his destination, although he seems like the sort of person who would check his emails constantly, wherever he was. But things went smoothly this morning; both children got dressed without incident, apart from a minor disagreement when Ella said her brother had drunk from the glass of water she has beside her bed. She then spent some time deciding how to adorn her hair, they ate their breakfast, and finally, by the time Mrs B arrived, we were all ready. Just as we were about to leave for school, the phone rang and Ella ran down to the kitchen to answer it.

'That was my daddy,' she said, coming back up the stairs. 'He's in America now and he's going to bring me a present when he comes back,' and she smiled to herself as she put on her wellington boots.

'What's your teacher's name?' I asked as we set off along Pembleton Crescent, with Ella keen to show me the right route to walk to school.

'Hannah.'

'Is that what you call her, Hannah? Not Mrs or Ms or Miss?'

Ella looked at me as if I were mad.

'And do you like her, is she kind?'

'She's kind,' said Ella, and she began to skip exaggeratedly down the pavement. 'But she doesn't like me.'

'I'm sure she likes you,' I laughed, pushing the buggy faster to keep up.

'Oh no she doesn't.'

'Why do you think she doesn't like you?'

'Oh, it's just one of those things,' and Ella gave a very grown-up brittle smile.

Bobby's nursery was bright and colourful, with porthole-shaped windows, but the young woman in charge didn't appear very interested in helping him settle in. She didn't bend down to talk to him or ask him how he was; she just told him to sit down at the table with the others and do some drawing. But Bobby went off happily enough; he's an utterly biddable sort of child.

Then I took Ella to school. She walked by my side until we reached the gates, when suddenly she sped up. 'See you,' she muttered, as if she was embarrassed to be seen with me, and she ran in.

'Ella, wait,' I said. Was this how she was used to leaving? Was there no hug, no kiss, no proper goodbye? I guessed her father rarely if ever took her to school, and that she'd grown used to a succession of babysitters and nannies. My mother would never have let me leave her like this as a child; there had always been a *love you*, a *see you later*, a *have a lovely day*. My mother thought that partings were something to be savoured, perhaps because of Dad. His death was so sudden that she always felt she hadn't said goodbye to him, hadn't said what she needed to before he was gone. In the end it happened so quickly and unexpectedly, and I was so young, that try as I might, I have no memory of him in hospital at all.

Ella ignored my call to wait, and ran right into the playground; she didn't seem the least bit reluctant to go into school, despite yesterday's letter. I heard a bell ring and caught a glimpse of her as she joined a haphazard queue. I waited until a teacher came out and led the children inside, and when I was sure she was safe and sound, I left.

The rest of the morning I spent organising my things, and keeping out of Mrs B's way as she furiously vacuumed the house. I tidied up the toys in the playroom next to Jonas's office, and then I went downstairs to prepare Bobby's lunch so it would be ready when I brought him back from nursery. I realised I was quite enjoying the sense of domesticity; of having a kitchen so large I could have danced the tango in it if I'd wanted to. As I moved around tidying up, I felt that number 68 Pembleton Crescent was nearly my own home now, and I thought about what I would keep and what I would change and rearrange if the house were really mine.

At midday I picked Bobby up from nursery and brought him home. He sat happily in his high chair eating his fish fingers and baked potato and salad, and then, without a word of protest, he went for his nap. When Mrs B popped out to the shops, I took the opportunity to explore the one room I hadn't yet seen, Jonas Murrey's bedroom. I opened the door a little cautiously, not sure what to expect, surprised that it wasn't locked and that it had never crossed his mind that this was a room I'd want to see. There was an oddly sweet smell, a little like marzipan, and I stood there trying to think what it was. Perhaps it came from one of the glass bottles lined up on a chest of drawers. Then I noticed that the far wall, instead of being plastered and painted white like the other walls, was simply bare exposed brick. It had been treated in some way – the bricks were glossy and clean – but it made the room feel industrial, like the inside of a warehouse. It was not a comfortable room; there was nothing on the walls, no paintings or photographs, no clues to family life. The glass in the windows was frosted, so it was impossible for anyone to either look in or look out. The king-sized bed was covered with a stone-coloured spread, and I looked at it, wondering how Jonas Murrey slept at night. Did he sleep on his back or his side, was he a sound sleeper, did he remember his dreams in the morning when he woke up?

I looked around the rest of the room, at the built-in wardrobe, an exercise bike, a row of lights on the ceiling. I walked across to the chest of drawers, picked up a small white jar of hand cream. The lid was stiff, the edges sealed with hardened lotion, and when I opened it and smelt the marzipan scent again, I wondered who it had belonged to. Then I put down the jar and opened the drawers. In the first were several packets of underwear, boxer shorts immaculately wrapped in piles of three, their plastic hangers still attached. In the middle drawer, under a pile of T-shirts, I found a small wallet of photographs, but none had anything I was looking for. The final drawer was empty but for a razor, with a black handle and a glinting blade, which looked unused. Maybe it was a present, something for the man who has everything.

I walked around the bed and opened the wardrobe, the door releasing with a metallic clicking sound. On the floor inside was a single red scarf, its edges bleached a little as if from the sun, and I picked it up and put it round my shoulders, admired myself in the mirror on the inside of the door. Could it have belonged to the children's mother?

I wondered why no one wanted to speak about her, and what this family and this house had been like when she was here.

Next I inspected a green tie hanging from a hook, imagining it knotted tight around Jonas Murrey's neck. I ran my hands along a row of suits, arranged according to shades of blue and grey. At one end was the green padded jacket Jonas had been wearing the first day I met him. I slid the jacket towards me and put my hand in the outer pocket. The material was soft and quilted inside, but there was nothing in there, no loose change or forgotten receipt. I thrust my hand into the pocket of the next jacket and was surprised to find a lighter, a heavy silver Zippo. I took it out and clicked open the lid, ran my thumb down the wheel, and at once it lit up, with a burst of flame and gasoline. Still I held the lighter in my hand. How easy it would be, I thought, if I moved it just a fraction closer, for all of this to go up in flames.

Then I heard Bobby cry out and quickly I threw the Zippo back into the wardrobe and returned to the doorway. 'You okay?' I called, closing the door behind me and hurrying to the children's bedroom. I expected to find Bobby lying down, perhaps having cried out in his sleep, but instead he was standing wide awake in his cot. 'I didn't know you were up!' I held out my arms, ready to lift him.

But Bobby refused to be lifted; instead he grasped the wooden bars of the cot. 'I want to go home. I want to go home now.'

'You are at home, Bobby.' Gently I prised his fingers from the wooden bars and put my arms around him, feeling the heavy wetness of a nappy that needed changing.

I heard a sound then, footsteps on the stairs, and I turned to see Mrs B in the doorway. 'What does he mean?' I asked, laying Bobby on the changing table, busying myself with finding a fresh nappy, trying to work out how long she'd been back. Had she seen me coming out of Jonas's room? 'Why does he keep on saying he wants to go home?'

'Don't ask me,' said Mrs B, and although I didn't turn around, I could feel her there as she stood in the doorway watching me.

CHAPTER SIX

Two little half-caste children aged five and seven, badly in need of a home. Generous maintenance and clothing allowance. Apply Hoodfield House, Widenham, Kent.

**Branch home newspaper advertisement,
2 September 1951**

How do you pinpoint the moment something happened in your life, when there is no one to tell you that it did? Memory is a fragile thing. It shifts as you age. It melts away when you try to grasp it. And sometimes it creeps up on you when you'd rather it didn't.

After my mam left me, I settled into life at Hoodfield House. There was no other choice. Children are adaptable, and I was no different. I had a drawer for my clothes. A metal locker in the playroom for my toys and books. A peg in the hallway for my mackintosh and grey woollen beret. And everything was labelled. Auntie Peal set great store by respect for other people's belongings, and we were not to touch anything that did not belong to us.

In the morning we rose early and made our beds with

hospital corners, as I still do today. Then we waited in line in the washroom, where even the littlest child was taught to take pride in clean hands and teeth and nails. The washroom floor was always wet in Hoodfield House, the taps dripped constantly, and we stood there, six children at a time, shivering in the cold. The other children meant nothing to me then. I had no friendships in the early days. I was in shock, and so were they.

After washing, we went downstairs to breakfast, taking our places at the long wooden benches and saying grace before we ate. Auntie Peal watched us carefully from her table to ensure we made proper use of table cutlery and didn't chatter unnecessarily. Then we did our chores, scrubbing and polishing the floors, cleaning the playroom. And we never dared to leave a speck of dust, for Auntie Peal came afterwards and checked our work with a clean white handkerchief.

On Sunday mornings we were marched to church, past the football pitch and down Station Road, stopping at the island bus stop before turning in to Market Square. I would look up the hill then, to the new estate and the patch of common where I longed to be allowed to play. We lined up outside the church and Auntie Peal told us that if we needed to cough then we should do so now. I sat there quietly on my pew, a Bible in my hand. The vicar told us to be thankful. He said God was the father of nobody's children. And that meant us. Then we sang *Jesus loves the little children, all the children of the world, black and yellow, red and white, they're all precious in His sight.* But I didn't feel precious, not one little bit.

For a long time after my mam left me, I kept a button under my pillow at night. I can't recall where I found it, but I thought it could be hers. There was something precious about that button. If I could keep it, then she would come back. I kept a watch out for her. I thought each day she would come. One morning I was looking out of the window when I saw a lady in a nice new coat coming up the drive. I held my breath. I waited for her to see me, anticipated the touch of her arms, a loving kiss upon my cheek. But it wasn't her. Another day I saw a figure getting out of a big black car. I was in the bedroom, looking down. I pressed my face up against the glass. 'Mam,' I whispered. But I already knew it wasn't her. Still, it took me a long time to realise she wasn't coming back. That I wouldn't be rescued. That I wouldn't be saved.

I did at last begin to make friends. We used to gather in the playroom, by the fire that had a big grille around it and where there was a scratchy square of carpet on the floor. Some of the children only ever wanted to play mummies and daddies, but I never wanted to do that. A few weeks before Christmas, and before the long summer holidays, Mr Barnet would put up a noticeboard in the playroom. He wrote the names of all the children who were wanted by their parents or their foster parents. Children ran there every day to look at that list. But not me, not after the first few times. I learned to keep my bewilderment to myself.

When I was five I started school, and that was when the bed-wetting began. It was a foggy September morning and we were made to walk down the middle of the road and not on the pavement like other children. I could feel the pinch of the leather boots against my toes, the soreness of my skin. Because the shoes weren't mine and didn't fit at all. Mr Barnet knew; he regularly examined our feet and noted down deformities. But he never called the doctor for mine. Mr Barnet was very fond of inspections. He lined us up weekly to examine our heads for lice. We stood in the playroom, in our stockinged feet, while he weighed and measured us. He was forever filling in forms and sending memos to headquarters. And he was forever receiving memos back, and filing them away in his big red book.

That morning we started school, the milkman was out doing his rounds and we skirted round his horse and cart left parked on the side of the road. We passed the rag and bone man, his barrow empty, and he shouted 'Ragboa!' in his doomsday voice and the other children ran away. But I stopped and stared and he smiled at me in a kindly way and raised his trilby like he knew it was a big day for me.

I thought it was all an adventure. I wanted to go to school because at the home they told me I was bad. 'You're a bad penny, Muriel,' said Auntie Peal. 'Is it any wonder nobody wants you?' At school I thought it might be different. But although I was nicely washed and had a red velvet ribbon in my hair, I was still the girl that no one wanted to sit next to. I was the one the other children's mothers told them not to play with. I was the branch home child who only wanted to be good.

At Hoodfield House I learned to keep my head down. I knew my place. I minded my manners. And sometimes I hated going into the world for the way people stared at me. Once or twice I heard remarks that I was beautiful. 'What lovely hair,' someone might say, 'so thick and curly.'

Then they would pat me on the head as if I were a favoured pet. But mostly people looked at me with barely concealed disgust. There were no other children like me in Widenham.

Still, I was better off than some of the others at school, the children who had never been left with strangers before. They couldn't cope without their mothers. When the teacher showed us to our desks and the mothers waited outside, looking worriedly through the small glass window of the door, then how those children howled. And I hated them for that, for having a mother. I hated the children with home-made sandwiches, or coins wrapped in paper to buy what they liked later. I could not bear it that they had the single thing that I didn't.

That first day we were given textbooks. But someone had already written the answers in mine. Then our teacher told us the rules. We were not to hurt other people or damage their belongings. We were not to interrupt an adult. We were not to cover up the truth.

At least I was stronger than the other children, because they knew nothing about public humiliation. They had never been punished in front of their peers. They were shocked when the teacher slapped them with the ruler. Or threw the board rubber against the side of their head. And they were the ones who fell sick in the playground afterwards, and the caretaker had to come with a bucket of sand.

I wanted to be good at school. I wanted to be a monitor, I didn't care what for. It could have been pencils or paint-brushes or the giant metal sharpener mounted on the teacher's desk. It could have been putting flowers in a jam jar of water. Or collecting the blue plastic crate of milk bottles and poking a hole through the silver foil caps with a straw. I just wanted to be chosen.

At story time our teacher read us *Noddy*. The other children laughed when she came to Mr Golly with his black face and wild white eyes and they all looked at me. And here I am at sixty-five and I can remember that as if it were yesterday.

When we returned from school, Auntie Peal inspected our uniforms and we cleaned our shoes and changed into our play clothes. And then, come rain or shine, we ran outside to the back of Hoodfield House, where the lawn led down to an embankment and the railway line. How I loved that time of day. We played chasing games, bats and balls; we slipped down the wooden slide and jumped over skipping ropes, we played marbles and hopscotch. We climbed the trees; we searched for goldfish in the pond.

Then it was dinner, and we came inside and ate our food. We cleaned our teeth and said our prayers and got into bed. And Auntie Peal stood at the doorway and said, 'Lights out,' after which she expected complete silence.

That night I first started school I woke in the dark to find the sheet sopping wet. I couldn't think what had happened. In the morning Auntie Peal pushed my nose against the mattress as if I were a dog. 'See what you've done?' she said. Then she made me stand on the landing with the wet sheet over my head. And when I cried, 'Where's my mam?' she put her face right into mine and said, 'I've told you, we are your parents now.'

It was not that she blamed me for the bed-wetting. She just assumed I had bad blood. And Mr Barnet did as well, each morning when he ticked my name in bright red ink to show what I had done.

I can sometimes still hear Auntie Peal, her footsteps

coming quickly up the central staircase from her sitting room below, the fast slap slap slap of them getting nearer. If my bed was wet, then the punishment was swift. And there I was, a little child badly in need of a home and individual affection. But who was the other child in this advertisement? If I was the five-year-old, then who was the seven-year-old? I didn't have any brothers or sisters, so I don't know who that could have been.

After the bed-wetting, then came the sleepwalking. I can see myself on one particular night, in my prickly white nightdress, walking into Auntie Peal's room and straight to the bed. Someone was in it. I thought it was mine, even though something about the room, its shape and its warmth, told me it wasn't. And I climbed on to the bed and snuggled next to the sleeping body that was there. The next thing I knew was a sharp kick on the shin and I was hurled from the bed and found myself flat on the floor. 'Nasty little girl,' said Auntie Peal, adjusting her hairnet. And there I lay; awake now, desperate for my mam, trying not to cry.

It must have been the year after I started school that I went to hospital. I had to have my tonsils out, and I was left there all alone for a week among the adults. No one was allowed to visit back then; people were far less senti-mental when I was a child. But one nurse gave me plasticine to play with, asked if I wanted to write a picture postcard to my parents, and if I were homesick, which of course I was. Did she not know I was in a home? Had they not told her about me? I remember lying there in that hospital bed, terrified that when Auntie Peal came for me, the kindly nurse might think she was my mam.

*　　*　　*

I put away the advertisement; store it back in my file. I'm expecting my daughter this afternoon. She comes every Tuesday and Thursday, like clockwork. She doesn't like to see me with my file. 'Mum,' she says, 'you've read everything in there a million times!'

I have always tried to shield her from things. I didn't want to burden her with the truth. All this time she thought she knew me. But what she knew was her mother, not the damaged child I used to be. Yet here I am at the age of sixty-five, still searching for my childhood, still wanting to know the full story. Some days it is as if I am crouching by a pond, my hands plunged in the water, looking for a fish that I know is there. And I can't find it; it is as slippery and elusive as a memory.

My daughter seems happier since she left her job. She's too competitive to last anywhere for long. When she didn't get the deputy head job, after six years at that school, she just upped and left. Another teacher was favoured over her, or so she said. I worry sometimes why she's so suspicious of other people's motivations, why she feels undervalued, as if her efforts are never quite given the recognition she deserves.

But then she has always been good at bearing grudges. Quick to suspect a betrayal. To jump to conclusions. She is just one of those people who can't forgive and can't forget.

CHAPTER SEVEN

It's Sunday, and this afternoon we had visitors. It was just after lunch and Bobby was napping when there was a knock on the door. Mrs B doesn't work on Sundays, and it took me a few minutes to get upstairs from the kitchen, but then, as I was about to open the front door, I could hear someone outside already in the process of putting in a key. 'Oh!' the woman cried, as we seemed to open the door at exactly the same time. 'So you are here! Don't think I'm checking up on you or anything!' and she laughed so loudly that the birds in the nearby cherry tree scattered in unison. 'I'm Shanice,' she said, 'Jonas's sister-in-law.'

She's a striking woman with soft caramel hair, and she was wearing a white linen trouser suit, gold earrings and a bracelet studded with blue stones. Her sunglasses had bright white rims and I wondered if she had other variations at home so she could change her glasses depending on what she was wearing.

Then I saw someone else was outside, a pasty-skinned man standing at the bottom of the steps wearing a University of Manchester T-shirt. He rested one hand apologetically on the railings, as if just before the front door had opened he'd been imploring Shanice not to use her own key. In front of him, on the first step up, was a girl about the same age as Ella. Her hair was tied back in a ponytail; she wore a pair of shorts that were too big for her and a crumpled green shirt. In her hand she clutched a small soft toy, which seemed odd for a child of her age. She glanced at me quickly and then looked up the steps at her mother, and the way she did this suggested that if there were any battle lines to be drawn, she would choose her father's side.

'So,' said Shanice, and in she came with the obvious intention of showing me that she was at home and that I was not. She led the way down to the kitchen, took off her sunglasses and put them on the table, walked a complete circle around the room and finally stopped at the fridge. I watched her as she did this; there was angriness in the way she treated the kitchen, as if she wanted to claim ownership of the house and was unhappy to find me there. She looked inside the fridge for a while and seemed unimpressed with the contents, then she took out an unopened bottle of mineral water, unscrewed the top, and sniffed it. She marched to the sink, opened a cupboard and took out a glass. Then she filled it, expertly, like a waiter, and licked her lips. 'Where's Mark?'

Her husband came into the kitchen, an anxious smile on his face. 'Sorry to burst in on you like this,' he said, his expression both sorrowful and guilty.

'Only we wanted to see, you see,' laughed Shanice. 'Hi there!' she said as Ella came into the kitchen. 'Aren't you going to give your auntie a kiss?' For a woman who'd been so at home just moments before, she now seemed awkward, and when she put down her glass, it rattled uncomfortably on the aluminium sink. Ella stayed where she was and shrugged in a deliberately rude way. There was a tension between them, as if neither quite knew how to behave, until Shanice stepped forward and offered her cheek and eventually Ella came over to kiss her. I thought they seemed wary of each other, as if Shanice wanted to show more affection but something was stopping her.

'Well.' She folded her arms and looked at me. 'Things have certainly changed around here. Jonas told me all about you.'

I smiled agreeably, but I wondered what words he'd chosen to describe me, what his opinion of me had been.

'And how are you settling in?'

'Very well, thank you, it's such a lovely house.'

'Yes, isn't it,' said Shanice with a glance at her husband. 'This is Cassidy.' She pointed at her daughter, who stood by the table with a vacant look in her eyes. 'She's Ella and Bobby's cousin. Obviously. And they all get on really well.' At this, Ella went immediately back outside to the garden. It was hard to tell if Cassidy was upset or not, because she didn't seem to register the rebuff. Either she was expert at hiding the hurt of rejection, or Ella's behaviour was just not something that troubled her.

'So,' said Shanice. 'You're the nanny!'

'That's me,' I said, suppressing a flash of resentment at the careless way she said this.

'And you're looking after Ella and . . .'

'Bobby,' I said, as she seemed to have forgotten his name.

'Bobby, yes. Cassidy often stays with her cousins, doesn't she, Mark? It is nice for them all to be together.'

Mark, who had sat down at the table and was studying his fingernails, didn't reply.

'So we were thinking,' Shanice said brightly. 'If we needed to leave her with you sometime . . . while I'm away?'

'In Milan?'

Shanice laughed. 'I'm sorry?'

'Ella said you often go to Milan.' I glanced outside, to check that Ella was still in the garden. Then, annoyed with myself, I took a cloth from the counter and began to wipe crumbs off the kitchen table.

'She wouldn't be any trouble,' said Mark, who looked as if this exchange had been rehearsed but he still wasn't happy with the situation. 'And we'd pay you extra, of course. It's just that Shanice is working day and night—'

'And,' said Shanice with a furious look, 'you're not working?'

'Yes, I'm working, but it's because you're—'

'No, Mark, it is not. We are both working, we have a child and she needs someone to look after her.'

'Well.' I smiled. 'That wouldn't be a problem at all.'

When Shanice and Mark had left, and I'd said goodbye to Cassidy, I took the children to a nearby park, where Bobby slid down a slide and Ella climbed a brightly coloured climbing frame. I watched as she ran along the narrow walkways and then threw herself down on to a green net, which shivered flimsily under her weight. Every now and again she looked down at me, hoping perhaps that I would be afraid and call for her to come down, but I stood there next to a poster inviting parents to 'Join a conversation about beneficial risk and detrimental safety' and waved and smiled as if I didn't have a care in the world.

At last the children were hot and tired; I took them home and by eight o'clock they were both in bed and fast asleep. I cleaned up the kitchen and went upstairs, stopping outside Jonas's bedroom. Gently I pushed at the door and went in. It didn't smell of marzipan this evening; instead it smelt as musty as his office. I went to the window, tried to look through the pane of frosted glass down on to the street below, wondering what Jonas thought about when he stood here like this, all alone in his bedroom in Pembleton Crescent. Did he ever put his own children to bed; did he ever worry about them during the night? And I was pleased at the thought that if someone in the street were to look up, a neighbour perhaps walking by, and they saw my figure standing here, they would think I was the new occupier of this grand house.

Mum rang this evening on my mobile. She wanted to know where I was, because no one's answered my home phone for four days and I didn't go round on Thursday. I told her what I told her a week ago and which she must have forgotten: I have a new job, I'm living in and I won't be home for a while. But where are you? she asked. Who are you working for? I tried to be vague, to change the subject by asking about her gym class, to apologise again that I hadn't gone round on Thursday. Because it's far too early to tell her what's happened.

It worries me sometimes, how intertwined we are. She has a busy life: she still works at the library two days a week, she has her book group and her evening classes; she has no need for distraction or company. But the only relative she has in the world is me. I've always gone to her about everything, she's always been there to listen and advise, and now I can't.

It also worries me the way she's begun making lists; everywhere in her flat are lists, on the noticeboard in the kitchen, on the mantelpiece in the living room, on the cabinet next to her bed. It's not just what food to buy or things she needs to do tomorrow or next week, but lists of things that have already happened, like notable dates and places she's been. On one list she's written the names of all the people she works with, and all the names of their children and partners too, as if she's desperate not to forget a single thing.

Mum, I said to her tonight, I'm not going to be home for a few weeks. If it's anything urgent, call my mobile. What are you up to, Rosie? she asked. I'm not up to anything, I told her, why would you think I'm up to something? Because I can't tell her yet, however much I might long to tell her, she can't find out just yet.

CHAPTER EIGHT

It's Wednesday, and Mrs B has been compulsively checking the post the past three days, convinced she's about to receive her first pair of free knickers. It seems a little odd that she's chosen to give her employer's address for such a personal delivery, but perhaps she doesn't want her husband to know. As yet no knickers have arrived, however, and she's beginning to mutter ominously about 'so-called friends' and how she spent a good deal of time choosing a lovely pair of knickers that weren't cheap at all. She says she suspects the chain has been broken and now she won't get anything. What I can't understand is why anyone would want someone else, even a friend, to buy them something as intimate as a piece of underwear.

By lunchtime it had started to rain and by late afternoon it was pelting down. 'I'm not going home in this,' said Mrs B as she made herself comfortable at the kitchen table. Ella was colouring, an activity she puts a lot of effort into, and Bobby was sitting quietly on my lap while I read him a picture book. When the phone rang he jumped, startled at the sound, and I stopped reading as Ella rushed to answer it. Then I watched as she carried the phone out of the room and spoke secretively on the stairs.

'Was that your father?' Mrs B asked when Ella returned to the room.

'Yes,' she said, sitting down. 'He says he misses me so much.'

'That's nice,' I said, feeling annoyed that he still hasn't answered my email, that he can't be bothered to reply or to ask to speak with me.

And still it rained, and I shivered at how dismal it began to feel. The kitchen lights were on but the walls were heavy with shadows from the hanging brass-bottomed pots, and when I looked out towards the garden, at the rain smashing against the door, I saw the world had lost its shape, reduced to misty smears of green and grey. 'I hope it's not going to be like this,' I said, 'for the rest of the holidays.'

'Good for the roses,' retorted Mrs B.

'Yes, but not for two young kids. Things always seem to slow down when it rains like this. It can get a bit oppressive, like something's hanging over you.'

'Ah.' Mrs B smiled and unbuttoned her cardigan. 'I thought I sensed something. Is that why you've come?'

'Sorry?'

'Yes.' Mrs B leant towards me and widened her eyes. 'I've always had great connections.'

'Connections?'

'Yes, connections with other people.'

'Right,' I said, surprised at the strange direction the conversation was taking. I was about to get up and put Bobby on the floor to play when Mrs B reached her hand across the table to stop me.

'Connections, Rosie, it's just something I can sense.'

'You can?' I resisted the impulse to laugh.

'It's just a gift, something I do for other people sometimes.' Mrs B smiled and removed her hand. Then she glanced at Ella, who had put down her pen and was sitting transfixed by her side.

'What is it that you do?' I asked, curious despite myself.

'She can hypnotise people,' whispered Ella.

Mrs B nodded. 'Only if they come to me.'

'And why,' I asked, 'would they want to do that?'

'Oh, there are plenty of reasons. There might be something they need to process . . . or to confess. Sometimes they think they might have been someone else in the past; a lot of people do.'

I laughed then, because I just couldn't help myself. 'So do you have a past life?'

'Me?' said Mrs B. 'I was the Queen of Tonga,' and she got up and went to the window, and I couldn't see if she was smiling or not.

'Hypnotise me!' cried Ella.

'No.' Mrs B turned and shook her head. 'You can't hypnotise a child, Ella, that wouldn't be right.'

'But you can hypnotise Rosie.'

I laughed again. 'No thanks.'

'If she wants me to I could.' Mrs B returned to the table and stood there, waiting.

'Go on,' said Ella, as if she was in the playground, egging on another child to fight. 'Hypnotise Rosie so she's a really cool nanny.'

'No, really.' I stood up, feeling cornered. The last thing I needed was someone to confess to.

'Let's do drawings, then,' said Ella. 'Get Rosie to do one of your drawings. Please, please!'

'Well,' said Mrs B, and I knew by the careful way she pulled out a chair and sat down that this was something they had done together before. 'How about you just take that piece of paper there . . . that's right. Ella, give her a pencil . . . no, not a pen, a pencil.'

So I took the paper and sat there, the pencil in my hand, and there was something trancelike about Mrs B now; she sat so very still, not a muscle moving, like a figurehead on the bow of a ship. 'Close your eyes.'

I closed my eyes, but lightly, feeling my lids fluttering.

'Are you inside or out?'

'Sorry?'

'I'm going to ask you a series of questions and as you answer them you draw on the paper. Are you inside or out?'

I squeezed my eyes shut. I could sense Ella opposite me, jiggling around in excitement, and I wondered if this were a good idea. 'Inside,' I said, and with the sudden urge to provide them with what they wanted, I began to draw on the page.

'Good. With other people or alone?'

'Alone.'

'Good. Are you in a room?'

'Yes,' I said, and all the hairs along my arms prickled to life, because suddenly I did have an image of a room; against the darkness of my closed lids I could see squares of light, faint outlines of shapes, and I had the strangest feeling of being somewhere else.

'Is it at the top of a house, or the bottom?'

'The bottom.'

'Is there carpet on the floor?'

'Yes, I think it's red.'

53

'Any furniture? Books on the shelves?'

'Yes, I think there are books . . .'

'Can you describe what you see?'

'It's a large room. With a very high ceiling. It's blue. I think there are pillars. With gold on top . . .'

'Yes?'

'It feels like there's something on my head.'

'Yes?'

I opened my eyes. 'That's it, really.'

'Hmmm.' Mrs B took the paper and studied it. 'See what you've drawn?'

I turned the page around and looked at it. I was expecting a meandering childish scribble, but instead I saw I'd produced a neat series of boxes, like an architect's floor plan of interconnecting rooms.

Mrs B stood up and rebuttoned her cardigan. 'Well then,' she said, 'I'd best be off.'

Then I realised that the rain had stopped, squirrels were shaking the branches of the tree outside and a burst of angry April sunshine lit the room.

CHAPTER NINE

Muriel is a pleasant-natured girl with a happy disposition.
She is making good progress with her reading and writing.
Branch home report, 22 October 1954

How can you know who you take after when you are
brought up in a children's home? There is no one to say,
look at her, she is mine. She resembles me. She has my
temper, or my ambition. My aptitude for reading or for
maths. And when there is no adult to call your own, then
you must adjust to those you are closest to. You just shape
yourself as best you can.

My daughter takes after me. Not her complexion as
much as her height, the shape of her head, her feet and
her hips. And she has a way of doing things that are mine.
A habit of standing when she's concentrating, her weight
to one side. A way of licking her bottom lip when she's
irritated and doesn't want to say so. And when she does
these things I can see myself in her. She has inherited these
mannerisms from me. But whether it is a case of genes or
whether it is because I brought her up, I'm not so sure.

Who did I take after, this pleasant girl with the happy disposition? Maybe I took a little bit of everybody who passed through Hoodfield House.

My favourite person was Mrs McGregor, the cook. She was a sturdy, white-haired lady with kind brown eyes and strong arms. 'No healthy child is good all the time,' she used to say when the other adults scolded me. 'Ach, it's just high animal spirits.'

Mrs McGregor seemed so old to me, a member of a completely different generation. But adults were very different from children back then. I can see her now in the kitchen at Hoodfield House, a place of bustling busyness. It was where I could forget the anonymity of the children's home and pretend she was my adult, until another child came in and spoilt it.

The kitchen was where she reigned supreme, in charge of our food, our sustenance. The silver-nozzled kettle was always whistling. A fresh pot of tea was continuously brewing. The huge radio on the sideboard was tuned to the Home Service. Sometimes Mrs McGregor called us in to *Listen with Mother*. 'Are you sitting comfortably?' asked the posh lady on the radio. 'Then I'll begin.' And how we sat and looked at that radio and were mesmerised.

The kitchen had a walk-in larder, its shelves lined with leftover wallpaper grown sticky to the touch. On the shelves were numerous tins, which Mrs McGregor had labelled to remind herself when she had bought them and which to use first. She didn't believe in extravagance; she couldn't bear to see anything go to waste.

The larder had a tiny little window, and a cold stone floor on which there were always several bottles of milk standing in a bucket of water. The other children often stole from the larder. Even when Auntie Peal installed a Yale lock, they just climbed in through the window. It was sweetness they were after, and often they would steal handfuls of currants, which were something I always disliked.

Mrs McGregor kept the kitchen very clean. The white wooden cupboards and the big range and cooker. The double sink with the shelf underneath, the washing powder and starch kept discreetly behind a curtain. The only thing I didn't like about that room was the blinds. They were striped red and white and made me think of the Punch and Judy shows we saw during our annual week in Clacton-on-Sea. Sometimes I was afraid that the big-nosed figure of Mr Punch would burst out between the blinds, looking for a defenceless baby to pick up and throw.

Yet although Mrs McGregor kept the kitchen very clean, the chequered linoleum tiles on the floor were always a dirty white and yellow, like stained urine. And the air always smelt of boiled haddock, though we only ever had that on a Friday. But Mrs McGregor sang while she worked, especially as she laid the food out on the table. 'Plenty herring, plenty meal,' she would sing, her voice as triumphant as if she were presiding over a feast for a queen, 'plenty peat to fill her creel, plenty bonny bairns as weel, that's the toast for Mhàiri.' And all there was on the table was bread and butter. We only rarely saw meat on that table. And we only ever had a chicken at Christmas. But Mrs McGregor sang as if the kitchen were full of food. 'Come on!' she would say. 'Don't dawdle, kiddies, tea's ready.' She saw us all as wayward puppies that needed to be fed. And everything she gave us was good for us, whether it was sugar in our sandwiches or salad cream.

Mrs McGregor could never forget the war years. She spoke often of the poor wee bairns rescued from bombed-out homes and brought to Hoodfield House. She couldn't forget the time she had spent three hours queuing for apples. And when sugar came off ration, she baked as if her life depended on it. But mostly her method of cooking was one of concealment, designed to hide the absence of meat or eggs, or other foods that were hard to find.

In the early evenings, her voice was softer. She would hum to herself before leaving for her home. She would sing so mournfully that even as a child it pained my heart. 'I've been a wanderer all of my life and many a sight I've seen, God speed the day when I'm on my way to my home in Aberdeen.' Because that's what I was, a wanderer without a home. And I so wished that Mrs McGregor would not leave us every evening and return to her own family. She was like a mother to me.

I learned to sing as well as she did. I could sing so well you would have thought I was a true-blue Scot. I could have been born and bred in Aberdeen. When I was eight, a well-wisher made a donation of clothing to Hoodfield House. I was given a blue and green tartan skirt. 'You look very bonny, Muriel,' said Mrs McGregor. And I was pleased, and felt at last there was someone I took after.

I have a photograph here, and I'm wearing that tartan skirt. My face is squinting in the sun. I am standing behind a group of six children, all with happy smiles. That was me, always trying to fade into the background. That's what I did to avoid Mr Barnet's eye. He thought I was a guttersnipe. He used to pounce on me sometimes when I came out of the playroom. He'd chase me right up the central staircase of Hoodfield House, laughing until he coughed so hard his tobacco tin fell out of his pocket.

Each morning he sat in the kitchen and read the newspaper and muttered about the Colour Problem. There should be a curfew, he said. The white woman who had her dress torn in half by police dogs had no one to blame but herself. She was nothing but a common prostitute for living with a wog. And I felt a tearing in my stomach then, because I knew somehow he was speaking about my mam. She had made a baby with a coloured man. That was why she didn't want me. My birth had been a disaster for her.

One morning Mr Barnet came into the bathroom. I was washing in the bathtub and I tried to cover myself. He had a big glass bottle of bleach in his hands. He opened it and poured a capful into the bath. I watched as the water turned milky and sour. 'There you go,' he said. 'That will help you blend in a bit more!'

Sometimes that smell takes me over now; when I bend down suddenly and stand up again, I can smell bleach inside my head. It seems to come from the back of my nose, and I can taste copper in my mouth, like I'm licking a battery.

Mrs McGregor rarely commented on what Mr Barnet said. But I knew they never much liked each other. They argued over everything. Mr Barnet liked his tea made in one big pot with milk and sugar. Mrs McGregor was of the opinion that any milk or sugar should be added afterwards. And every Christmas they fought fiercely over the tree. Mr Barnet favoured the Norway spruce. Mrs McGregor said that as far as she was concerned, Christmas was a normal working day. But still, she'd prefer the indigenous Scots pine.

One year in particular I remember. Mrs McGregor put on her best frock, and despite what she said about Christmas, she took me shopping in town. We went from shop to shop on Widenham High Street. The butcher's, with sides of bacon hanging from a hook; the grocer's, with open sacks of shining prunes; the baker's, smelling sweet and homely like vanilla slice.

The bags grew heavier and heavier, until at last we stepped outside for the final time. The day was frosty, the air smoky from chestnuts roasting over red-hot coals. We stopped by the two-wheeled cart and the man winked at me and gave me a chestnut. I took it, burning, in my hands. I split the shell, as Mrs McGregor showed me, and bit into the creamy belly underneath, and I was lost in a richness of taste. A group of carol singers passed us then, lanterns waving at the end of long thin poles. A girl in a smart tweed coat and matching mittens held on to her mother's arm. And I put my hand in Mrs McGregor's and pretended she was mine. Christmas was coming. I had a roasted chestnut in my mouth. I was loved.

'What's that?' asked the girl, and pointed at me.

'That,' came her mother's reply, 'is a Yank's kid. I don't know why they don't send them all home.'

I didn't grasp the significance at first, not then. I thought she meant the home in which I lived.

Then the mother made a face of disgust and looked at Mrs McGregor. 'And that,' she said, 'is a nigger-lover.'

Mrs McGregor didn't speak, but she pulled sharply on my hand. And it frightened me, because I didn't know what the mother meant. Where was my home? Where did she want to send me to?

*　　*　　*

It seems to me that children in homes do one of two things: either they try to trace their parents, or they don't. There is no in-between; either you do or you don't. And except for one time, I never did. Maybe I was a coward. Because what would I have said to my mam if I ever found her? 'Did you ever think of me, did you ever expect to see me again?'

But my daughter has long wanted to know. Over and over again she has asked, 'Don't you want to find out about your parents?' I'm whole as I am, I have told her more than once. I don't need to know about *them*. I have you. But her curiosity is insatiable. And when she fails to find what she is looking for, that doesn't stop her, not one little bit.

Something is going on, I'm certain of it. I haven't heard a word from her since Sunday. I don't know what job she has that she needs to live in. I don't believe she would return to teaching, not now. I have no idea where she is. And if things go wrong again, then who will be there to pick up the pieces?

CHAPTER TEN

It's Saturday, and this afternoon I decided to take the children on a trip, Ella and Bobby and their cousin Cassidy. I thought if I invited Cassidy then if her parents do need to drop her off one day, at least she'll already feel reasonably comfortable with me. Her father brought her round after lunch and seemed pleased I was taking the children out. I suggested some fresh air would do them good, and this was exactly the right thing to say because Mark nodded enthusiastically the way someone who's clearly very unfit approves of the idea of others taking an interest in their health. He suggested we go to Hampstead Heath, and when I said I wasn't quite sure how to get there, he offered to take us in his car, dropping us off on a busy road next to a row of tennis courts. We set off in no particular direction, Bobby in his buggy and Ella and Cassidy walking on either side. The girls chatted away and shared the snacks I'd brought, until I thought Shanice was right and perhaps they were good friends. It was only when we got to Kenwood that things changed.

But first we walked past the tennis courts and an

immaculate bowling green, then along a neatly paved path that led around a small children's playground. We stopped at some ponds, where we watched dogs splashing for sticks, and then two boys sailing a model boat, before following a path up a muddy hill. 'I want . . . I want . . .' Bobby chanted from his buggy, without ever saying what it was that he wanted. At the top of the hill the path forked in several directions and I stopped in front of a gated entranceway, wondering which way to go. 'Come on,' I told the girls, enjoying the fact that I could choose where we went, and we turned on to a pathway darkened with trees and holly bushes. It seemed secluded and a little wilder than what we'd seen of the rest of the heath, and I pushed the buggy quickly, Bobby laughing as he bumped along. A few minutes later we came out on to an open meadow where picnickers, optimistic about the weather, sat in small groups on the grass.

'Who lives there?' asked Ella, pointing up the crest of another hill to the cream facade of what looked like a large stately home.

'I wouldn't have thought anyone does now,' I told her, taken aback by the sudden sight of such a grand house, 'but there was probably a lord or lady there once.'

Still Ella looked at the house. 'I wish I lived there.'

'So do I.' I laughed. My phone beeped then and I took it out, saw a text from Amina asking how I was. I thought about replying, but I could see Bobby wanted to get out of his buggy and so I put the phone back in my pocket, lifted him up and watched him totter off, struggling to keep up with the girls. The children played for a while on the lawn, which Bobby dreamily rolled himself down, and then we walked along a wide pathway in front of the house.

Up close the walls were decorated with pillars and swirling flowers, but the paint was yellowish and had peeled in parts like sunburnt skin. It felt as if we were promenading, that everyone had turned out in their Saturday best in order to stroll along, to see and be seen, and I was pleased that although we'd only been together for a week, we appeared to be as much of a family group as anyone else.

A small child on a wooden bike with no pedals scissored her legs along the path, giggling. People walked leisurely with their dogs, two men carried blue cool boxes under their arms, and everywhere was the sound of shoes crunching on the surface of sand and stones, so it almost seemed as if we were on a beach.

'Okay, I'm making an executive decision,' declared a tall man, towering over a group of people all wearing orange cagoules, 'that we're going this way.' I watched them walk down the steps to the meadow, and I thought of Jonas Murrey and how he might lead people like this, and as I looked back, I realised that someone must have stared out of this house once, and this would have been their very own lawn.

We left the house, passing tall curved windows like a giant conservatory, and stopped at a small metal archway, so short that as I stepped forward I could feel strands of ivy brushing against the top of my head.

'This is spooky,' Ella said, and she picked up a stick and ran quickly through, trailing it noisily along the sides. She rushed out on to a large area of grass, where the children chased each other in and out of clumps of brilliant pink rhododendrons and between low-hanging magnolias, stopping at a tree with flowers that waved like white handkerchiefs. We walked down a pretty pathway, through patches of shadow and sun, and under a tree with weeping branches that shivered like seaweed. Then we passed through another archway, as dark as a tunnel, heavy with sturdy creepers that had entwined themselves around the metal framework, thick and bulbous like tubers torn from the earth.

And then, inevitably, it began to rain. So I put Bobby back in his buggy and called for the girls, and as the sky erupted with thunder we ran round to the front of the stately home. I pushed the buggy in through a set of wooden doors, and then we came into an entrance hall. I urged Bobby not to make a fuss, but faced with the sudden silence, he was utterly quiet.

It was quite busy inside; many others had had the same idea as us, to get out of the rain. 'Let's go and look around, then,' I suggested. Ella seemed happy with this, although Cassidy looked uncertain. She had a way, I thought, of turning in on herself, of appearing to go along with what everyone else wanted to do but at the same time to be somewhere entirely different herself. 'Which way shall we go?' I asked, but Ella had already run off, and Cassidy and I followed her. The girls headed left and into a shiny-floored passageway with doors on either side. It was quiet here as well, but for the sound of footsteps and floorboards creaking from above, the occasional jangle of keys in someone's pocket. Still I followed the girls, this time into a room with marble pillars, again with doors in both directions. I heard the spluttering mechanical sound of someone on a walkie-talkie; a guard walked by in a blue uniform and a crisp white shirt. I followed the girls as they turned into a larger room with carpet on the floor.

Everywhere were signs of wealth and antiquity,

chandeliers and chaises longues, gilded paintings of gentlemen and ladies on the walls. I saw Ella stop by a shiny wooden chair with a 'Please do not touch' sign, just a small yellow card that looked almost home-made, and then off she ran again. Now we were in a generous-sized room with burnt-red walls, where a dozen or so people wandered aimlessly, wearing raincoats and rucksacks, murmuring gently to themselves. A French couple, each clutching a bottle of water, stood chatting arm in arm in front of a chaise longue, a green rope slung across the cushions to stop people from sitting on it. From another room came the sound of a baby's cry, and the couple turned around with tight smiles at the intrusion.

I bent down to give Bobby his drinking cup, and when I looked up I saw the girls were standing in front of a large oil painting. Pleased they'd found something that interested them, I came closer. 'Do you—' I began, but Ella jumped and turned around and her startled expression reminded me of the way Jonas Murrey had swung around in his chair when I'd first been shown into his office. Surprised at her reaction, I studied the painting; clearly something had captivated her.

It was an outdoor scene of two young women; the one in the foreground was bathed in a horizontal shaft of light, making her skin as luminously white as the bodice of her dress, and in her hair was a wreath of rosebuds. In one hand she held an open book and her other hand reached out, resting perhaps on the young black woman behind her. Everything about the woman in the background suggested a forced mischievousness, her smile and the way she held one finger to her cheek. Her body appeared to be in movement; she balanced a bowl of fruit in her hands, as if she was about to dash off and out of the painting. Her dress, like the other woman's, looked silken and elegant, but on her head she wore a white turban with a feather poking out, and this made her seem deliberately exotic and out of place.

I looked again at the touch between the two women. The white woman definitely had her hand on the black woman; at first it was as if she were pushing her away. But then I saw that there was some affection being portrayed between them, that they were even perhaps holding hands. I read the small box of text below the painting; this was Lady Elizabeth Murray and Dido Elizabeth Belle.

'Who is she?' Ella asked. 'Why is she at the back? Is she a servant?'

'I've no idea,' I said, impressed by the way Ella had picked up on the positioning of the women and what this might imply.

'Is she dead?'

'I would have thought she died a long time ago.'

'Did she have a husband?'

'I don't know.'

'Did she have children?'

'I would guess she might have, why?'

'Well, where is her family?' Ella looked around the room; there were no paintings on the walls showing anyone resembling Dido Elizabeth Belle. 'Did she have a mum?'

'She must have had a mum.'

'So where is she, then?'

'I don't know, Ella, but I'll try to find out.'

I turned as a group of elderly women came into the

room, each clutching a guidebook, followed closely by a young guide. 'Right!' he announced a little breathlessly. 'We're now in the breakfast room. This is Lady Hamilton . . . and she was painted by Romney. It's fair to say she was the most painted lady in Europe . . . and you can see her beauty here!' The guide threw out an arm, pointing at a painting at the far end of the room: a woman sitting before a spinning wheel, swathed from head to toe in white, one finger idly pulling on a string of cotton. She looked like she hadn't done a day's work in her life, or at least she wasn't paying much attention to her job. 'Later,' said the guide, his voice hoarse, 'she met Lord Admiral Nelson, okay . . . and fell into his arms and they had a child and all hell broke loose.' The guide paused for a moment, then he moved to a smaller painting and began to talk about Constable.

I pushed the buggy to a small round table in the centre of the room. There were several open folders and I picked one up and began to read about Dido Elizabeth Belle, scanning the pages quickly, with one eye on the girls. I read that she was born in 1761 and that her mother was an African named Maria Bell, who lived in the Caribbean, where she may or may not have been enslaved. Maria was on a ship captured by the Royal Navy and she came, or was brought, to England, where she gave birth to Dido, whose father was a Royal Navy officer named John Lindsay.

I turned a page. Dido's mother had apparently disappeared without trace, and Dido had ended up with her father's uncle, the 1st Earl of Mansfield, at Kenwood. It wasn't known if her father had ever visited her, but she grew up here with her half-cousin Elizabeth.

I looked around the room. So Dido had lived amid this

wealth and luxury, but far away from where her mother had come from. She'd been forced to start life in a new home, and I wondered if the family had cared for her, this illegitimate girl without a mother, and why her father had turned his back on her and never visited. Just like my own mother, I thought, hundreds of years later and in different circumstances, but abandoned for similar reasons. I was just thinking about the sadness and indignity of this when, from the corner of my eye, I distinctly saw Ella slap Cassidy on the hand.

'Ella!' I cried, pushing the buggy back to the painting. 'What did you do that for?'

'She was touching it,' said Ella, not at all apologetic.

'That doesn't mean you can slap her!'

'You are not allowed to touch the paintings,' Ella said, as if she were the guard.

'I'm hungry.' Cassidy bent down to retrieve her soft toy from where she'd left it earlier in Bobby's buggy.

'They were cousins, you know,' I told Ella. 'These two women in the picture. And Dido did have a mother; she was called Maria.'

Ella ignored me; she was still glaring at Cassidy. 'How can you be hungry? You just ate on the way here!'

'Come on,' I said quickly, before a fight could erupt. 'Let's try another room.'

But Ella was angry that Cassidy had touched the painting, and even angrier that I hadn't told her off, and she followed me with an air of great injustice. 'Why don't I get a say?' she complained as I pushed the buggy through the doorway and hesitated at the entrance to a large empty room. Then, on impulse, I turned right, and there we were, back in the entrance foyer.

Immediately the girls set off in exactly the same direction we'd gone before, along the passageway like two demented mice in a maze, only this time at the marble-pillared room they stopped by a set of open wooden doors on the left. I followed them to the threshold of an unusually shaped room with a high, ornately decorated blue ceiling. At the entrance were two white pillars, paved at the top with gold, facing an identical set of pillars at the far end of the room. The carpet was red as a tongue and on either side a series of short gold posts were slung with pink rope. I had a sense of objects in shadow, a desk, perhaps an instrument of some kind, but I didn't pay them much attention. Instead I was drawn towards a long curved wall where all I could see were books.

Ella nudged me with her elbow. 'This is it, isn't it, Rosie?'

And she was right; this was the room I'd described to Mrs B. I felt a sudden wave of dizziness, as if I'd stepped into someone else's life. Here was everything I'd seen when my eyes were closed: the red carpet and the gold-topped pillars, the high blue ceiling and the books. Still I stood there, not understanding how I could possibly have described something I had no knowledge of ever having seen before. Had I seen a picture of this room somewhere, in a book or on TV perhaps, and remembered it without knowing?

Ella slipped her fingers into mine, and there was a sudden hush in the room as if the visitors in the rest of the house had been obliterated. Then I let go of her hand and began to walk towards the books. As I did, I caught fragments of myself in the mirrors on the walls, a glimpse of my arm, the side of my raincoat, a sliver of hair. I felt an urge to reach the books, to touch their soft leather spines, the colours dulled over the years into deep sea green, forest brown, burnished gold. And then, as I was only a metre away, I heard a woman's voice, '*Excuse* me,' and I saw that I was blocking the way, and that Bobby was fussing and about to lunge out of the buggy.

The rain had stopped and we went back outside. The trees dripped around us, splashing wetness on the paving stones, and in the distance a rainbow appeared in the sky, as faint as watercolour paint. I let Bobby out of his buggy and off he ran, desperate to keep up with the girls. But Ella ignored him, marching off ahead of us, back round the house and across the now empty, sodden lawn. Once or twice Cassidy tried to catch up, but Ella was having none of it, and as she walked off down the dark holly-lined pathway, every now and then she stopped and seemed to say something, as if she were speaking to someone at her side.

'Ella, slow down,' I called.

'She can't hear you,' said Cassidy, putting her hand on the handle of the buggy next to mine. 'She's talking to her imaginary friend.'

I saw Ella reach the end of the pathway and look quickly from right to left as if deciding which way to run.

'Ella!' I called. 'Will you *slow* down!' And suddenly I didn't want responsibility for a fractious girl whose moods changed as quickly as the weather. I wanted to be alone and to think about the room I'd just been in and how I'd been able to describe a place I'd never seen before. 'Ella!' I cried. 'Will you stop where you are!'

She did stop then; she waited until we'd almost reached

where she stood and then she turned and shouted, 'Why should I?'

Next to me I felt Cassidy cringe at the sound of Ella's voice, while from the buggy Bobby started to whimper.

'You're not the boss,' Ella screamed. 'You're not my mum!'

CHAPTER ELEVEN

When we got back from Kenwood I left the children watching TV in the playroom while I went down to the kitchen to make them a snack. Mrs B was busy cleaning the windows; she had her back to me and she was working hard, spraying with one hand and wielding a cloth with the other. The air was filled with a salty ammonia smell and the sound of the glass squeaking set my teeth on edge.

'Can I ask you something?'

Mrs B continued her job, and the fact that she still had her back to me made it easier to ask. 'Where is Ella and Bobby's mother?'

Still Mrs B sprayed the window. Finally she put down the cloth and turned around. 'I wondered when you'd ask me that. It's a very sorry story. Isabella wasn't well.'

I sat down, unsettled by the fact that Mrs B was speaking in the past tense. 'She was ill?'

'She was very ill and I don't mean physically. I would say it all started around six months after Bobby was born.'

'What did?'

'When she fell ill.' Mrs B sighed and picked up the cloth,

bunched it tightly in her hand. 'It had happened after Ella was born, but it hadn't been so bad then and everyone said it was just a case of the baby blues. But with Bobby it was different.' She stopped and looked around the kitchen, as if reluctant to continue. 'She tried to carry on, because that's how she was. She wanted everything in the house to be perfect, she always did. But she couldn't sleep, she couldn't eat . . . and she didn't really tell anyone because, well, she didn't want people thinking she was a bad mother. I suppose you could say everyone thought she wasn't the type.' Mrs B stopped again and glanced at the doorway, apparently worried that someone might be listening. 'If there is a type. Although she was always very sensitive. The doctors said it was post-natal depression, she was supposed to be going into a unit, then Mr Murrey came back—'

'From where?'

'From wherever he'd been. He was away a lot at the time. I don't think he really knew what was going on. He decided to take her away for the weekend, to Oxford, where she was from . . . I think it had got to the point where she just couldn't take it any more.'

'And?'

'And that's where she did it.'

I ran a finger along the edge of the table, felt my nail press into the wood. 'What?'

'She jumped off a bridge.' Mrs B turned back to the window, as if the conversation were over.

'A bridge?' I watched her spray the glass again, felt sickness rise in my throat, as I realised this was why no one talked about the children's mother. She hadn't left Jonas, he hadn't left her, she had thrown herself off a bridge. This was why no one mentioned her; they just didn't know what to say. I thought of Jonas's bedroom and how barren it was, perhaps because he just couldn't bear to have anything in there that reminded him of his wife. And her name was Isabella. Ella must have been named after her mother.

I stood up, about to ask if the children knew what had happened, when we heard the sound of Bobby crying.

'I told you,' Ella was saying as she came down the stairs. 'I told you not to touch the TV.'

I felt awkward then as she came into the room; the fact that I knew about her mother when she might not didn't feel right. Perhaps the adults had kept the truth from her. 'Do you want some juice?' I asked.

'What's wrong?'

'Nothing.' I smiled. 'Nothing's wrong. Just you must be thirsty. You all must be,' I said as Cassidy came into the kitchen as well. Ella opened the fridge and took out a carton of juice, and I marvelled at her poise, at how this nine-year-old child was able to behave in such a self-controlled way when surely she must be overwhelmed with confusion and loss.

'Why are you watching me?' Ella turned from the fridge. Then she saw Mrs B was in the room and she ran over to the window, tugged on her cardigan. 'Guess what? We went to Kenwood and we found the room that Rosie drew. It was just like she said it was.'

'Well,' said Mrs B, putting down her cloth. 'Did you really?'

'Yes,' said Ella, 'and we saw the lady.'

'What lady was this?'

'The one that Rosie used to be. She looks like her. Her name is Dido.'

'Don't be silly,' I said, and I went to the counter, took some rolls out of the bread bin to make a snack.

'Really she does,' said Ella insistently. 'And Rosie's going to find out everything about her because we don't even know where her mother is.'

I heard Mrs B sigh, and I stood there, with a roll in my hand, not sure what to say.

'So you found the room you drew?' asked Mrs B.

'It was just a room,' I said, uncomfortable at the way she was looking at me. 'There wasn't anything special about it.'

'If you say so,' said Mrs B, and she smiled and gave Ella a wink.

CHAPTER TWELVE

Bobby is grief-stricken. It's Easter Sunday and his beloved guinea pig has died. The cat must have got into Jonas's office sometime in the night, because when Bobby asked to see his pet this morning, we found the door open, and the poor creature lying lifeless in its box. Perhaps, as Jonas had warned, the very presence of the cat had been enough to give the guinea pig a heart attack and I wondered if it was me who'd mistakingly left the door open.

Ella is strangely unmoved. She seems irritated by the fact that Bobby won't stop crying, and more interested in when she'll be allowed to eat the Easter eggs that Mrs B has left for her. I've promised him that this afternoon we'll organise a proper burial and make a memorial, but I'm reluctant to bother Jonas with the news, although Bobby is insistent we tell Daddy.

I've still not spoken to Jonas, or had any message from him, since I started work. Each time he's rung in the past ten days, Ella has picked up the phone and he hasn't asked for me. I still don't know what the problem might be at her school, or what Jonas intends to do about it. Ella can be bossy and confrontational, but there's also a brightness and a cleverness about her that her teachers must have noticed. I don't think many children her age would have studied a painting with the concentration she displayed at Kenwood.

But she's been difficult today; she's not as easy-going as she was in the beginning, and her outburst on the heath yesterday seems to have sparked a change in her. This afternoon, after I'd been calling her for a while, I went upstairs with Bobby on my hip and found her in my room, sitting on my bed. I stood there annoyed, because there's something intrusive about finding someone on your own bed, even a child. 'Ella, when you go into someone's room, you need to ask . . .'

'You haven't made it properly,' she said, getting up.

'What?' I put Bobby down on the floor.

'You should have a blanket over the sheet.'

'People make beds in different ways, Ella.'

She didn't comment, but held out her elbow as she went past, knocking my arm quite painfully. Gone was the child who'd slipped her hand into mine at Kenwood and whispered, 'This is it, isn't it, Rosie?' Now she clearly resented me. I worried whether it was possible that she'd overheard my conversation in the kitchen with Mrs B; maybe that was the problem.

I was about to ask her what she'd been doing in my room when we heard the doorbell ring. When I went downstairs, I found a remarkably tall woman with harshly suntanned skin and bleached blonde hair standing on the doorstep.

'Oh,' she said accusingly. 'I was beginning to think no

one was at home.' Then, instead of introducing herself, she began to speak in a sharp, self-important voice, as if she was not used to being contradicted. 'It's about the committee. We haven't heard anything from Jonas and our meeting is next week.'

'I'm afraid he's away.'

'So who are you?'

'I'm the nanny.'

'Well . . .' The woman eyed me as if deciding whether I was trustworthy. 'I suppose you could stand in for him. It's numbers that are important. Next Tuesday, seven fifteen.'

'And what committee is this?'

'The Pembleton Crescent committee,' said the woman in a humourless fashion. 'Number twelve. Next Tuesday, seven fifteen.'

A few hours ago I found Ella in my room again, and this time she'd brought Bobby. I'd put him to bed with his milk and left Ella watching TV in the playroom while I'd tidied up downstairs, but when I came up to check on Bobby, I found his cot empty and both children in my room. Ella was sitting at my desk, all the drawers open, a mess of things on the floor. I stood there, aware that she was testing me, but feeling unable to rise above it. This was my room, the only space that was mine, and I'd told her not to come in without asking. I looked at the things on the floor – a pair of my socks, my hairbrush, a novel I'd intended to read – and I wondered where my diary was. Had she found that as well, and if she had, would she have read it?

'What *are* you doing?' I snapped in my best classroom voice, the sort of voice it's necessary to use when you set some work, leave the room for a moment and come back to find a handful of children wandering around disturbing everyone else. 'I told you, Ella, you need to ask before—'

Ella got up from the chair. I thought she was going to argue with me, but instead she walked slowly towards the door, moving in such an awkward fashion, her arms held stiffly by her sides, that I wondered for a moment if she was even conscious of what she was doing.

'Ella!' I said, sharply.

As she reached the door she appeared to remember where she was, or perhaps my voice had startled her back to life, because she turned to me with a friendly smile and asked, 'Then why did you go into my daddy's room?'

'Sorry?'

'If you have to ask before you go into someone's room, why didn't you ask to go into my daddy's room?'

'Well, Ella . . .' I frowned; I'd thought she'd been asleep the night I'd gone into Jonas's room. 'He asked me to check if—'

Ella smiled. 'But you haven't spoken to my daddy.'

'No,' I said briskly. 'He emailed me. Now go and get ready for bed.'

She did as she was told and I turned my attention to Bobby, still sitting on the carpet. 'Come on,' I told him, 'back to bed.' He let me pick him up without a struggle and I followed Ella down to the bedroom. I waited while she changed into her nightie and went to the bathroom to fill up her bedside glass of water, and then when she'd got into bed with a loud deliberate yawn, I settled Bobby back in his cot. I checked on them a couple of times, and on the way upstairs a little later, I looked into their room again and found them both asleep.

* * *

I spent the evening on the internet, looking up Dido Elizabeth Belle, something I'd been too tired to do last night. I read a little about the history of Kenwood: when the house had been built and why, a description of its architecture and collection of paintings. I read about Dido's great-uncle Lord Mansfield, who was Lord Chief Justice during a famous slavery case in which he'd declared that under English law one man could not own another. I found an extract from the diary of an American visitor who'd dined at Kenwood in 1779, and who wrote that 'a Black' came in after dinner and sat with the ladies, before strolling with the others in the garden. She wore a high cap, he wrote, and 'her wool' was 'much frizzled in her neck'. There was no mention of the turban I'd seen in the painting. The American found Dido 'pert enough'; he reported that his host Lord Mansfield 'has been reproached for shewing a fondness for her – I dare say not criminal'. I read the passage again, wondering what he meant by *not criminal*, and what he was implying about Lord Mansfield's relationship with Dido Elizabeth Belle.

I continued switching from one website to another, part of me hoping to stumble across something that would be familiar: another room perhaps, a name, or a picture of someone I might for some reason recognise. I thought about what Mrs B would think. Would she say that I remembered the library so clearly because in a past life I'd been there too? The very idea is ludicrous, but still I stared at a copy of the painting of Dido and her cousin, wondering if Amina might know anything about Kenwood that could explain how Dido's adoptive family had treated her. It was too late to reply to her text from yesterday, so I sent an email apologising for my silence and asking if she knew anything about the family who once lived on Hampstead Heath. Then I got ready for bed, feeling annoyed at all the time I'd spent looking up Dido Elizabeth Belle when it's a distraction I really don't need. But as I stood in front of the mirror brushing my teeth, I thought about how Ella had so enjoyed looking at the painting. She'd really wanted to know who Dido was, whether she had married and had children and what had happened to her mother. She was interested in family relations, and as I rinsed my mouth and put my toothbrush on the side of the sink, I saw that this could be useful; it could be a way for me to encourage her to find out more about her own family. Because after all, I've been here for nearly two weeks and I've been so immersed in looking after the children that I haven't even started to do what I came here for.

CHAPTER THIRTEEN

Muriel has passed her eleven plus. She will be going straight to the grammar school.

Branch home report, 15 August 1957

How does a person find any real beginnings or endings when they grow up in a children's home? Children arrived at Hoodfield House, their characters and personalities largely in place. Nothing was said about where they came from. Not a word about their parents or their background. But you came to love them like family. And then they were gone.

That is how it was with Susan. She was left at Hoodfield House when she was nine. Her mother said she couldn't cope. People could do that back then, hand their child to a home. Sometimes it was because of an emergency. A mother in hospital. An invalided father. A sudden eviction. Some only stayed for a short time; they were visited by their parents and taken out for treats. But Susan stayed for two years. And no one ever came for her.

I had heard Mr Barnet on the telephone saying, 'Don't

send us any more coloured kids.' But then they sent us Linda, and shortly afterwards Susan. I had become expert by then at overhearing grown-up conversations. That was how I heard that Linda's mother had died and no one else in the family would take her. They were too afraid of what the neighbours would say.

Linda didn't stay for long. She came in the summer, a tiny scrap of a girl. She was so frightened of the sun, she would run and hide indoors because she didn't want her skin to get any darker. At mealtimes, and much to Mrs McGregor's displeasure, Linda would use her finger to wipe at her plate and then lick it slowly, long after the taste had gone. Sometimes, when Mrs McGregor wasn't looking, she sneaked a finger into the cooking pots as well. And then one day, she was gone.

But when Susan arrived at Hoodfield House, I stopped the bed-wetting and my sleepwalking too. Maybe it was because she was in the bed next to me and that was a comfort. Right from the start we were delighted with each other. We pretended we were sisters. We didn't look alike in either complexion or size. She was small and pretty, with a butterfly mouth and a dancer's gait, while I was tall and awkward, and preferred to hide in the shadows. But still, people at school believed us. Because all the other children were white.

We worked very hard to find similarities between us. And if you look for similarities between people, you will find them. We began to mimic each other. What we chose to draw on the brown paper covers of our exercise books. The way we ate our food. The position we slept in at night. Maybe we just had the need to feel the same as someone else.

Pink was our favourite colour; that was evidence of our sameness. We both loved marmalade, especially the bitter little strips of peel. And our favourite animal was the polar bear. On Saturdays we put our pocket money together and bought sweeties that only we would share.

On summer days she carried me on the crossbar of her bike. We went all the way to the common, where we sat by the grand old oak tree and looked down over the fields of wheat. In the winter, when it snowed – and it always seemed to snow in winter – we made sledges from milk crates. Then we slid down the back lawn of Hoodfield House to the embankment. One spring morning we found a little wild rabbit in the grounds. It was speckled grey and brown, with a tail as white as ice cream. We made it a bed of grass and fed it dandelion leaves. We were so happy to have that rabbit. But a few days later, when we went to feed it, it had died.

I remember it rained hard that afternoon, and Mrs McGregor did something very unusual. She sought permission for us to watch the television. It was a new thing then, and the homes were under instructions not to solicit gifts of televisions from well-wishers. But Auntie Peal had certainly solicited hers. And she didn't like us watching it at all. She said the variety programmes were vulgar, and it could only be switched on with her authority. Then we had to wait while she turned the knob on the cabinet and the television made a humming noise and eventually came to life. Mrs McGregor was usually of the opinion that children should be out and about playing during daytime. But on this day it was raining hard, and perhaps she knew how upset Susan and I were about our rabbit.

I don't recall what we watched that afternoon. I can

only see us on the carpet, feel Susan's outstretched legs beside mine. There we were, just the two of us. In Auntie Peal's sitting room. Watching television while the rain poured down outside, as if we were sisters.

Susan stayed at Hoodfield House until we sat our eleven-plus exam. I vividly remember that day. There was such a feeling of worry in the classroom. We were under strict instructions not to look at any other child, not to so much as turn our heads to left or right in case we were accused of cheating. We'd had it drummed into us how important the exam was and everyone was nervous, especially Susan. Because although she always got good marks, and her books were covered with silver stick-on stars, she just couldn't do examinations.

But I sat behind her and I found it soothing, the quietness in the classroom. The blackboard with nothing on it but the date. No one running around, no one shouting. Not even little Jimmy Cox, the son of the local policeman. We all sat very still, our examination papers face down on the desk. I bent my head and held my pencil to my lips, and I can feel that now, the hard pink rubber at the end encased in a thin band of metal that gave way with a surprising softness when I bit on it.

'You may begin,' said the teacher. And we did. I liked the English questions the best. I think that was when my love of English first began. I liked the sets of words, when you had to choose the odd one out, or sort out the mixed-up letters to find the proper word. And I liked the general knowledge questions too, because sometimes they were tricky and the answers weren't clear and I enjoyed that.

There was one question in particular I remember. A

woman had fallen into water and was almost drowned. She was dragged out by a man, but she did not thank him. Was it because she never felt thankful for small things, or because she did not know the man well enough? Did she not thank him because she was feeling better, or because she was still unconscious? After some thought, I chose 'd'. The drowning woman hadn't thanked the man because she was unconscious. That had to be the reason. Why else would she not thank a man who had rescued her? Unless she hadn't wanted to be rescued, unless she had deliberately tried to drown herself. But that wasn't given as an answer. I had to choose the right one, and so I knew it was 'd'.

But as for Susan, first she ticked one answer and then she changed her mind. I watched her from behind, as she took a pin out of her hair and pinched it apart with her teeth. I longed to tap her on the shoulder and tell her 'd'. But she was changing her answer again and Mr Jones slapped her with his ruler for fidgeting.

The day they read out the eleven-plus results in morning assembly we sat crowded in the school hall, legs crossed, waiting. Our headmistress Mrs Featherstone watched us, her eyes beady behind her horn-rimmed glasses. Only a few children had passed; the rest were distraught. Then they had to go home and tell their parents. Even some of the very clever children had failed, like Susan. But I had passed. No one could believe it. Because branch home children never, ever passed, especially not the likes of me. And I so wished Susan had as well, because she deserved to, maybe even more than me.

The day after the results, we were sitting side by side

in the kitchen dipping chips into eggs when Susan's mother appeared. Susan got up from the kitchen table. She said thank you to Mr Barnet and Auntie Peal. Then she just collected her things and walked out. She didn't look behind her as she left Hoodfield House. She didn't shed a single tear.

But I watched her, from the kitchen window. I peeked out between the Punch and Judy blinds. I saw her walk along the gravel pathway with her mother. I saw her open the big black gate. I saw her mother stop and adjust her daughter's beret. And then they were gone.

For some children, growing up in a home gives them a fear of abandonment they can never shake off. But I always expected abandonment. I expected it and I was prepared for it. So when Susan left, I wasn't that surprised. But I would like to know what happened to her, the girl I pretended was my sister.

After Susan had gone, I went to the grammar school, a big dark building in what had once been a button factory. It had a good reputation and attracted girls from far and wide, and I was proud to attend. Each morning I had a mile-long walk along Station Road, swinging my leather satchel, careful to keep my uniform clean. I walked all the way to the bus stop opposite Molly's Café. Then I caught the bus to school. I was so happy to leave the home behind. But anxious because I had no friends at the grammar school.

Mrs McGregor had left Hoodfield House that summer. Auntie Peal and Mr Barnet followed shortly after. A married couple moved in to run the house, Mr and Mrs Appleyard. They liked to have couples in charge of the branch homes by then. Mr Appleyard was stern like Mr Barnet, but not as cruel. Mrs Appleyard was so inconsequential she could have been a ghost.

And I am ashamed to say that was when it happened. One winter's morning I arrived at school before the other children. There was no one in our form room. It was silent but for the spitting of the radiators. The air was dim and full of floating chalk dust. I walked around, lifting up the lids of the other children's desks, just high enough that I could peek inside. I stood in front of the teacher's table and pretended I was telling everyone what to do. And then I saw it. It was on the edge of the table, a small tapestry purse embroidered with flowers. I picked it up and clicked open the metal kiss clasp. I put my hand inside, felt the cool satin lining. I grabbed a few pennies. I knew what I was going to do. I was going to buy the other girls sweeties. I was going to try and buy new friendships, now that Susan had gone. I had the pennies in my hand; I could smell the metal warming against my skin. I was deciding where to put them when Mrs Mumford walked in. A formidable lady, always dressed in a flowing black gown, she caught me red-handed.

I was marched along the corridor and up the stairs to the headmaster's room. Then I was given five strokes on my arm for stealing. 'This hurts me more than it does you,' said the headmaster, his upper lip wet with sweat. I watched as my name was entered into the punishment book, heard the scrape of the pen across the page. *Muriel Wilson – thief.* I can see those words now, as clear as anything. That was me. A thief. Then I was sent back to Hoodfield House with a note that said I was lucky not to have been expelled. I can feel that letter in my hand, the sense of shame that hung over me all the way back to the home. Because I hadn't meant to steal. I had always tried so hard to prove that I was good. I had been quiet and mild-mannered. No matter what anyone said to me, I had never answered back. And now everyone would know I was bad.

CHAPTER FOURTEEN

It's Easter Monday, and Mrs B popped in this morning to see how we were all getting on. Ella seems calmer today, as if the exchange in my bedroom never happened and I hadn't found her up there going through my things. It unsettles me, how easily she can pretend everything is fine. I'd hoped to ask Mrs B more about the children's mother, but Ella was in the kitchen, so I washed the dishes while they chatted, thinking of Amina and the email I'd received this morning in which she promised to see what she could find out about Kenwood.

Once Mrs B had left, I asked Ella if she'd like to bake a cake, and happily she got out a recipe book, a carton of eggs, some margarine, sugar and flour. I set Bobby on the floor with his building bricks, while Ella took out a set of weighing scales and a large ceramic mixing bowl. The outside was golden brown and decorated with diamond-shaped panels, its edges dented as if it had been worn smooth over years of use.

Ella put on an apron and began to measure out the ingredients.

'You're very good at this,' I told her as I watched her spoon margarine into the bowl.

'I know. I used to—'

'You used to?' I asked, wondering what she'd been about to say and whether this was something she'd once done with her mother.

'Nothing,' Ella mumbled. 'I'm going to get some nuts.' She went to a cupboard at the far end of the kitchen and began to hunt through its shelves, and as she did, I saw she had her head to one side, murmuring as if to someone just behind her shoulder.

'Ella,' I said softly, 'who are you talking to?'

She didn't reply, but stopped murmuring and stood there staring into the cupboard.

'Is it your imaginary friend?'

Still she didn't reply, so I went over to where she stood, but as I did she quickly shut the door and moved along the wall, opening another cupboard.

'You know what,' I told her, 'I used to have an imaginary friend when I was your age. Actually I had two; their names were Billy and Joey.' It was true; it was something I had totally forgotten about until Cassidy had told me about Ella's as we'd hurried after her outside Kenwood. I thought of the two boys now. I couldn't think where they'd come from, or when or why I'd invented them, but I remembered the way they'd accompanied me in my periphery vision, always by my side. I used to show them how to do things, how to build a den in the living room, how to make recipes of sticks and mud, and then at some point they'd just disappeared. 'They used to come everywhere with me,' I told Ella, as she put her hands in the cupboard, searched among the things inside. 'I used to talk to them all the time.'

'Well.' She slammed the cupboard door shut. 'You must have had no real friends then.'

'Oh, I did have friends,' I said, walking back towards the table, aware that I sounded defensive. 'I had plenty of friends. And children who have imaginary friends are usually very bright. So do you have one? Because if you do, then I'd like to meet them.'

'Well you can't.'

I remembered then how much I'd resented Mum and other adults asking me about my two imaginary friends. I felt I was being mocked, that they were being intrusive, that my made-up boys were my private affair, or perhaps it was because I knew they weren't real. 'What does your imaginary friend look like?' I asked.

'She looks just like me,' said Ella quickly, 'but she has black hair to here,' she pointed to her neck, 'and even though she's scary sometimes, I still like her.'

'Scary?' I stopped in the middle of the kitchen and stared at her. 'How do you mean, scary?'

'Oh, she just gets angry sometimes, but I still like her.'

'What does she get angry about?'

Ella shrugged. 'Here's the nuts,' she said, and she held out a packet of broken walnuts and shook it up and down in her hands.

As she put the packet on the table next to the other ingredients, I wondered if it was Ella's imaginary friend who'd made her run away from her father the day I saw him taking Bobby to the doctor's. Was it the imaginary friend who'd made her run across the carpet with the open pair of scissors, who'd told her to slap Cassidy as she stood in front of the painting at Kenwood, and then urged Ella to run off down the holly-lined pathway?

Maybe she'd invented this friend so she could have someone to talk to about her mother. But then again, she might just want to use the idea of an imaginary friend to put the blame for her behaviour on someone else.

'Guess what?' she asked, sitting down at the table. 'My friend knows what I'm thinking before I say it, and I know what she's thinking before she says it.'

Well of course she does, I wanted to say, because your friend is you and you are your friend, and as Ella continued to make her cake, I thought how a child could go a little crazy thinking things like this.

Once the cake was in the oven, Ella went up to the playroom, and a few minutes later the phone rang. I picked up the receiver, about to say hello, when I heard the sound of a man's voice, a tentative 'Honey . . . ?' I thought for a second it was a wrong number when suddenly Ella's voice came sharp and clear down the line: 'Daddy!' I knew I should hang up then, that at any moment one of them might realise I was listening in, but instead I covered my mouth with one hand to silence my breathing. Jonas was telling Ella something about his trip, that he would be back reasonably soon, and I heard her sniff as if she were about to cry. Then Jonas asked, 'Is Mrs B behaving herself?' and Ella laughed and began telling him in a rush about what she was watching on TV. Carefully I put down the phone. So he does care, I thought. He might not have any interest in answering my email about her school, but he does care about his daughter, he can tell when she's upset.

This afternoon, Shanice came by to drop off Cassidy and I opened the door to find her dressed head to foot in green.

'What a beautiful coat,' I said.

'Isn't it?' Shanice looked pleased. She's one of those rare women who enjoys a compliment; she didn't respond with 'Oh, this old thing' or 'It really doesn't fit me any more.' Instead she clearly thrives on being told that something she has is beautiful, presumably because she likes the idea that people envy her, that whatever it is that's being admired, you would like it too.

'It smells lovely in here,' Shanice said as she came into the kitchen.

'We've been baking.' Ella sounded a little boastful.

'Well isn't that nice?' But Shanice's smile was false, and the way she looked around the room, at the freshly made cake cooling on the rack and the ingredients that had yet to be put away, suggested that the scene of cosy domesticity irritated her. She walked towards the table and I saw her rest a finger on the mixing bowl for a second, before pushing it away.

'Do you want to lick it?' asked Ella.

'No thank you.'

'Mmmm.' Ella pointed at the cake and looked at Cassidy, a challenge in her eye. 'Doesn't that smell yummy?'

But her cousin just sat down at the table, picked up a fork and began to help herself to some broccoli left over from lunch.

'I've never seen her do that,' said Shanice, as her daughter speared a particularly large piece and put it in her mouth. 'She never eats her vegetables with me.'

'Oh well,' I said, moving the plate nearer to Cassidy. 'Children are always changing their tastes.' Cassidy made a point of swallowing the broccoli, and then reached for another piece, and it seemed so deliberate the way she did this, as if food has formed a convenient battleground between her and her mother. Shanice can't force Cassidy to eat something, and her daughter knows this; it is one thing her mother can't control. I looked at Shanice; saw a fleeting expression of distress on her face. 'I used to hate things when I was small that I love now,' I told her. 'Avocados, for example.'

Shanice nodded; she seemed to accept this. 'And where was that?'

'Sorry?'

'When you were small, where was that?'

'London.'

'You were born here?'

'Yes,' I said, and I realised it's been a long while since anyone has asked anything about me. Maybe Shanice has more curiosity than I'd thought, and given the chance she's not as self-centred as she appears.

'Well . . .' Shanice looked around the kitchen, her eyes drawn back to the bowl. 'I should be back about seven.' She gave her daughter a half-hearted wave. 'Do hope that's okay.'

CHAPTER FIFTEEN

After her mother had left, Cassidy asked to see where the guinea pig was; Bobby had told her it had died but perhaps she wanted to see the evidence for herself. So I let the children into Jonas's study, where Cassidy inspected Guinea's empty box and Bobby showed her his wilting memorial flowers. Ella refused to join them and stood impatiently in front of the photographs hanging from the picture rail.

'This is a pretty one, isn't it?' I asked, pointing at the elderly couple sitting on the swinging chair. 'Who are they?'

'That's my great-grandpa,' said Ella.

'Is it really?' I smiled to myself and ran my finger along the frame. 'And where does he live?'

'America, that's where my daddy's from.'

'He's my great-grandpa too,' muttered Cassidy, still crouched on the floor, perhaps not wanting to come anywhere near the hanging photograph after the slapping she'd received at Kenwood.

'No he's not,' said Ella. 'He's my daddy's grandpa, not yours.'

'What's he like?' I asked.

She looked uncertain. 'Why do you want to know?'

'I'm just interested, Ella, in your family. Do you ever see him?'

'No.'

'Well that *is* a shame. It must be nice to have a great-grandfather.'

'Why, don't you have one?'

'I don't think many people have a great-grandfather.' I turned and smiled at her. 'You're very lucky. So when was the last time you saw him?'

'Can't remember.' Ella shrugged as if this didn't matter but she looked as if there was a worry beginning to form in her head.

'Is he too elderly to travel?'

'Yes,' she said, so quickly that I knew she hadn't really thought about this.

'So do you write to him?'

'No.'

'Well that's a shame. It's good to stay in touch with family.'

'I want to write to him,' said Ella, and she looked at Cassidy as if daring her to say she wanted to too. 'I'm going to email him today on Daddy's computer.'

'Do you think your great-grandfather uses a computer? Maybe you could just write him a proper letter, with some drawings as well. Do you know his address?'

'Yes, it's in my address book, I got it for Christmas. He lives in Florida. That's in America where my daddy's from. And do you know what his name is?'

'No,' I said lightly. 'What's his name?'

'Rooster!' Ella laughed and nudged the photo with her

hand so that it swung precariously against the wall. 'My great-grandpa Rooster!'

This evening Shanice failed to turn up when she'd promised, and it wasn't until nine o'clock that Mark finally arrived to collect his daughter. 'Oops!' he said, stumbling a little on the doorstep. 'Don't tell Shanice!'

'Cassidy's fallen asleep in the playroom,' I told him, as if I hadn't noticed he was partly drunk. 'Why don't you come down and have a coffee and—'

'Sober up? Good idea.'

Mark sat down at the kitchen table while I made his coffee, and as I did he started to hum to himself, a strange tuneless sound as if he'd forgotten there was anyone else in the room. I wondered what he'd been doing that had made him collect his daughter so late, whether he'd been out celebrating with friends, or drinking alone at home.

'Couldn't Shanice come?' I asked.

'She's working late.' Mark laughed. 'Again.'

'It must be difficult,' I ventured. 'Trying to balance work and family.'

'Oh you don't know the half of it.' Mark tapped the table with his fingers. 'She was going to come, but something apparently came up. She thinks because I work from home I can just leave everything at the drop of a hat.'

I gave a sympathetic smile and handed him his coffee.

'And sometimes . . .' Mark stopped and blew on his cup, 'she does find it hard coming here.'

'To this house?' I looked at him in surprise, because Shanice hasn't shown any reluctance about coming to 68 Pembleton Crescent since I've been here; in fact she seems to relish it. Then Cassidy walked into the kitchen, her hands hanging by her sides, looking reproachful and exaggerating her sleepiness. At once Mark held out an arm and she fitted herself under it, and he kissed the top of her head and rubbed her back with a loving, protective touch, like a father should, like all fathers should.

'You smell of beer,' she said.

Mark laughed. 'Out of the mouths of babes. Don't worry, I'm not driving, we're walking.'

I went upstairs to get Cassidy's coat and bag, and came back to find Ella had joined her cousin at the table. She had squeezed herself in behind Mark and his daughter with her head bent down between them as if she wanted to become part of the hug. But then I realised she was standing like this because she was whispering. 'It was Rosie,' I heard her say. 'She killed Guinea.'

I stopped where I was; I could see Cassidy was on the verge of tears, but Ella simply nodded and whispered, 'I *saw* her kill Guinea.' When she looked up, she showed no reaction at seeing me there; there was no glimmer of guilt, no suggestion that she'd just been caught telling a ridiculous lie. Did she want to upset Cassidy or shock Mark, or did she think this was a way to get me in trouble?

Mark smiled and stood up, holding out his hand for his daughter, and I took them upstairs and said goodbye.

'Can I have hot chocolate before going to bed?' asked Ella, and when I didn't reply she demanded, 'Can I?'

'No,' I said, 'I don't think you can,' and I watched her stomp up to her bedroom, muttering over her shoulder.

CHAPTER SIXTEEN

It's Tuesday, and this evening, before I left for the Pembleton Crescent committee meeting, Ella asked what she could do while I was gone. 'Why don't you write to your great-grandfather?' I suggested, 'That might be nice. If you write to your great-grandpa Rooster.' So obediently she ran off to get her address book, a large hardback book covered with flying birds, and I was surprised to find it full of addresses, when most nine-year-old children barely if ever write a letter these days.

Ella insisted I read out the address so that she could label the envelope first.

'Rooster Murrey,' I read, 'Mount Royale. Ajax Drive.'

'How do you spell "Royale"?'

'It's with an "e" at the end,' I told her. 'It sounds like quite a grand place.'

'Yes, because my great-grandpa's very rich.'

'Is he really?' I asked as I watched her writing, her head bent over the envelope with studied concentration. I was curious to know just how rich he was, how he had made his money and what exactly he spent it on. 'How do you know he's very rich?'

But Ella didn't answer. 'Read the rest of the address,' she instructed.

'Tallahassee,' I said, 'Florida.'

'What's wrong?' Ella asked, looking up. 'Your voice went all funny.'

'Don't be silly,' I said, and I spelt out Tallahassee, and then I read out the zip code and told her to write United States of America.

'There,' she said. 'All done. Now we can send it to *Florida*.'

'Lovely,' I said. 'Well done.'

After Ella had started on her letter, and with Mrs B having volunteered to look after the children, I left for the committee meeting. At first I felt oddly liberated leaving the house, as if I was escaping from being a mother for an hour or so. I wouldn't have to think about whether the children had had enough to eat, whether Bobby needed his nappy changing, whether it was time for Ella to go to bed. But I also felt a little irresponsible leaving them, even with Mrs B – perhaps particularly with Mrs B – and the moment I closed the door and went down the steps without the buggy, it was as if I'd forgotten something. Then, as I set off down Pembleton Crescent, I realised I hadn't taken my keys, and this made me stop on the pavement, struck by a sudden irrational thought: what if I came back and they wouldn't let me in? What if I returned in an hour or so and I didn't have my keys and they refused to open the door? I hesitated, wondering whether to go back, but then I put my hands in my empty pockets and continued down the road.

* * *

Mrs B had told me where Felicity lived, the tall, brisk woman who'd come round on Sunday: in a house at the other end of the crescent with an added attic and garage. I knocked on the door and looked up at the rakish fellow whose stone face adorns the doorway; I've become so used to seeing this face over Jonas Murrey's door that I've almost forgotten he exists, but this evening he looked distinctly like a gargoyle.

Then I saw there was a note on the front door, telling visitors to go straight down to the basement. The flight of steps was short but steep and the wall narrowed suddenly as I reached the bottom and there was a strong smell of mildew. Through the partly open glass door I could see the meeting was already in progress. A dozen people, mainly women, sat around a long table, so long that there was barely space to pass at either end. There were bottles of wine, both red and white, on the table, and several large ceramic bowls of snacks. I knocked on the glass door, called hello and went in, wondering if I'd got the time wrong, and if I hadn't, then why they had invited me to come after everyone else.

As I went further into the room, no one moved. Then Felicity cast a look at a short elderly woman with a bright blue scarf around her neck, and she stood up and fetched me a chair. I had to squeeze myself past several women to reach the chosen spot, and because my chair was placed just out of the circle of other chairs, when I sat down I was not quite included in their gathering. I folded my arms together tightly, annoyed at the way I was deliberately being made to feel excluded.

'We're just finishing things off,' said Felicity. In front of her she had several sheets of paper and I could see she'd been busy scribbling with a thick black pen. There were no doodles, no idle patterns of aimless flowers; instead she'd drawn up a list of bullet points, with words underlined or boxed in. A woman at the far end of the table began outlining the problem with parking restrictions in Pembleton Crescent, and as she did, the elderly woman with the blue scarf whispered, 'Would you like some wine?' I nodded and she poured a very small amount of red wine into a glass and handed it to me. This seemed to cause a chain reaction around the table, and several women drew a bottle nearer and poured the remains into their glass, as if they feared that now I was here there would not be enough to go round.

'Now then,' said Felicity. 'We've come to antisocial behaviour.'

'There's a whole group of them!' burst out a woman to my right. 'They're in hoods—'

'Hoodies,' corrected her neighbour.

'And they lounge around at the corner. We just don't feel safe any more.'

I looked along the table, wondering who these hoodies were, until I realised Felicity was looking at me expectantly.

'Has Jonas briefed you?' she asked, pen poised.

'I'm sorry, no.' The people around the table exchanged looks.

'But,' said Felicity, 'haven't you spoken to him?'

'Not recently, no.'

'Is she Mrs Murrey?' I heard a woman whisper from somewhere to my left.

'No,' said Felicity. 'She's just the nanny.'

I felt my cheeks grow hot then, like a child who suddenly

becomes the centre of unwanted attention, and I shifted angrily in my chair. I'd given up my evening to come here, only to be dismissed as 'just' the nanny, and I gripped my wine glass, resisting the urge to lean over and slap Felicity in the face. 'So,' I said, trying to keep my voice steady. 'What was Jonas going to do?'

'Well,' she snapped. 'If you'd bothered to speak to him, then we would all know that,' and she sighed and scribbled angrily on her paper. 'Now then, we need a venue for our garden party in the summer and the host will need to do the catering. Any offers? No? Well I'll leave you all to have a think about that one.'

I returned home to find Mrs B standing at the open door, wearing her coat and hat. She shot out of the house the moment I came in and so I had no chance to ask what Jonas's thoughts might have been on antisocial behaviour. I walked upstairs a little wearily, and as I went into my bedroom I saw two letters carefully placed exactly on the centre of my bed, weighed down with small stones that must have been taken from the garden. Ella obviously wanted them to be the first thing I would see when I came back. One had been written by Bobby, a series of blue and yellow pen lines, perhaps made under his sister's instructions, while Ella's letter was another matter entirely, her handwriting firm and clear, each letter perfectly joined to the next. 'Dear Great-Grandpa Rooster, I'm so lucky to have a great-grandpa like you! And would you like to come here and see me because not many people have a great-grandpa and it's been so long since I saw you and family is very important you know . . .' She'd filled nearly an entire page and then she'd signed off with a flourish and drawn little stick figures at the bottom.

I read the letter through to the end and then read it again. It was perfect; her great-grandfather would have to have a heart of stone not to be moved by this. She'd even included him in the picture at the bottom; he was the figure with a walking stick and a bubble coming out of his mouth saying, 'I live in Florida!'

I sealed the envelope shut and held it in my hands, staring at the address, trying to imagine the man who lived at this place. Would he receive Ella's letter, and if he did, would he answer it? Finally I propped it up on my bedside table ready to be posted tomorrow.

I was just about to get ready for bed when I heard a sound from downstairs. I guessed it might be Ella, eager to know what I thought of her letter. I went down the stairs, treading softly and stopping at the doorway to their room. Bobby was breathing deeply, his arms flung out on either side of his cot, but Ella's bed was empty. Perhaps she was in the kitchen, I thought, sneaking an ice pop from the freezer, or maybe she'd gone to the bathroom. I was so busy thinking this that as I went down the next flight of stairs I didn't see the shadowy figure in the hallway at first. But there she was, fully dressed, with a rucksack on her back, reaching up to open the front door.

'Ella!'

She didn't appear to have heard me. Her body showed no reaction at all; instead she continued trying to open the door that I had Chubb-locked after Mrs B had left.

'What are you doing?' I asked, loudly now.

She heard me then, I could tell, but still she pulled at the door. I wondered what she'd packed in the rucksack:

clothes or food or whatever provisions she needed for wherever it was she thought she was going. 'It's locked,' I told her. 'Come on, let's get you back to bed.'

Ella did turn round then, her expression full of panic. 'I'm going to be late!'

'Late for what?' Perhaps she had the day wrong, perhaps she thought it was morning and she was late for school. 'Ella, please.' I went forward and touched her on the shoulder. 'It's the middle of the night, you need to go back to bed—'

'Go away!' she screamed, and I could see that she was awake now and not confused at all. 'I don't want a babysitter any more!'

'Ella, calm down and tell me what you're doing.'

'Ring my daddy. *Ring* him and tell him to come home!' and she whirled round in the hall, pushed past me, ran up the stairs and slammed her bedroom door.

CHAPTER SEVENTEEN

When I went down to the kitchen this morning to prepare Bobby's bottle of milk, I found Ella already at the table, quietly eating a bowl of cereal. 'Everything okay?'

Ella put down her spoon. 'It's gone all soggy.'

'You probably put too much milk in. Did you sleep all right?'

Ella nodded.

'After I found you in the hall?'

Ella looked at me, picked up the bowl and drank the rest of the milk.

'Do you remember? You were in the hall, with your rucksack on, and you were trying to go somewhere. Where were you going?' When she didn't answer, I took the chair opposite her and put down the email I'd printed out. Late last night I'd emailed Jonas Murrey about the committee meeting, and this morning he'd actually replied. *Rosie, Felicity Hamilton is a deluded woman with a lot of time and very little to do. Suggest you avoid her. Jonas.* I'd read it a few times, looking for clues. He hadn't started with 'Dear Rosie' or 'Hi Rosie', and I was slightly taken aback at the way he'd used my name. But I'd smiled at what he said about the committee woman; it was brief but mildly witty, and it made me feel better about the meeting and the way I'd been treated. I wondered about the history between Felicity and Jonas, but more than that, I wanted to know why he hadn't replied to my earlier email about Ella's school.

'What's that?' asked Ella.

'It's an email from your father. So, what was going on last night?'

For a moment I thought she was going to demand that I ring him again, but instead she just pushed away her bowl. 'Aren't you going to get Bobby up?'

So this was how she wanted it to be; once again we were supposed to pretend that nothing had happened. 'I liked your letter,' I said carefully. 'To your great-grandpa.'

Ella's shoulders relaxed and she looked pleased. 'It took me a really long time.'

'Yes, I could see that. It was beautifully written. We'll post it this morning, on the way to the park.'

'How long will it take to get to America?'

'I'm not sure, a few days.'

'So when will I get a letter back? Next week?'

'You could do,' I said, not wanting to raise anyone's hopes.

'How does it get there, by aeroplane?'

'That's right.'

'So when will I get a letter back?'

'Like I said, I don't know.' Impatiently I opened the fridge, took out the milk and poured it into Bobby's bottle. Then I turned on the kettle and waited for it to boil. 'So, about last night, what was going on?'

'Nothing.'

'It wasn't nothing, Ella!' I put Bobby's bottle in half a cup of hot water and stared at her seriously. 'You had a rucksack on your back and you were trying to leave home in the middle of the night! That's . . .' I was going to say dangerous but something stopped me. 'Do you even *remember* what you were doing?' Then Bobby shouted out from upstairs and I called back that I was just warming his milk, and when I hurried up to the bedroom with his bottle, he took it greedily. I lifted him out of his cot, breathing in his sweet early-morning toddler smell, feeling the heaviness of his little body on my hip, enjoying his unquestioning acceptance of me, the way he allows me to care for him and never asks who I am or where I came from or what I'm doing here. As we reached the hallway, a rubbish truck began to rumble along the street outside, I could feel a gentle tremble in the floorboards, and then we heard the sound of a motorbike starting up. Suddenly Bobby stiffened.

'What is it?' I asked.

'Don't like it.' He took the bottle from his mouth and held it out as if it tasted bad.

'You don't like it? Maybe you're too big for a bottle now.'

'No!' he howled. 'Don't like it,' and he pushed his head hard against my chest.

'Is it the motorbike? There's nothing to worry about, Bobby, it's just a motorbike.'

I carried him downstairs, and although he still seemed upset he let me put him in his high chair and went back to drinking his milk.

'You're such a crybaby,' said Ella, taking a banana from the fruit bowl.

'Don't be mean,' I snapped. 'He was just afraid of the motorbike; everyone's afraid of something.'

'What are you afraid of?'

'Me?' I laughed.

'Yes.' Ella started peeling her banana. 'What are you afraid of?'

'Well . . .' I looked at her, saw the familiar glint of challenge in her eyes. 'I'm afraid of children who tell lies.'

'It wasn't me.' She said it quickly and then put her head down as if she wished she hadn't spoken.

'It wasn't you who what?' I looked at her, knowing immediately what she had done. It was Ella who'd let the cat into her father's study; it was her who was responsible for the death of poor Bobby's pet. Maybe she'd been up during the night, wandering around the house, and had left the door open. Then she'd lied and blamed me to cover up her guilt. 'Did I tell you I had a letter from your school?'

Ella looked up, but didn't reply.

'They say they want to have a chat with your father.' I picked up the banana skin from where she'd put it carelessly on the table. 'What do you think that's about?'

'Dunno.'

'You said once that your teacher, Hannah, doesn't like you. Is it about that at all?'

'I don't *know*,' she said, getting down from her chair.

'Well then,' I said, 'I think it's about time we found out.'

And instead of looking worried, her expression was immensely pleased.

CHAPTER EIGHTEEN

> Muriel Wilson is very keen on lodgings. She says she desires
> a greater sense of freedom.
>
> **Branch home report, 15 May 1962**

How do you set yourself into the world when there is no
one behind you to urge you on? When you have no one
who believes in you, no one to offer any encouragement.
Then you must rely on yourself. And that is what I have
always done.

The day I left Hoodfield House, Mr Appleyard called
me into his office and had me stand in front of his desk.
I can see myself now in my school uniform. The thin black
skirt pinching my waist, the green and yellow tie around
my neck. He got up, reached under his chair and put a
suitcase on the desk. It was the colour of blancmange,
with a soft top and hard sides. He opened a drawer, took
out a bible and laid it on top of the suitcase. Then he
handed me a sheet of paper.

'Your birth certificate,' he said.

I looked at it, because I knew I was supposed to. It was

a thin yellow sheet criss-crossed with bright red lines. It gave my name and birth date. It said where I was born. It gave my mother's name. There was a signature and an address. But where my father's name should have been, there was nothing. Just a thin black dash. Was this it? I thought. Was this all anyone knew about my life?

I wasn't that surprised that his name wasn't there. I had never given him much thought. It was like I had never had a father. I didn't know anything about him. I didn't know his name. Or what he did. Or where he was. But as I stared at my mother's name I thought, as I often did by then, why couldn't my mam have kept me? Other women must have managed, even if they hadn't been married. They still kept their child. Why had she never claimed me? Had there really been no alternative? Had I been so bad that she didn't want me?

I pictured her the day she had left. Her camel-hair coat. Her handbag and matching gloves. I thought of how she had tucked the sheet under my chin and promised to be there when I woke up. Only she wasn't. And that was why I was standing in Mr Appleyard's office at the age of sixteen, with no one to help me go into the world.

I said thank you, folded up the certificate and stood there, waiting.

'Any plans?' Mr Appleyard asked, not that he cared if I had. He was a man with no real sense of occasion. And he had had enough of me by then. I was no longer the easy child I'd once been. The pleasant-natured girl who would give anyone a cuddle. The girl who had only wanted to belong and be good. I had grown resentful about a lot of things. Why they had never found me foster parents. Why I had had to spend my life at Hoodfield House. I was an adolescent now, full of hormones and anger. I wanted to leave. I wanted my own place with a real desperation. So I told him. After my A levels, I intended to go to university and study English.

Mr Appleyard laughed. 'You should look for a clerical job, Muriel.'

That was what the educational adviser had said, when he'd come to Hoodfield House. He had suggested I obtain factory work. When I said I didn't want factory work, he said training as a nursery nurse or clerical work might be a possibility. And when I explained what I really wanted to do, he had looked at me in disbelief. 'You should be thinking about employment opportunities, young lady. Although I have to say, in your case there are very few openings for jobs . . . entailing contact with the public.' The educational adviser had stopped then, waited until I had understood. 'We wouldn't want you to risk rebuffs by setting your heart on something when you will almost certainly have to be content with an alternative.' But I wasn't content with an alternative. I wasn't content at all.

Later that day the new assistant matron, Miss Cleary, a kindly lady who had been at Hoodfield House only a few months, called me to her room. She was young, with heavy backcombed hair like a glossy balloon, and long pink nails.

'So you're leaving us today.' She made a sad expression with her mouth. 'And Mr Appleyard, he's given you your birth certificate? If there is anything you wanted to know, you can always ask me.'

Miss Cleary had not spoken to me like this before and I sensed that she wished she had. The rules were changing by then. Staff were allowed to know more about the histories of the children, although the children themselves were still kept largely in the dark. I stared at Miss Cleary's bouffant hair, mumbled something about my mam.

'Yes, your mother. Her name was Dorothy Wilson and she was from Whitehaven. That's in Cumberland. She was very young when she had you. And your father, he was an American soldier.' Miss Cleary looked down at her nails. 'A coloured soldier. From Louisiana.'

I stood there, rooted to the spot. Because no one had ever said anything about my father before. There was never any suggestion that I even had a father. Except that one Christmas afternoon when the little girl's mother had said I was a Yank's child and should go home. How did Miss Cleary know where he was from? And Louisiana, it sounded like a girl's name. It sounded like a nice warm place. Was he there now, was that where he lived? But unable to ask the questions I really wanted to, I thanked Miss Cleary and got up from my chair.

'Even though you're leaving our care,' she said as I reached the door, 'remember you're still a member of the family.' Then she handed me a stamped addressed envelope and said I should keep the home up to date with any news.

I went back to the bedroom and opened the suitcase Mr Appleyard had given me. There were so many pockets and compartments inside. For a moment I was happy and full of anticipation. Then I saw that one of the pockets had been torn. There was a stain on the lining, so dark it almost looked wet. But I put the birth certificate and the bible into the suitcase, along with my clothes, my allowance and my meagre belongings, and I left.

Lodgings had been arranged for me. I was to rent a small room in a house belonging to a landlady named Mrs Kettle. I had seen the room. There was a bed, a table, an upright chair and a gas fire. And it was all mine. For the first time in my life I wouldn't have to share with anyone.

So I walked out with my suitcase, trying not to look behind me at the gloomy biscuit-coloured walls of Hoodfield House. For however much I wanted to leave the home, I was still attached to the place. It was all I knew. It was where I'd spent my childhood. Made my friends. Dreamed my dreams. Conquered my fears. It was where I'd played with Susan, and pretended Mrs McGregor was my very own adult. It was where I'd learned to survive. And now I was leaving, going into the world all alone.

Once I had finished college and left Mrs Kettle's house, I moved to London with my friend Barbara. I was still hoping to earn the money for university, applying for jobs that no one wanted to give me. And it was then that I tried, for the first and only time, to find my mam. One day I took my birth certificate from where I kept it at the bottom of my old branch home suitcase, and I looked at it and made a plan. It was an autumn day, with a dusting of leaves on the streets, when I took a bus to St Mary's Hospital in Paddington. I stood beneath the entrance bridge before the large iron gates, watching people pass by. Nurses in their smart uniforms. Ambulance drivers and deliverymen. Reluctant patients and anxious visitors. All busy with their work and their lives. And it seemed so pointless. Because I didn't know what I would learn about myself or my mam by seeing the ward where I had been born. What questions could that possibly answer for me?

A week later I took another bus, to Maida Vale, to my mother's address on my birth certificate. I walked along a long tree-lined avenue. The houses were white-pillared and handsome. But then they stopped and there were two derelict homes and a new high-rise block. The house number I wanted was gone. In its place was a carpet shop, with slabs of carpet samples in the window, as brown as discoloured meat.

I tried to imagine the house that had been there and how my mam might have lived. Had she come whistling down the path in the evening, glad to get home and out of the cold? Had she opened the door in the morning, happy to start a new day? Had she ever woken in the night thinking about the daughter she had left all alone in a children's home? I tried to remember anything of my life before Hoodfield House. And I couldn't recall a single thing.

I still can't, however hard I try. It makes me think of a party I once went to as a child. At the beginning of the party I saw the child's mother wrapping presents for the lucky dip. I saw her wrap one particular prize. It was a shiny little yellow notebook with its own matching pen. And I wanted that prize with all my heart. But when I put my hand in the lucky dip box and rustled around in the torn-up newspaper, I couldn't find it. Each time my fingers found a prize, I could tell, by the shape and the weight, that it wasn't the one I wanted. I knew it was in there somewhere, but I didn't know where. The other children grew annoyed. They began to complain. They wanted to take their turn. And so I was forced to pull out a small rubber ball that I didn't want at all.

It is the same when I try to remember my life before

the age of four. My mam before she left me. Those memories must be here somewhere. It is finding them that is the difficulty.

That day outside the carpet shop, I felt a sadness that has never really lifted. It was the heavy weight of not knowing who I was. But I went back to the flat I shared with Barbara, sat down on the sofa and turned on the television. I remember the news that day. It was the race riots in America. I watched with horror as people were sprayed with water. Charged with horses. Beaten with batons. Shot with guns. I saw their houses and their businesses burn. Lifeless bodies carried away. And I thought, I might never know where my mam is. But is my father there, is that where he is?

I had a phone call from my daughter this morning. I asked her how she was and she said she was fine. Then I asked her where she was and she sighed. 'I've told you, Mum, I have a new job and I'm living in.' Yes, I said, but where? 'London,' she said. I asked her where in London. 'Does it matter?' she asked. And I thought, yes, it certainly does. 'In north London,' she said. 'You wouldn't know it.'

She said she wanted advice. She's looking after a little girl and boy. She thinks the girl might be sleepwalking and isn't sure what to do. I told her sleepwalking is fairly common and not to worry too much about it. 'You used to sleepwalk, didn't you, Mum?' And I told her yes, but that was a long time ago. 'But how did you stop?' I said I didn't know, but that I had a very close friend and that seemed to help. I asked if the girl remembers in the morning that she sleepwalked, as I usually didn't. I said if other people knew, it could be very embarrassing, as it had been for me. Then I asked what the girl's mother thought of the sleepwalking and my daughter said there was no mother, only a father.

I asked her if she wanted me to come round. 'No,' she said at once. 'I can cope.'

I have no idea why she's being so mysterious. What is going on that she can't tell her own mother? Just try not to wake the girl, I told her, or restrain her. Just make sure all the windows are locked, that there's nothing she might stumble on or break, and that she can't come to any harm.

'Of course she's not going to come to any harm,' said my daughter. 'Why would you say that?' And then she said she had to go and hung up.

CHAPTER NINETEEN

It's Saturday, and this morning I had another email from Jonas Murrey. *Rosie, re Ella's school, yes you can go in. Jonas.* There's no explanation as to why he's finally decided to answer my earlier email and it doesn't give me much to go on in terms of what the actual problem is. It also irritates me the way he says I *can* go in, as if I've been asking permission to do this, rather than the truth, which is that the school has been asking *him* to do something. But when school starts on Monday, I'll find out what it is that Ella's teacher wants to speak to him about.

The past few days have passed relatively quickly. Ella hasn't shown any more signs of sleepwalking and I haven't seen her talking to her imaginary friend, but I've made sure all the windows are locked at night, as Mum advised, including the one in my bathroom which I usually keep a little open. I've also insisted that the glass of water Ella has beside her bed has been replaced with a plastic mug, just in case she breaks it by accident.

*　　*　　*

Cassidy came round this afternoon after I rang to invite her swimming. Shanice arrived wearing a beautiful red pashmina, and she was laden down with an expensive waterproof swimming bag containing a costume, a thick soft towel, a pair of pink goggles, a small packet of earplugs and brand-new miniature bottles of shampoo and shower gel. She'd also packed a Tupperware box with slices of carrot and cucumber, which she made a point of showing me, saying, 'And these are because she seems to eat her vegetables with you.'

'Will you be picking her up?' I asked.

'No, her father will today. If he remembers.'

'It must be hard,' I said, putting Cassidy's swimming things on the table. 'Juggling a business and a family.'

'Oh.' Shanice gave a tense laugh. 'Not all of us can stay at home and just . . .' She looked around the kitchen, her expression a little embarrassed. 'What I mean is, we women are very good at multitasking.'

'Yes,' I agreed, 'although sometimes I think that's only because it's forced on us.'

Shanice looked at me with interest, as if impressed by the fact that I'd made a valid point; she even seemed about to engage me in a proper conversation, but then her mobile rang and she pulled it out of her handbag. I watched as she began circling the table, speaking rapidly into her phone. As she walked she began to unwrap the pashmina from around her shoulders, and then she flung it over a chair. Finally she waved at her daughter, and she was up the stairs and gone, still talking on her mobile phone.

We walked to the swimming baths and the children seemed excited at the outing. But while Cassidy happily changed in the communal area, ripping off her T-shirt and struggling out of her shorts, Ella was surprisingly self-conscious. She insisted on having her own cubicle; she spent some time making sure the curtain was fully closed, and she was furious when Cassidy pulled it back some ten minutes later to ask if her cousin was ready.

At last Ella came out. Cassidy was wearing a new blue Speedo, but Ella's suit was childish and decorated with purple fish, and she obviously hasn't been swimming for so long that no one has thought to see if her costume still fits.

'It's tight,' she hissed as we made our way to the pool, and she pulled on the straps, which I could see were already making dents in her skin. 'Everyone's going to be looking at me.'

'It'll be fine for now,' I said, 'and we can get you a new one later.'

The girls dived into the water – I had the feeling Ella wanted to submerge herself as quickly as possible – while I waded in with Bobby on my hip. I put him down gently in the shallow area and he bobbed around in his water wings like a jellyfish. I was just trying to teach him how to kick his legs when I realised the girls had gone. The pool was crowded, a mass of sleek-haired children and flying limbs, and I panicked for a moment. Then I saw Ella on the far right-hand side of the pool, walking up a flight of stairs that led to a long yellow zigzagging chute. I saw her stop and I thought she was waving at me until I realised Cassidy was behind her and she was urging her on. I saw Cassidy stop suddenly and hold on to the railings. She was blocking a group of children behind her; she must have lost her nerve. I called out to her to come down, but when she started walking up the stairs again, I pulled Bobby on to my back and swam to the area where the chute ended.

I could see, in the fibreglass walls, the shadow of someone coming down, and then Ella shot out, feet first, laughing. But she didn't stand up, although she must have known what would happen next, because Cassidy was right behind her. Her cousin came down in an awkward position with her knees stuck out, and she banged into Ella with an open-mouthed scream. Still Ella didn't move, so I stood up in the shallow end and shouted, 'Ella! Get up so Cassidy can get up!' but the pool was so noisy I wasn't sure if she'd heard. 'Ella!' I cried as I struggled to get out of the pool. Any sympathy I'd felt earlier had gone, and I wondered whether the problem at school might be that Ella was a bully. Because that was what she'd just done: she'd bullied Cassidy into doing something she was afraid of; she'd forced her up the stairs and down the chute. I didn't know if she only did this with Cassidy, because she knew her cousin wouldn't fight back, or if she did it with other children as well. I wasn't sure if she'd made Cassidy go down the slide as revenge for the way her cousin had opened the curtain of the changing cubicle, or if it was more than this. Maybe Ella was jealous of Cassidy because her cousin had a mother and she didn't.

'When does the post come today?' Ella asked as we got on to the bus.

'I'm not sure, why?'

'Do you think when we get home my great-grandpa Rooster will have written to me?'

'It's only been a few days, Ella,' I said. 'Let's be patient.'

∗ ∗ ∗

At five o'clock, to my surprise, both Shanice and Mark arrived at Pembleton Crescent. 'You could have asked,' said Shanice as I opened the door. I couldn't think what she meant at first, until I looked down and remembered I was wearing her pashmina. I'd been in the kitchen making the children a snack after swimming, and I'd just picked it up and draped it around me. Ella had seemed pleased; she'd stroked it for quite a while and said it suited me. For a second I thought Shanice might be flattered that I had it on, that it showed just how much I admired her clothes, but evidently not. Instead she clicked her fingers and held out her hand and waited while I took off the cashmere shawl and handed it back.

'I'm so sorry,' I said. 'I was cold.' And then, when I turned at the top of the stairway, I saw Shanice hold the pashmina quickly to her nose. I wasn't sure if she knew I'd seen her, but I found myself walking noisily down the stairs, my shoes slapping on the boards. Did she think I was dirty? Did she not like my smell? Did she not think a nanny should be wearing her precious clothes?

'Hey there,' Shanice called to her daughter. 'Did you have a lovely time?' Cassidy looked at me, perhaps about to mention the chute, but then she nodded. 'Can I watch *Doctor Who* later?'

'Ask your father.'

Mark smiled and sat down. 'I'm the babysitter tonight.'

Shanice slammed her hand on the table. 'How *can* you say that?'

'What?' Mark looked bewildered.

'That you're the babysitter, when you're her *father*! A mother would never say that. She would never say she was babysitting her own child!'

Mark hung his head, began humming quietly.

'So,' said Shanice, looking at me. 'Have you heard from Jonas?'

'Yes, I had an email—'

'Oh, an *email* . . .' Shanice pulled angrily at the shawl around her shoulders.

'Honey,' said Mark, and he held out one hand as if to calm her, but when she glared at him, he put it down.

'Not a phone call, then?' Shanice looked around the room, her voice increasingly shrill. 'Not some actual human contact?'

Ella came sidling up to me, perhaps sensing that her father was being criticised, and tugged at the hem of my shirt. 'I'm hungry.'

'Well,' said Shanice, 'I'm sure your babysitter will make you a lovely snack, won't she?' and she grabbed Cassidy's swimming bag and marched out of the room.

After they had left, Ella and Bobby went to the playroom while Mrs B cleaned the kitchen, and when I heard the phone ring and then stop I resisted the urge to pick it up, assuming Ella was speaking to her father. I watched as Mrs B began dusting the vast table with a brush attached to her vacuum cleaner, moving steadily in the direction of the grain. 'You know what you said about the children's mother?' I asked, and at once I saw her back stiffen. 'Where were the children at the time? Were they there?'

'No.' Mrs B turned off the vacuum cleaner. 'The children weren't there.'

'Where were they?'

'Well . . .' Mrs B bent and dipped a cloth into a bucket

of soapy water, slowly wrung it out. 'Shanice said she would look after them . . .'

'She was supposed to look after them here?'

'That's right.' Mrs B grunted slightly as she wiped the wet cloth across the table. 'But in the end I did.'

I watched her as she dried the table with a clean cloth, thinking of what Mark had said, that sometimes Shanice found it hard coming here. I'd been puzzled at his comment, because every time she came she tried to show me the place was hers, flinging her clothes around and opening the fridge and pacing around the kitchen. Now I could see that maybe she wanted to make her mark on the house because she feels she let her sister down. She wishes she had looked after the children that weekend and every time she comes here she must remember what she'd promised to do. Maybe she'd never even known how ill Isabella really was, and her anger about this house wasn't directed at me at all; it was because it belonged to Jonas and she hated him.

I thought of how Shanice had found us baking and how annoyed she'd seemed, how irritated at the scene of cosy domesticity. She'd rested her finger on the edge of the mixing bowl and then pushed it away as if it offended her. Because she'd come into the house to find me, the babysitter, in her sister's place, baking with her niece just like her sister used to do.

'Do the children know?' I asked. 'What happened to their mother?'

Mrs B didn't reply. She opened a jar, dipped the end of the cloth into the wax.

'Did they go to her funeral?'

Mrs B shook her head.

'But don't they ever ask what happened? They must do, especially Ella. What have they been told?'

'Mr Murrey,' said Mrs B, her lips tight as she began to rub the wax across the table, 'will not talk about it. Which is his prerogative, don't you think?'

CHAPTER TWENTY

I was glad to get the children to bed tonight so I could have the place to myself before Amina arrived. She texted me last night to say she'd found some information about Dido Elizabeth Belle. 'I'll come to you,' she wrote, and without really thinking straight, I'd sent her my address. I bought some wine and made a pasta sauce the way she likes it, with plenty of chorizo, and I enjoyed being in the kitchen and making an adult meal for once. I turned the lights down, put on some music, laid the table and made everything look pretty and welcoming, as if it were my home and I was proud of it.

'Hello, doll!' said Amina when I opened the front door. 'Nice house!'

'Do come in,' I said in a posh voice, and Amina laughed. I watched as she came into the hallway and looked around, inspecting the prints on the wall, peering closer to see if there were any titles or dates. Ever since we first met on our teacher-training course, I've always liked the way Amina is so alert to her surroundings. Her love of local history and her hobby building family trees for people means she can't look at an image without wanting to know more about it.

'So whose house is this?' she asked.

'It's a nanny job.' I took her coat, a favourite grey army jacket with silver buttons, and hung it up. 'Didn't I tell you?'

'No.' She looked at me cautiously. 'You didn't tell me. So this is where you've been hiding. You okay?'

'I'm fine,' I told her, leading the way down to the kitchen. I put the pasta on, opened a bottle of wine, and we started chatting. Amina wanted to make a trip to Cornwall; mutual friends had a wedding planned for next summer, and it felt good to talk about someone else for once. An old group of us used to meet up regularly, but since last winter I've fallen out of touch with everyone, except Amina.

'So how did you get this job?' She put the hessian bag she always carries with her on the table.

'It was advertised,' I told her, busying myself with draining the pasta, wanting to make it sound as if it was just coincidence that I'd ended up here at Pembleton Crescent.

'Does it pay well?'

'Better than school,' I laughed.

Amina looked at me with sympathy. 'Are you glad you left?'

'Definitely.' I handed her a plate and asked what she'd found out about Kenwood.

She took a pile of photocopied articles out of her bag, and then a book, its cover showing a glorious summery photograph of Kenwood and the lawn. On the flyleaf inside, in childish blue pen, someone had written *6th June*

1998 with Nana B and it was lovely. The grandmother must have bought the book as a memento of their time together, then the child had grown up and the nana had died, and the book had been sent to a charity shop or jumble sale where Amina had found it. It seemed sad that a day that had meant so much had now been forgotten, that the book had been given away along with the memory.

'What is it you wanted to know?' Amina started to eat, and then she picked up her wine glass and held it as she always does, with both hands.

'Oh, it's just for the children I'm looking after. Bobby's two and Ella is nine, and I took them there last Saturday and Ella was fascinated by one of the paintings.' I flicked through the book, past images of floor plans and earls, bedchambers and stairways, until eventually, in the final few pages, I came to the painting of Dido Elizabeth Belle. 'This is the one.'

'Yes, I looked at that. Dido's an interesting figure.'

'Isn't she?' I said, pleased Amina thought so as well.

'London's first black aristocrat, according to the book, daughter of a Scottish baronet and a Cuban woman.'

'Was she Cuban? I thought she was African.'

Amina put down her glass and leant across the table, pointing at the picture of Dido and her cousin. 'No one knows really why this was done, or even who painted it, but it looks like whoever did do it had two goes.'

'How do you mean?'

'Dido's costume is from a later date than her cousin's, so there was probably already a portrait of Elizabeth and then someone wanted the two of them together. The original had the cousin with her arm held out, so the second time around the painter had to fit Dido in there as well.'

'That's why it looks so awkward.' I stared at the picture, remembering the day I'd seen the portrait with Ella and how out of place it had seemed in that grand Kenwood room. 'I thought her cousin was pushing her away.'

Amina laughed. 'Why would you think that? That's so like you!'

I shrugged and closed the book, began to eat my meal. 'What do you think happened to Dido's mother?'

'I don't know, doll. There don't seem to be any records on her.'

'Do you think she was a slave?'

'Probably. It seems like she was on a Spanish vessel that was captured by the British.'

'Then she came here and gave birth to Dido?'

'That's not clear. From what I've read, Dido might have been born in the Caribbean and her father brought her here later. There is an English baptism certificate apparently.'

'And is her father's name on the certificate?'

Amina shook her head. 'I don't know.'

'So there's nothing? Just a black dash across the page?'

'Well I don't know, Rosie, because I haven't seen it, but—'

'And so Dido ended up with her father's uncle?'

'That's right.'

'Then what did the father do?'

'He went back to sea.'

'So he didn't give a shit about his daughter, then.'

'Rosie!' Amina looked shocked at my outburst. 'He was in the Royal Navy, that's what he did. He must have cared enough about her to put her in the care of his uncle. If she was born in the West Indies, he could have just left her there, couldn't he? And if she was born here, then he could have just fobbed her off with anyone. She was illegitimate and her mother was black; what rights did she have? And if that had happened, then we'd never have known anything about her.'

'But how did Dido live, do you think?' I finished my food, put down my fork. 'Were they nice to her? Were they kind?'

'Well, this,' Amina pointed at the book, 'says she was treated as part of the family.'

I laughed. 'But she wasn't, was she?'

'No,' Amina said carefully. 'My guess is she had a sort of twilight position, neither servant nor family. Maybe you could ask to see the documents at Kenwood. She apparently had some influence over her great-uncle when he made a landmark ruling in a famous anti-slavery case.'

'Yes, I read about that.'

'Although she would have been tiny at the time.'

'And what happened after her great-uncle died?'

'That I don't know.'

'And her father never even visited her.'

'How do you know that?'

'Said it in a booklet at Kenwood, that it wasn't known if he ever visited her.'

'Well he must have visited his uncle; he would have seen her then.' Amina pushed away her plate, picked up her glass and drank her wine. 'Why are you so interested anyway? Are we on another genealogical wild goose chase?'

I took her glass and filled it up again. I was aware of how much she'd helped me last year. I thought how patient she'd been with my endless questions, my overriding need to know, my futile never-ending search. Then I saw she was staring at me and I put down the bottle, realised it was empty.

'So what's going on? I haven't heard from you for God knows how long; you email me out of the blue, and then you're here . . .' She raised her eyebrows, gestured round the kitchen, and I knew I was crazy to ever have invited her round. 'How many times have I texted you in the past five months? I was getting worried.'

I was about to say I hadn't got any messages, but she knew I would have seen them. 'I wasn't . . .' I hesitated, trying to think what words to use. 'I wasn't feeling too good.'

Amina looked concerned. 'Why didn't you tell me?'

'Oh, it was nothing. Some sort of . . . I don't know, but it laid me low for a while.'

'I would have come round.'

'I know,' I said. 'Thanks,' and I stood up and gathered our plates.

'So who is it you're working for?'

'He's some sort of lawyer, very wealthy.'

'I can see that.' Again Amina looked around the kitchen, at the gleaming surfaces, the expensive furniture. 'And what does she do?'

'There isn't any she. It's only him.'

'And he doesn't mind you inviting friends round?'

'No.'

'It's a long way for you to come from Clapham every day. What time does he come home?'

'I live in,' I said, putting our plates in the dishwasher.

'You what?'

'I have a room upstairs.'

'What, with the father here as well?'

'He's away. In America.'

'America? So it's just you and the kids in this big house?'

I smiled as if this wasn't something to be worried about, put a tablet in the drawer of the dishwasher and slammed it shut.

'And what about the kids? Can I meet them?'

'They're asleep.'

'Wake them up, then.' Amina laughed.

'Next time,' I said, and I turned on the dishwasher and the kitchen filled with a loud churning sound.

CHAPTER TWENTY-ONE

This morning I took Bobby to nursery and Ella to school, and both seemed glad to be back to their old routine, with Ella running off the moment we got to the playground gates. I went to the school office to ask to speak with Ella's teacher, to be told she's on a course until Thursday, and then I decided to go to Kenwood, because ever since our first trip I've thought about going back, but on my own this time rather than with the children. I didn't have long, I had to be back to pick Bobby up at lunchtime, so I set off quickly, catching a bus to the tennis courts where Cassidy's father dropped us the other week.

It was windy on the heath, as if the world was on a tilt and all the trees forced to lean to one side. The noises of city life seemed to be picked up on the air and blown away, and once or twice I thought I heard Ella calling for me, when it was only the muffled cry of a crow. I walked the way I'd gone before, and as I passed a pond I heard a watery clapping sound and caught a glimpse of white through the railings as a swan skated the surface, rose up and was gone.

I turned right and made my way up the muddy hill, where a woman sat motionless on a bench. In the distance I could see a man with a pack of dogs, different shapes and sizes and colours, all sniffing and meandering in the long grass, and I wondered what this place had been like hundreds of years ago. Were there animals here then, boars perhaps, or deer, and roaming hunting parties of Georgian gentlemen, and would Dido have cared for their horses, or prepared the meat from whatever animal was killed, and would she have taken part in the feast that followed?

The pathway to Kenwood seemed gloomier today, dark and dank and overgrown, and just before I entered it, I looked behind me at the tip of the London skyline, shimmering like a far-off fantasy island. The holly leaves glistened and the air was still; sunlight filtered through the trees, making dappled patches on the pathway. It was so still that I flinched at the sudden flight of a magpie between the trees, and the denseness of the bushes to my left played with my sense of perspective. I couldn't tell how far back the landscape went, how many layers there were before the woods ended.

Then the path became more even and less overgrown. I walked into a blast of sunshine, and while I knew what I was expecting, it was still impressive the way the cream walls of the house could just be seen at the crest of the hill.

Kenwood felt very different on a Monday morning; there was no one promenading on the pathway, and I was more cautious this time; I didn't need to rush to the front of the house, eager to get children out of the rain. I walked through the archway that Ella had said was spooky and then followed the path round to the front pillars and in through the doors. There was no one at the entrance desk, and I stopped and looked at the books and leaflets on display, before setting off in the direction I'd first followed Ella and Cassidy.

The house seemed less grand this morning, the walls drabber, the furniture less imposing, and however wealthy the surroundings, it felt more like someone's actual home. I could almost picture a roaring fire in the fireplace, hear the patter of a servant's feet upon the shiny wooden floor as she brought a tray of coffee to her mistress.

I made my way to the room with the painting of Dido. It was quiet and empty: no breathless guide, no other visitors. I stopped and looked at the portrait, at the way Dido had one finger to her cheek, as if bringing attention to the colour of her skin, and I thought of what Amina had said, that Dido had been added to the portrait because someone wanted the two girls together. I wondered what she had thought of the artist's decision to paint her like this, whether she had liked the way she looked, if she'd found the image flattering or false, or whether she'd ever seen the picture at all.

After Amina had left last night, I'd gone through the articles she'd brought. One called Dido a 'famous black beauty' and said her mother had been discovered on a ship held captive; another called her 'the mulatto', and described her mother as 'a black' who'd been taken prisoner by the man who would become Dido's father. It stated this simply, with no acknowledgement of the potential horror this implied, if she had been a prisoner and Sir John Lindsay had made her pregnant. Had she had any choice? Was he her rescuer and he'd set her free, or was she still enslaved?

Perhaps this was why I'd slept badly, endlessly plunging in and out of troubled dreams that I couldn't quite remember when I opened my eyes. And I'd tried not to think about Amina's questions: who I was working for, whose house it was, and how I'd got the job. It had been careless of me to ask her round. I'd been so pleased when she'd told me she'd found out about Dido that it was only after she arrived that I'd realised what I'd done.

I stood staring at the painting. I thought about how Ella had said I looked like Dido, and I tried to imagine what it would have been like to live in this house with its gilded mirrors and chandeliers, to have strolled its rolling lawns, a million miles from London's dirty streets. I could almost see myself doing this; feel the sweep of a long dress against my legs, the rustle of petticoats underneath.

Then I came to the library and stopped, looking up in awe at the high blue ceiling, because however ridiculous it seemed, there was something that made me feel I knew this room, that impelled me to walk towards the curved wall of books. I didn't know if I would be allowed to touch them, but I wanted to find out; I wanted to know how it would feel to pull one from the shelf, how the pages would smell when I opened them, what the story would be inside.

I thought of Mum, how even when I'd outgrown bedtime stories, she'd always wanted to choose a book and read it to me. She would tell me which story had been Dad's favourite, and sometimes I would let her get on the bed with me and open the book and start reading in her bedtime story voice. But other times I hadn't, and I felt sorry now for all the evenings I'd said no, I didn't like that book, I was too old or too tired, I could read to myself. Then from somewhere in the house a clock began to chime, and I knew that if I didn't leave to fetch Bobby, I would be late.

Before I left Kenwood I asked the man at the entrance desk whether it would be possible to see any documents relating to Dido Elizabeth Belle. He said he believed there was an account book, but the curator was on maternity leave. If I left an email address he would ask someone to get in touch. 'We don't allow original documents to be handled, except under supervision,' he said.

'Of course not,' I replied. 'I'd be very careful.'

Still he didn't look sure.

'It's for a school project,' I said. 'I thought it would be very educational.' And he smiled now, so that I knew this was the right thing to say.

The wind had died down as I walked back across the heath, and I stopped and sat on a bench for a moment, enjoying the silence. I thought about Dido and whether her adoptive family had let her read the books in the beautiful library, and then I thought of Mum, a motherless child in a children's home with no one to read her bedtime stories at all.

CHAPTER TWENTY-TWO

It's Wednesday, and this morning we had a surprise in the post, just as we were leaving for school. Ella saw it before I did and shouted, 'Look, it's for me!'

'Let me see,' I said, as she crouched down to pick a postcard from the doormat.

'No! It's mine!'

'Yes, but let me just see . . .'

She held up the postcard and I saw she was right: there was a blue airmail sticker and an American stamp, and it was addressed to Ella Murrey at 68 Pembleton Crescent. 'I told you!' she cried. 'I *told* you my great-grandpa Rooster would write to me!'

'Well isn't that lovely?' I sat down abruptly on the stairs, began helping Bobby into his coat, but my hands were clumsy and I couldn't seem to work out how to get his arms into the sleeves. I couldn't believe it. It's been barely ten days since Ella sent her letter, and her great-grandfather is obviously so keen to communicate with her that he's replied by return of post. 'Hang on!' I snapped unfairly, holding Bobby by the arm. 'Just stand still.' I forced myself to concentrate, to work out what went where, but when I did finally manage to get his coat on, I realised I'd done up the buttons in the wrong order and had to start all over again.

'I got a card!' said Ella, waving it in front of my face.

'So what does it say?'

'I don't know.' She handed me the postcard. 'It's not very good handwriting.'

I looked at the card; the front was colourful, a swirl of palm trees and flowers, cartoon alligators and holiday-makers on a beach, while on the other side the writing was spindly and slightly smudged. I touched the stamp on the right-hand corner, pressing my fingers down on the serrated edges where they were coming unstuck, thinking about the man who had put it here, who had taken the time to go to a shop and buy a pretty postcard for his great-granddaughter, to address it and stamp and post it, to send it all the way here.

'Read it!' said Ella.

Still I looked at the card, not quite able to take it in. 'It says, "Dear Ella, thank you for your lovely letter, I was very happy to get it. What beautiful handwriting you have! How are you and your little brother? Please write me again."' Then great-grandpa Rooster had signed his name and in bold capital letters he'd added an email address.

'You see!' said Ella triumphantly, looking over my shoulder. 'He does have email!'

'Well indeed he does.' I stood up, took my coat off the hallway hook and quickly zipped it up. 'Let's go.'

'But I want to email him now,' said Ella, throwing down her school bag.

I hesitated, looking at my watch. 'No, we'll have to do it later, there's no time now.'

'But—'

'I know, Ella, I know, but we can't do it now or we'll be late. Put the card in your school bag and let's go.' Then I opened the front door and stood on the steps, feeling as nauseous as if I'd just lost my balance.

Ella seemed exhausted when I brought her home from school this afternoon. 'I'm hungry,' she said as we came into the kitchen, so I made her a peanut butter sandwich, cut an apple into slices, and gave her a glass of juice. She ate in silence, and then she took the postcard out of her school bag and put it on the table.

'So,' I said. 'You can email your great-grandpa now if you'd like?'

'I'm too tired.'

'Well then, let's leave it for later. What homework do you need to do?'

'Maybe I will email him,' said Ella.

We went into Jonas's office and I opened the window and looked down on to the garden, where Bobby was helping Mrs B water the plants. Ella sat down in her father's chair. She rested her hand on the mouse, and when the screen lit up, she clicked on the internet icon. 'Have you got your own email address?' I asked.

'No, my daddy lets me use his.'

'Really?' I asked, surprised that her father would let her use his own address.

'Yes.'

'Wait!' I said, as she started to type, my voice louder than I'd intended, realising that Jonas could, if he chose, see all her correspondence. 'Why don't we make a new one just for you, a private email address with a really good password, just for you and your great-grandpa?'

'Why?' She looked up at me suspiciously.

'Well . . . because that way we won't be bothering your father.'

Ella waited while I created a new account; we set up the password and then she opened up a message box and I helped her to type in her great-grandfather's address. 'There you go,' I said.

'What shall I say?'

'Just say, you know, that you got his postcard and how much you love it. Ask him how he is, tell him what you've been up to at school, how much you miss him . . .' and I waited for a moment, resisting the urge to correct her as I looked over her shoulder.

It's Thursday, and Ella has sent her great-grandfather three emails since yesterday. Despite the time difference, he's managed to reply to every one. Not only has he sent her a postcard and answered her emails, he's even suggested they contact each other using Skype. This afternoon I asked if she wanted to send a picture of herself, and we chose a class photo we found on the desktop of her father's computer and I showed her how to attach it. 'I'll have to come over and see you for myself,' her great-grandfather responded at once. 'You look very cute. Lol!'

'Why has he put "laugh out loud"?'

'It could mean something else . . .' I paused. 'It could mean "lots of love".'

'He's coming to visit me!' said Ella.

'Hold on,' I said, leaning over the back of her chair. 'He doesn't actually say that.'

'Yes he does, look, he says, "I've been thinking I would like to make the trip while I still can. You are right, Ella, family is very important."'

Impatiently I moved away from Jonas's desk. 'Tell him you'd really love that. In fact, why don't you ask him when he'd be able to come?' Then I walked to the window, and as I looked down at the garden below, at Bobby and Mrs B, I thought, how *dare* he? Just what does Rooster Murrey know about the importance of family?

CHAPTER TWENTY-THREE

Muriel Wilson has notified us that she is to be married. A card has been sent.

Branch home note, 23 September 1970

How do you know when someone loves you, not for what they think you are or hope you are, but for the person you have never shown to anyone else before? That is how it was with Donald Grey. I met him first on a rainy September day in 1969, in a tea room on Tottenham Court Road. It was where I took my lunch break from my secretarial job. I spent my days typing letters for other people, just as Mr Appleyard had predicted. At lunch I had a cup of tea and a bun. I was always counting my pennies. I liked to sit at a small table near the window; people seemed to take less notice of me there. I could watch all of life passing by, as if I was invisible, which by then I thought I was. I had given up on university. I had failed to find my mam's house. I had lost my old enthusiasm for life.

The tea room was so busy that when Donald Grey came by, he stopped and asked politely if he could join me. I said he could. Then I pretended I had had enough of my bun, and got ready to leave.

'Please,' he said. 'I didn't mean to chase you away.'

I had stood up by then, and although I felt foolish, something made me sit down again. Donald Grey was wearing an unusual coat, dark blue with a black velvet trim. His face was pale and square and framed by black sideburns. There was something solid about him, solid and trustworthy. He beckoned the waitress over and ordered a savoury pancake, and her eyes flicked disapprovingly between the two of us. She didn't like the look of me; she didn't think we should be sitting together at all. But I didn't care, because I saw the pleasure with which Donald Grey ate his food, and I felt a flush through my body. And when he asked if I came here often, it made me laugh.

We met several times after that. At first I questioned his motives, as I'd been brought up to do. Did he really like me, or would he one day walk away? And if he did like me, then why? I didn't think there was much about me to like. And whenever something went wrong – when Donald once lost his wallet, when we arrived at a cinema to find the film already showing – I felt guilty, as if I were to blame.

Then one day, after a long walk in the park, I sat on a bench and said I was tired.

'Do they hurt?' he asked. 'Your shoes?'

I nodded and slowly unbuckled my sandals.

'Oh God,' he said in disbelief. 'What has someone done to you?'

It was years of wearing shoes that didn't fit me that had done it. Boots that pinched my skin, that made me bleed. But I hadn't told him why this was. That it was a childhood spent wearing someone else's shoes. That I was a bastard, brought up in a children's home. That Mr Barnet had never called the doctor for me. That I was an unwanted child.

I had avoided Donald's questions about family. I had said nothing about my childhood, for fear he would think less of me. But that afternoon in the park, I thought I might tell him, as he knelt down and rubbed my aching feet in his hands. I had tried for so many years not to look at them. I thought if I didn't look at them, then maybe I wouldn't notice. The thick hardened skin. The toes pressed unnaturally together. Except for one, swollen in the middle, like the head of a hammer.

'How did this happen?' asked Donald.

And I looked down at him, kneeling there on the grass, and I told him.

We married on 30 September 1970. I was twenty-four. I wore a cream dress, with a white rose in my hair. I would have liked someone to be there at the register office. I would have liked a witness of my own. I wanted my mam to see me on a day like this. Her daughter, fully grown. In love and about to marry. I had sent a card to Hoodfield House. I didn't know who to address it to. But I wanted them to know that somebody wanted me.

Donald asked his friend Paddy Carson to be witness, with his girlfriend whose name I can't recall. He chose to wear an Afghan coat that had seen better days. There was seating for thirty people in the oak-panelled room, standing room for ten more. And there were just the four of us. Donald wanted it to be a small affair. Paddy took the photographs as well, because I so wanted pictures of our day.

The next day I moved out of the flat I shared with my friend Barbara and into Donald's. He liked to say he was a man of independent means. His Southwark flat was small but he owned it himself, bought with the proceeds of his clock repair business. You'd be surprised at how many people like to buy a well-repaired clock, said Donald. He had no family with whom he was still in touch; his parents were both deceased, and I was disappointed about that. I wanted to be a part of someone's family. But then I knew we could make our own.

We went to Clacton-on-Sea for our honeymoon and stayed in a boarding house with a good view of the pier. The house was run by a motherly lady called Mrs Patience, who took an instant shine to us. Each morning when the tide was out we walked along the sand, like wet sticking plaster beneath our toes. We held hands and watched boys hunting for crabs. We bought ice creams from the girls who pushed the trolleys up and down the prom. We kissed as the waves caressed our feet.

In the afternoons we walked along the pier, passing family groups. Couples with their children. Little babies in prams pushed by grandmothers. In the distance came the rumbling sound of the roller-coaster ride. And one day we saw a Punch and Judy show, the tall box and stripy curtains towering over the excitable children on the sand. I watched them, thinking of the blinds in the kitchen at Hoodfield House. How it was here at Clacton that I'd first seen a Punch and Judy show and how afraid I'd been.

We wrote postcards every day; that was what you did back then. I sent one to Barbara, and to two friends in the office. But the person I really wanted to send a card to was my mam.

Three months later, I went to the lady doctor. She reminded me of Auntie Peal. A thin face and a harsh, disapproving manner. But I tried not to let that bother me as she told me what I already knew. I was pregnant.

'Let's talk about your medical history,' said the doctor.

I shifted nervously on my chair. Even though I had my clothes back on now, I still felt exposed.

'Any history of heart disease in your family?' She sat there, an official sheet of paper before her on the table.

I told her no. There was no heart disease.

'Not your father or mother?'

'No,' I said in a very quiet voice.

'Both parents alive?'

I nodded, not able to speak, and she looked at me and frowned as if I was being difficult.

'And their parents, any heart disease?'

I told her no, I didn't think so.

'Any history of high blood pressure in the family?' She sighed and looked up, waiting for my reply.

Again I told her no.

'Diabetes?'

And each time I said no, I grew more and more upset. I wanted to be dismissed. I longed to be told that I could go. Because of course, I had no idea of my history at all. I did not know if my parents were dead or alive. If they were ill. If there were any diseases they might have handed down to me. I knew of no uncles or aunts, siblings or cousins. I had no knowledge of where I came from. And I hated that lady doctor for asking the questions I could not answer.

I had no one to give me any advice after that. No one to say eat this or don't eat that. No one to say, don't worry, Muriel, just stay in bed and have a nice cup of tea. I had no one except Donald.

I went to the hospital in a state of blissful ignorance, which was just as well. I remember in particular a sense of whiteness and of metal. The iron rafters. The aluminium trays. The beds on wheels like those at Hoodfield House. No one said anything to comfort me. No one said anything to me at all. A nurse came in and pushed up her sleeves and put an instrument on her head. She pressed it against my stomach, listened to my baby's heartbeat. I looked at the large buttons on her lavender dress. They reminded me of something, large and shiny as mother-of-pearl.

I let them do whatever they wanted. I was good at that. I'd had many years of being pushed around. They shaved me and bathed me and broke my waters. They put me on a stretcher, barely covered me with a sheet. They treated me like a naughty schoolgirl. Showing me the scalpels they would use on me later. Rolling me on to the delivery table. Cranking up the bed. Strapping me down with a belt. Fitting my legs into stirrups.

Another nurse came in. She smelt of cigarettes. I heard the scrunch of her apron as she walked across the room. 'Oh get on with it, Mrs Grey,' she said.

Donald was there throughout, although they didn't want him in the room. He held my hand, said, 'There, there.' And once, when he made to move away from the bed, the nurse snapped at him, 'You just stay there at the head end, young man.'

I remember how the nurse looked up as the doctor came in. 'This one doesn't want to come out,' she said. And I thought, she does, she does want to come out. Because even then, I knew in my heart it was a girl.

I lay there on the table, felt a vibration in my bones. My baby's shoulders turning, her flesh rotating deep inside mine. Then my body sobbed and she was born. I had pushed her out. I heard the first sound of her, a plaintive cry as the nurse blew on her face. And I looked at her. Skin so pale. Eyes as blue as forget-me-nots. She didn't look like me. Surely this baby wasn't mine, this blue-eyed girl? For a moment I thought I had the wrong baby. And if she didn't look familiar to me, if I didn't recognise her, then who did she look like?

I put out a finger, touched her gently on the nose. Did she look like my mam? Was there something in my baby that took after my mam? I looked at Donald, saw tears in his eyes. I stopped myself from crying as well, because I would never know who she looked like, if she resembled anyone in my family. And I so didn't want that to spoil the proudest moment of my life.

Then the nurse put her to my breast. I watched her begin to suck. I felt how well she fitted on to me. I stroked her thin fine hair. I saw her eyes flutter. And I knew that she belonged to me. No one could take her away from me. She was mine.

I spent ten days in hospital after that. At night they put Rosie in the nursery with the others. But in the day she was by my side. And at last I had someone who was mine, someone of my own to love and to cherish. To cuddle and to spoil. My daughter wouldn't need a number chain-stitched into her clothes. She wouldn't have to share a bedroom with five other girls. She wouldn't need a locker for her things. Or a single hook for her coat.

She wouldn't have to ask the questions I had always wanted to ask. She would know where she came from and who her parents were. Because we would be there, every day, beside her. She would have a proper home where she could bring her friends. It was where I would be waiting. Ready to defend her. To see what she wanted. To ask how she'd spent her day. She would have me, her mother, at home. And the only thing that troubled me was whether I would know how to give her all the love she needed.

CHAPTER TWENTY-FOUR

It's Friday, and when I went to collect Ella from school today, I had to wait ages in the playground, wondering where she was. I stood near the steps, watching the children streaming out, a group of boys play-fighting, two girls with blonde hair so long it stretched halfway down their backs. Then finally an adult appeared, a neat-faced young woman wearing silvery pointed shoes, and to my surprise she headed straight to where I stood.

'Hello!' she said, her tone overly bright. 'You must be Ella's carer. I'm Hannah. Could I have a word?'

I knew that look: the polite tightness of her smile, the falsely apologetic tone of a teacher about to confront a parent with something her child has done. This had been me, countless times, hovering in the playground, trying to catch a parent. Some would defer to my authority and believe me without question, but with others there was a flat denial, a disbelief that their child could be anything but perfect, an arrogance in their attitude towards me, just a primary school teacher.

'Of course,' I said, and I lifted the buggy up the steps,

hoping Bobby wouldn't wake. I followed Hannah along a crowded corridor and into a classroom. Above the teacher's desk I could see a familiar-looking list of targets and achievements, but there were very few examples of children's work on the wall, except for leftover Christmas decorations. Then I saw Ella sitting on a chair at the far end of the room, beneath a large yellow noticeboard, empty but for a calendar.

'I tried to catch you yesterday,' said Hannah, although as far as I knew she hadn't. 'I was hoping to speak with Ella's parents?' and she very deliberately closed the door.

'Her father is away.'

'Ah,' said Hannah. 'And her mother?'

I dragged a mini plastic chair from one of the tables and squeezed myself into it, feeling annoyed. Surely Hannah would know about Ella's mother; how could she be so insensitive as to ask?

She blushed then, as if realising her mistake, and perched herself on the edge of a table. 'I did think things had settled down. But this week has been particularly . . . difficult.'

'Oh,' I said. 'What seems to be the problem?'

'It's more of an ongoing issue . . .' Hannah fiddled with a thin gold chain around her neck. 'She won't sit on the carpet at registration like the other children. She appears to have some difficulty when it comes to telling the truth and can be very disruptive. And *that* doesn't make it any better.' We both turned then and looked at Ella. This morning her hair had been tightly plaited as it always is and decorated with clips, but at some point since I'd left her she'd taken out the clips and freed and combed her hair so it now formed a short glorious Afro halo around her face. 'It's just too big,' said Hannah.

'Sorry?'

'Her hair!' Hannah flapped her hands in a distressed fashion. 'It's too big.'

'Too big for what?'

'It's against school regulations and she knows that.'

'And what are the school regulations on hair?' I knew of course that schools have different regulations, some stricter than others. In my school, any child with long hair had to have it tied back, and no one was allowed to either dye it or shave it into patterns, but I'd never heard of a ban on Afros.

'According to the regulations, which we do make available to all parents and carers, pupils' hair must be smart and short . . .'

'Really?' I asked. 'Because a few minutes ago, I saw two girls with remarkably long hair.'

Hannah ignored my comment, '. . . and hygienic.'

'Hygienic?' I almost laughed. 'Why does her hair seem unhygienic to you?'

Ella's teacher sighed as if this was irrelevant. 'It sets a very bad example for the other children. It's just not appropriate.'

'Appropriate for what? It's her hair. It's part of her body. It won't get in her way and it looks very smart to me.' I looked at Ella again, thought of the first day I'd taken her to school and how she'd said her teacher didn't like her, and sitting there in the classroom I saw that she was right. It does happen sometimes: there can be a child in a class who you try to treat as equally as all the others, yet there is something that makes you mistrust and even dislike them. It is personal and instinctive; it could be they remind you of someone, it could be the whine in their voice or the fact they always have a runny nose, but whatever the reason, a teacher must never show her dislike. And Ella's teacher had, I could see this; she didn't like Ella and the matter of her hair was simply an excuse.

'It's not just that,' said Hannah impatiently. 'Other children's work has been defaced . . .'

I looked at Ella and she stared back, showing no sign of worry or guilt.

'I have attempted,' said Hannah primly, 'as her class teacher, to talk to her about all of this. It's in clear violation of the home–school agreement.'

I stood up then, infuriated at her bureaucratic manner, and held out my hand. 'Come on, Ella, I think we need to go home and talk about this.'

If I thought Ella would feel triumphant about the scene in the classroom, I was wrong. As soon as we left the school gates she seemed to deflate; she had nothing to say in answer to any of my questions, and instead walked silently beside me as I pushed the buggy. I wondered why she hadn't told her father what was going on, or whether she had told him and he hadn't taken any interest. If she had really been so troublesome at school, then why hadn't he done something about it, and why hadn't the school forced him to? I thought the way she wore her hair was an act of defiance – she knew her teacher didn't like it; it was a very deliberate way of undermining her authority – and I couldn't imagine how she had ever managed to replait it before she came back from school.

After we got home and were settled in the kitchen, I offered her an ice pop and she sat down at the table and slowly took off the wrapper.

'It's strawberry, your favourite. I asked Mrs B to get you some.'

Ella looked at the ice pop, as if she had no idea what it was.

'Are you okay?'

She held the ice pop to her lips. 'I just wish . . .'

'You just wish?'

'That I had a mum.'

'Oh sweetheart, I'm sure you do.' I reached over and squeezed her hand, unable to think what to say. Outside in the garden we heard the hosepipe spurting water into the paddling pool and Mrs B and Bobby chattering, oblivious to what was going on inside. Then Ella did the strangest thing: she leaned across the table and pressed her forehead firmly against mine. 'Do you ever get that feeling when you have to tell someone something and you don't know if you want to but in your head you're like, go on, tell her, and then you can't think of anything else?'

'Yes,' I said. 'I know exactly what you mean.'

We sat there, our foreheads still touching, and I thought how hard she must have tried, in all the days I've been here, not to talk about her mother. She had been suppressing her thoughts; and I knew that the more she had fought them, the more they would have come into her head, like trying to submerge a rubber duck in a bathtub: the more you push it down, the more it keeps on popping up. Perhaps her father had told her not to talk about her mother; maybe he naively thought it would be better this way. Mrs B had said he wouldn't speak about Isabella's death, so this might have forced Ella to remain silent as well; she couldn't talk about her mother because no one else did. I thought about how there was nothing of Isabella in the house, no sign except for the single photograph in Jonas's study. Ella didn't seem to have any evidence of who her mum had been; there was someone in her past she couldn't talk about, and it was her own mother.

I remembered the years after Dad had died, how Mum had spoken about him all the time, as if speaking about him would help keep him alive or somehow make sense of what had happened. She had put so many photos up on the wall: the two of them standing on the steps of the register office the day they were married, my father sitting on a rock during their seaside honeymoon, me as a baby swaddled protectively in his arms.

My mobile pinged. Someone had sent me a text, but I couldn't look at it now. From outside I heard Bobby laughing and the clattering sound of the watering can being put on the patio floor. Then I saw that Ella was crying and I stood up and wrapped my arms around her, felt her body heave with tears. I didn't know what I could say to make things better for her; because there is nothing as unbearable as the sound of a child sobbing, not because they've broken their toy or failed to get their own way, but because their heart is broken. Still I held her, feeling utterly helpless in the face of her grief. 'Tell me about your mum,' I said.

She drew away from me then, and for a second I thought I'd made a dreadful mistake, that maybe she didn't have any memories, that perhaps she couldn't remember her mother at all.

'She was very soft,' Ella said, her voice trembling.

'Was she?'

'And she never got angry. She liked to make chocolate cake.'

'She did?'

'Really good chocolate cake. With nuts. She used to kiss me on my belly button.' Ella smiled, but then her lips began to shake and I felt her start to cry again.

'I want to know all about her,' I whispered, holding her in my arms. 'Whenever you want to tell me, I'll be here to listen. You can tell me anything you want. It's good to talk about people, to remember them. And I know it doesn't help much, but you have your dad, and your brother and—'

Ella looked up at me, her cheeks wet. 'And I have a great-grandpa.'

'Yes, you do, you have your very own great-grandfather.'

And she stopped crying and picked up her melting ice pop.

CHAPTER TWENTY-FIVE

Ella went to bed very early last night, and when I took Bobby out of his cot this morning, she was curled tight on her side, still asleep. When she did wake up she appeared subdued and reluctant to be alone; instead she followed me around the house, not saying much, but shadowing me from room to room.

I'm still thinking about what to do on Monday. Her teacher has obviously handled things badly; it's ridiculous to fight with a child over a perfectly natural hairstyle. Someone needs to stand up to a teacher who finds an Afro unhygienic, and if Jonas won't, then it will have to be me. And if what she says is true, if Ella has been telling lies or defacing other children's work, then clearly something is wrong, but perhaps they have no idea how vulnerable she really is.

Yesterday evening I emailed Jonas, putting it as simply as possible: I've met with her teacher and the school is concerned about his daughter's behaviour. What does he want me to do? So far he hasn't replied.

* * *

Just before lunch, Felicity, the Pembleton Crescent committee woman, came round. I was in the playroom with the children when she knocked on the door, and I looked through the window to see her standing there. For a moment I was going to ignore her, but then I changed my mind.

'Felicity,' I cried as I opened the door. 'I've just spoken to Jonas and he says *whatever* you want to do about anti-social behaviour you have his absolute support. And he would like to offer his house for the garden party, for which he is happy to provide all catering,' and then, still smiling, I shut the door. It's childish, I know, but still enjoyable, because if Jonas Murrey can't spare the time to answer an email from me, then I will take it upon myself to make up anything I want.

After we'd eaten lunch, I suggested that Ella might like to see if she had a new email from her great-grandfather, and to her delight, she did. I stood behind her as she sat in her father's chair and waited until she'd opened the message.

'He's not coming!' Ella wailed, looking round at me with tears in her eyes.

I stared at the words on the screen. He was unsure about making the trip, he said; he was eighty-eight and it was a long-haul flight. He would think about it some other time. 'That is a great shame,' I told Ella, trying to keep the fury from my voice, because just two days ago he'd said he would come, he'd raised our hopes, and now he'd changed his mind. 'You were so looking forward to him coming, weren't you?' I said to her. 'And after all, a promise is a promise. Why don't you tell him—'

But Ella was already typing a reply.

'Shall we go to the park?' I asked when she'd sent it off.

'No, I want to wait.'

'It's still morning over there; maybe he hasn't got up yet.' But a few minutes later we heard the ping of an email in her inbox and quickly Ella opened it. He'd been thinking things through, said her great-grandfather, and she was absolutely right, a man should stick to his promises. He would come after all. 'I am going to book a flight for 25 May,' he wrote. 'Lol!'

'When's that?' asked Ella, leaping up from the chair.

'It's just in a few weeks,' I told her. 'In fact, that's the day before your father comes home,' and I looked at the picture of Ella's great-grandfather on the wall, sitting happily on his swinging chair on a summer's day, a jug of lemonade on the table, his arm possessively around his wife. So you are coming, I thought. Any day now you'll be in this house, and then we'll see just how important promises are to you.

This afternoon Shanice and Cassidy came round. I haven't seen them since Mrs B told me that Shanice had been supposed to look after the children the weekend Isabella died, and I was prepared to be more understanding when she came striding in and flung her things about the house, but Shanice remained on the step. I noticed she was wearing the same red pashmina and I thought this a little unusual for a woman who changes her outfits every day.

'Would you mind?' she asked, patting Cassidy on the head. 'Only I have an appointment,' and she nudged her daughter into the hallway.

'Of course,' I said. 'Ella's in the playroom. She's watching TV.'

'She won't let me watch what I want to watch,' mumbled Cassidy.

'Yes she will, I'll tell her to.'

But still Cassidy stood there, oddly defiant for once.

'Right!' said Shanice. 'I must get to this meeting.'

I watched as she headed outside to her car, where on the back seat I could see a large bunch of flowers wrapped in cellophane.

'Come on,' I told Cassidy. 'You can watch what you want while your mother's at her meeting.'

'She's not at a meeting.' Cassidy stood stubbornly in the hallway. 'She's gone to the cemetery.'

From the playroom I heard the faint sound of a cartoonish laugh, and I stepped forward, closed the partly open door. So Shanice was going to the cemetery to visit her sister; that was why she had the flowers. I thought of the last time she'd been here, when she'd seemed so angry to find me wearing her pashmina, and suddenly I felt sure that it had belonged to Isabella and that was why she was wearing it again today. She'd held it to her face then not because she didn't like my smell, but because there was a scent in there she treasured and all she was doing was clinging to a memory of her sister. I looked down at Cassidy, wanting to plead with her not to tell Ella where her aunt had gone, but she turned away from me and asked, 'Can I watch what I want on TV?'

'Of course you can,' I said.

Then Cassidy opened the playroom door, and I watched as she jumped on to the sofa and Ella shifted slightly, allowing Cassidy space, and without taking her eyes from the TV, linked her arm through her cousin's.

CHAPTER TWENTY-SIX

Muriel Grey (née Wilson) has notified us of her husband's funeral. Condolences have been sent.

Branch home note, 25 July 1974

How do you know the right way to mother, when you have never been mothered yourself? That day we came back from hospital I was so full of trepidation I didn't know what to do. If I were feeding my baby right. The correct way to hold her, bath her or change her. I didn't know if I should let her cry at night, or whether to go to her. I feared I would overcompensate, that I would smother her with all the love I had never had.

But Donald believed in me. He thought I knew instinctively what to do. And, in time, I did. I learnt to trust myself. To cuddle her when she needed me. To comfort her when she cried. To watch with pride as she learned to crawl, to walk and run. I watched her greedily as she ate her food. I savoured every word she spoke. They were the happiest years of my life.

Donald was a model father. Often Rosie only wanted

him. 'Daddy!' she would cry if she had hurt herself. 'Daddy!' she would howl, if ever I had told her no. And I was jealous sometimes, that she only wanted him. But happy too, that he was there for her.

On Sunday mornings we would lie in bed together, Rosie snug between us. Donald would sing, 'There were three in the bed and the little one said, "Roll over."' And he would pretend to push Rosie till she hung over the side, laughing so hard the blood rushed to her head. Then he would get her dressed and put her in the pram and take her to the park. 'You have a lie-in,' he would say, for he always looked out for me. In the week he would make sure we had everything we needed before he went into his workshop. And even then, while he was busy with his clocks, he kept an ear open for his child. In the evenings he would emerge again, wanting to hear about everything we had done, to make plans for the weekend, for the holidays, for our future.

Donald was never a sickly man. He used to say he was as strong as an ox. And he was. Then one day he complained of stomach pains. It was mild, he said. There was no need to call the doctor. The next day the pains were worse. He needed an operation, the hospital said, it was routine. There was nothing to worry about. I took him grapes and Lucozade. I told him I was taking Rosie out for the day. And by the time they found what had ruptured, it was too late.

I blamed myself, of course. I should have known something was very wrong. And I blamed the doctors and the nurses, because they should have known, even more than me.

Rosie didn't understand. How could she? She was only a child. I tried my best to explain, as we went home from the hospital. But how do you explain the unexplainable to a child? I tried to keep her father alive. I encouraged her to talk to me, to tell me all her fears. But instead she invented two imaginary friends, and would only speak to them.

I sat so many nights in the workshop room where Donald had repaired his clocks. I felt safe in there. The warm smell of oil, the golden cases, their numbered faces. I liked the gentle sound of the old alarm clocks, the way the wall clocks beat faster than a human heart. I looked at his instruments lined up on the workbench. The files blackened with use. The saws and the lathes and the shiny-topped screwdrivers. The Anglepoise lamp that had given him just the right amount of light. He had so enjoyed taking things apart and then putting them back together again. There they were, waiting for him to come back and repair them. And so was I.

Rosie lost her father at such a young age, and that may explain a lot of things. She always was an inquisitive child, full of questions. And as she got older she never understood why I could not answer them. She didn't like it that I had no mother or father. She was upset when I told her I had grown up in a children's home. I told her it was lovely there. I had so many toys, so many friends. I had pocket money and sweeties, new clothes and books. I had laughter and love. And she believed me then. But still she had her questions, and the older she grew, the more she asked. 'Don't you want to know who your parents were?' I told her I had no need to know about what had brought me to the home. I said there was no way to find my mam or father. No records existed on me.

Then a few years ago, she saw a programme about branch home children on the television. She rang me up excitedly that night, 'There are files, you know, Mum. There are files on everyone. Why don't you get your files?' And after that, she just did not stop asking.

CHAPTER TWENTY-SEVEN

It's Monday morning, and after dropping Bobby off at nursery, I decided to take Ella with me to Kenwood. On Saturday I had an email to say that while the curator is still on maternity leave, her assistant could offer me an appointment today. So I rang the school, saying Ella was not feeling herself this morning and as a result she would not be going in. When I told her we were going to find out more about Dido Elizabeth Belle, she seemed genuinely excited. I wasn't sure if I should keep her from school, but I thought some time together would do us both good.

We took a bus to Hampstead Lane, and after passing a sign for a visitors' car park we went through a big wooden set of gates in front of a small gatekeeper's house. Then we turned on to a sloping pathway, paved with gravel and lined with old-fashioned street lamps, their cast-iron stems like twisted liquorice. As we walked down the hill, I could almost picture a carriage coming along here hundreds of years ago, carrying important visitors, the horses trotting faster as they arrived at the house at the end of the path. I wondered where Dido would have been, whether she would have been among the welcoming party standing on the steps, or if she would have been kept firmly in the background.

We waited for a few minutes at the entrance desk and then an elderly woman with cropped white hair came down to meet us. She didn't say much as she led us through a door behind the desk and up a narrow set of grey-carpeted stairs, but I felt Ella and I were special, that we were being allowed into an area of the house not generally open to the public. It was almost like we were part of the family, that we were about to go behind the scenes. The curator stopped at the doorway to an attic room, crowded with tables and boxes, where two women sat in front of computers, the windows behind them showing a rolling view of the heath.

'So, I believe you wanted to see any mention of Dido.' The curator sounded busy, as if we'd interrupted her and she had other things to do. 'You said this was for a school project?'

I felt Ella turn and look at me, and quickly, before she could interrupt, I nodded and said, 'That's right.'

'It's an unusual request.' The curator walked to a small table on the left and handed me several sheets of typed paper. 'This is the transcript of all the references to Dido in the account book written by Lord Mansfield's niece. The first one you'll see' – she put on a pair of tortoiseshell glasses that she had hanging around her neck and peered at the page – 'is when she started getting a quarterly allowance.'

'What does that mean?' asked Ella.

The curator gave a slight smile; she seemed pleased now at Ella's interest. 'It means they gave her money.'

'They did?' I asked, surprised.

'Yes, the Mansfields gave her an allowance from the age of around nineteen, and she also got presents at Christmas and on her birthday. If you add everything up, Dido received around thirty pounds a year.'

'That's not much!' said Ella.

'Oh, it was then; a kitchen maid's annual salary was only eight pounds.'

'What did her cousin get?' asked Ella.

'Elizabeth got an allowance of a hundred pounds, and I would guess more on her birthday and Christmas too, though these amounts aren't recorded.'

'That's not fair!'

'No,' agreed the curator. 'It isn't. But the two girls were very close and it's well known they used to walk arm in arm. Now this . . .' she crossed to another table and began unwrapping several sheets of white tissue paper to reveal a thick book covered in green felt, 'is Lady Anne's account book. She kept it from 1785 to 1793 and it contains all the household expenses.' The curator took a pair of thin blue surgical-looking gloves out of a box and handed them to me.

'Why does she have to put those on?' asked Ella.

'To stop the oils from her hands getting on the paper. It is very old.'

I pulled on the gloves, thin and sticky like sausage skin, sat down at the table and gently opened the book. The first few pages of the parchment-coloured paper were blank, but then there was a date, January 1785, and on the right-hand page a list of items and amounts, all written in careful cursive writing. I ran my gloved finger down the list, not touching the page, reading out the entries. A couple of shillings had been given to poor musicians, Daniel's wife had received a shilling for feeding turkeys, money had been paid for the delivery of letters and for the purchase of a bottle of ink. Then, on the fourth page, I saw her. 'Look,' I told Ella. 'It says Dido's quarterly allowance is due on October the fourth. She got five pounds.'

'And what does that say?' Ella pointed to an entry below.

'It says . . . four pounds was spent on dogs' meat.' I leant back in the chair, aware of the sound of a woman tapping on a keyboard behind me, feeling disappointed that the money the Mansfields had given Dido on her birthday wasn't much more than what they'd spent on buying meat for their dogs.

'Look,' said Ella. 'It says Dido again.'

'Yes,' the curator agreed. 'That's five shillings for drawing Dido's tooth. That means she had a tooth extracted, which would have involved calling in the dentist. And do you see that one? It says Dido was given asses' milk . . .'

Ella giggled.

'. . . that cost three pounds. That was very expensive and meant she must have been ill.'

So they did care for her, I thought. The Mansfields might have only given her a fraction of what they gave her cousin, but when Dido was ill they had called the dentist, they had bought her asses' milk, they really had looked after her. 'Where did Dido sleep?' I asked.

'Well I'm afraid that I don't know. The house has changed quite a bit over the years, but the usual practice would have been for small children to sleep in the same room as their nursemaid, possibly on the top floor.'

'Not with their mum?' asked Ella.

'No, never with their mother.'

'Why?' Ella looked upset.

'Well that's the way it was. It was the nursemaid's job to look after the small children. When Dido was older, she might have shared a room with her cousin, then when Elizabeth married and left Kenwood, she might have been given a slightly better room. It's hard to know.'

'And where would she have eaten?' I asked. 'With the servants or with the family?'

'She would have eaten with the nursemaid when she was young, and maybe some of the other servants. By the time she was around fifteen, she may have dined alone in a little parlour, waited on by junior servants. But this is just my guess.'

I turned the page, thinking of my mother and all the years she'd spent in the children's home, how she'd always insisted she'd been part of one big happy family. She'd had everything she'd always wanted, she'd been well looked after, and yet now of course I knew she'd never been treated with individual love. She'd been set apart from other children who had their own families; she'd never known where she'd come from or the history that had brought her there. I wondered if it had been the same for Dido, alone in the world, without a mother, and with a father who'd simply left her and gone back to sea.

I turned the pages again. The year was 1793 and Dido was the very first entry; her quarterly allowance was due. Then suddenly the journal stopped, and page after page was blank. I sat there for a moment, before standing up and stretching my neck from side to side.

'Is there anything else you'd like to know?' Carefully

the curator closed the book and wrapped it back up in its tissue paper.

'What happened to Dido later in life?'

'Well, she was quite a wealthy woman by the time she left Kenwood. Lord Mansfield left her a substantial amount in his will,' the curator took off her glasses, 'and so did her father.'

'He did? He left her money in his will?'

'Yes, I believe the exact words were "a thousand pounds in trust to be held for Elizabeth and her half-brother John".'

'Elizabeth?'

'In other words, Dido.'

So perhaps Amina had been right: if Dido's father had left her money in his will, then he hadn't forgotten her or disowned her; he'd remembered her and left her an inheritance. I wanted to ask if the curator thought he'd ever visited his daughter at Kenwood, but maybe now, with Ella by my side, wasn't the right time.

'Can I look at that?' asked Ella, pointing to a large blue vase on a shelf by the window.

'As long as you don't touch it,' smiled the curator, and when Ella walked off across the room, she rested her hand lightly on my arm. 'What a beautifully behaved child you have; she's a credit to you. You must be very proud of her.'

'I am,' I said, and for a moment I could almost believe that it was true, that Ella was mine, that she was the child I'd never had. I looked at her standing patiently in front of the vase. How grown up and self-contained she seemed, when only a few days ago she'd been sitting at the kitchen table, convulsed in tears because she didn't have a mother. 'Do you know anything else about Dido's father?' I asked.

'He had a bit of a reputation,' said the curator, her voice low.

'In what way?'

'I believe there were unproved allegations about attempts to grab land in Florida.'

'Florida?' asked Ella, who had obviously heard every word that had been said. 'That's where my great-grandpa lives!'

CHAPTER TWENTY-EIGHT

Muriel Grey (née Wilson) has asked for a copy of her file.
June is to contact her.
Head office access request, 21 January 2009

How do you know what is true and what is false when you come to read a file about your life? You think you know what happened; however bad your memory is, you're still certain about some things. And then suddenly, at the age of sixty-five, you are not.

It started one afternoon three years ago. I was in the Co-operative, two weeks before Christmas. I was standing in front of the dairy section, intent on examining the ready-made desserts. Rosie was coming round after work. I was lost in thought about what to buy, only vaguely aware of an elderly white-haired lady beside me. She was leaning on a shopping trolley, wearing a double-breasted woollen tartan coat.

'Sorry, my dear,' she said. 'Could you just get that for me?'

As I reached up for a blueberry cheesecake on the top

shelf, I could feel her looking at me. She frowned and put her head to one side like an owl. 'Well, if it isn't Muriel Wilson.'

And her voice! That soft Aberdeen way of speaking. It took me back across all those years as if it had just been yesterday. Everything melted away from me then. The walls of the supermarket. The shelves of food. The stacks of tins. Everything but the face of my old friend. The cook from Hoodfield House.

'Mrs McGregor?' I picked up my wire basket from where I had dropped it on the floor, felt a faint taste of bleach at the back of my throat.

'Oh, call me Morag.'

I had never thought of Mrs McGregor as having a first name; no one ever called an adult by their first name back then. I searched her face, looking for the lady I had known, the adult I had pretended was mine.

'You look well,' she said.

'So do you.'

Mrs McGregor laughed. 'You should see me with my make-up on.'

She suggested we go and have a cup of tea. So we paid for our goods and left the supermarket and stopped at a nearby church. The doors were open for a Christmas bazaar. Inside, the wooden pews were lined with books. Metal rails were hung with cast-off clothes. In a small alcove room a lady in a green apron was serving tea. We settled down at one end of a trestle table, with our tea and a plate of mince pies, and smiled at each other.

Mrs McGregor explained she was visiting a friend in London, a pensioner who needed a helping hand, as pensioners often do. She said this as if unaware that she herself was nearly ninety. Her friend was feeling better, she said, and now she was away back home. She'd been buying supplies for a farewell tea. 'So, Muriel,' she said, 'and how have you been?'

I told her a little about my life. She nodded and said, 'Good lass' a few times, before telling me about herself. 'Are you not going to eat one?' She pointed encouragingly at the plate in front of me. I thought of how she used to lay the table at Hoodfield House and sing her songs and call us, saying, 'Come on, kiddies, don't dawdle.' So obediently I took a mince pie and bit into the crumbly pastry. And as I did, I had the dreadful realisation of what was inside. I felt the stickiness of the currants in my mouth. I looked around for a serviette but there was none. So I swallowed and reached quickly for my tea.

'Muriel?' asked Mrs McGregor.

I nodded, tried to smile. I watched two young women come into the room, showing each other what they had bought. I put down my cup, wiped at the mark it had made on the tabletop. 'Whatever happened to Auntie Peal and Mr Barnet?'

Mrs McGregor sniffed, watched as I added more sugar to my tea. 'I don't know about Auntie Peal, but I heard the old troll died a long time ago.'

'He did?'

'No great loss to the world,' said Mrs McGregor.

'And what about Susan?'

'Susan?'

'Yes, Susan. She was my best friend.' And I thought about how clever she had been, how we had been delighted with each other and pretended we were sisters.

'I don't recall a Susan . . .'

'Yes you do. Our beds were next to each other. We did everything together; we were inseparable.'

Mrs McGregor gave me a sympathetic look.

'You let us watch television the day our rabbit died.'

'Did I now?' Mrs McGregor smiled.

'Then Susan failed the eleven plus and her mother came for her.'

Mrs McGregor sipped her tea, her eyes a little glazed. I could see she didn't remember. 'And have you ever tried looking for your parents?'

I told her I hadn't, but that my daughter frequently asked me to. Mrs McGregor said she thought it might be a good idea. 'They let you know now, you know, about your parents, not like in the old days.' And that's what made up my mind. After a lifetime of not knowing, I would ask for my file.

Rosie was the one who contacted the home's head office. I can hear her now, on my hallway phone. 'Yes, I'm sure it's a long process,' she said, her voice cold and impatient. 'But this is my *mother* we're talking about. Of course she's given her consent!'

Then she gave me an inquiry form to sign, and sent it off with my passport. A few weeks later, I had a call. 'Mrs Grey?' asked a nicely spoken lady. 'This is June, from head office.' I felt afraid then, as I stood in my hallway, my shoulder pressed hard against the wall. I listened as she confirmed my name and date of birth. All the years I'd been at Hoodfield House. She told me I was on the waiting list. And I said, 'Thank you,' and held my breath.

She explained that people often thought they had every-one's file on a shelf. That all they needed to do was pick it up. But the reports were on microfilm, she said. They would need to print them off and put them in order. It would take quite a while. Was I happy with this? I said that I was.

The months went by; winter turned to spring and then to summer. I hoped they had forgotten all about it. But then I received a letter in the post. I was at the top of the list. They were going to research my records.

Rosie was with me, the morning when the social worker lady rang again. I was asked if I still wanted to go ahead. I was warned it could be painful and disturbing. I was to think carefully about who would support me when the time came. And I held the phone tight, lowered my voice. 'Does it say everything, in my file?'

'Not everything, Mrs Grey, just what the adults recorded at the time. Would you like me to take something out? We can always do an edited version if you—'

'No, no,' I said, not wanting to cause any trouble.

'And would you like us to post it, Mrs Grey, or will you be coming here to visit?'

Rosie had come out into the hallway by then, and she stood next to me, listening. She nudged me with her arm and said, 'Tell them we're coming to visit.'

CHAPTER TWENTY-NINE

It's Monday evening and I'm sitting in the kitchen of Pembleton Crescent. The children are asleep; the garden is bathed in darkness. I'm thinking of what we saw this morning at Kenwood, the account book with the entries about Dido Elizabeth Belle, the bare details of her life; it's made me think of the day I took Mum to head office, when finally we saw her file.

I'd got out of bed that morning, and when I'd opened my curtains all I had seen was nothingness. The street outside was wet, but there was no rain. The sky was white as gauze; there were no individual clouds, no sun. I'd stood there looking out, thinking it's not supposed to be like this; a significant day needs dramatic weather.

Mum was silent as we got the bus to the station, where the escalators and platforms were crowded with commuters who all seemed to be wearing black and grey. We sat side by side as the train whirred and swayed across London and I focused on the feet of the people opposite us, the long brown shoes of a businessman, the scuffed trainers of a teenager, the dainty animal-print pumps of a woman who looked like she was going to a party. I stared out of the train, at the backs of people's lives: blinds closed against a window, a battered bike on a balcony, overflowing bins at the rear of a supermarket. The more I shifted around in my seat and crossed and uncrossed my feet, the stiller Mum became.

She let me lead the way when we got off the train and caught the tube, and we rattled along and breathed in the stale warm air, and I felt sorry for her; I could sense her anxiety and this made me irritable, so that each time she said, 'Is this our stop?' I said, 'No, Mum, I told you . . .'

Finally we arrived at the station and I could smell the wood smoke of a bonfire and see a smattering of autumn trees, their leaves as red as beetroot.

We came to a busy roundabout. Ahead was a church and on the right a row of modest houses, and there it was, the home's headquarters: a grey concrete building, dirty and stained like a multi-storey car park.

We gave our names to a woman at reception and were directed across a yard to a smaller building, where we were asked to wait in a room with a kitchen and a seating area. A couple of times women walked past the doorway, efficient smiles on their faces, not looking in at us too closely, nothing too probing, and I wondered how often people came here asking for their files.

I sat down on a sofa next to a glass-fronted bookcase, its shelves stacked with photo albums, red and green with golden embossed squares, relics from the days when people printed out photographs and kept them filed away for the future. I read the labels on the spines: '95 Reunion, Australia, Canada, Birmingham, Village Fete, Special Outing Windsor Safari Park. On the counter of the bookcase was a box of tissues, one pulled out all ready to be used, and for the first time since we'd left home that morning, I felt a stab of misgiving about why we'd come.

Then the social worker appeared, a short woman in a soft green dress with a plastic-covered ID card pinned to her chest saying 'June'. She had a freckled nose and large wide eyes and she seemed confident, like a woman not often troubled by self-doubt. She shook our hands and asked if we'd like to have a look around first, saying that old boys and girls often liked to have a tour of the old cottages. I didn't want to – this wasn't why we'd come; this wasn't where Mum had lived – but we went outside, crunching a layer of acorns underfoot, to a pleasant lawn shaped like a village green. In the past, said the social worker, over a thousand children had lived in one of several houses on these grounds.

'I remember this!' said Mum, and she stopped suddenly beneath one of the trees. 'I remember coming here.'

'For what?' I asked. 'I thought you lived in Kent?'

'Yes, but sometimes I think we came here. I remember this lawn, these houses . . .'

The social worker nodded. 'You probably came here for Founder's Day, Mrs Grey.'

Mum smiled. 'Yes, that was it. Founder's Day. All the girls had flowers in their hair and there was lots of dancing.'

She looked pleased as we followed the social worker to a house at the edge of the green, and we waited while she unlocked the door and let us in. 'There would have been twelve girls in this cottage,' she said as we joined her in the hallway. 'Of course it's much smaller than a branch home, but it's laid out just as it would have been in the 1950s.' She opened a door on the left, showed us into the dining room, small and cold with a wooden floor and two long benches, a table laid with empty plates and shiny knives and forks, like a stage set waiting for actors to arrive and a show to begin.

'Oh!' Mum held her hand to her throat. 'I remember having to Ronuk a floor just like this!'

'Ronuk?'

'That's what the polish was called, Ronuk.'

The social worker smiled. 'People have very clear memories of all the chores they had to do, although it wasn't much different from children in their own homes; jobs were part of family life then.'

I stopped myself from questioning whether this was true, because Mum looked so happy standing in the middle of the room, looking at the shiny floor as if admiring her own handiwork.

'Are the children's bedrooms upstairs?' she asked.

'Yes, would you like to see them?' The social worker closed the door to the dining room and led us across the hallway to a set of stairs.

Mum stopped and held tightly on to the wooden banister.

'Are you okay?' I asked.

'I have never felt better,' she said, and she stroked the stair post and then looked down at her hands as if expecting something to be there.

Eventually, after showing us around the rest of the house, the social worker took us back to the main building and into what she called a meeting room, with a speckled carpet marked here and there with old brown stains of coffee or tea. I could hear a soft ticking sound coming from a nautical-looking clock above the door, and there was another noise as well, a faint persistent humming like a far-off generator. The windows were covered with tight venetian blinds, but through a small gap I could glimpse the village lawn, grand old oak trees and slivers of midday sunlight, and I felt claustrophobic all of a sudden, as if real life was outside and continuing without us. I looked around, at four wooden-framed chairs with faded pink upholstery, a table in the middle of the room on which was a hard-bound file as thick as an old phone directory.

'Would you like tea?' asked the social worker.

Mum nodded and sat down, and I sighed at what I saw as yet another way to delay the inevitable. What I wanted was to see the file; that was why we were here, to find out about my mother's life and the parents she had never known.

The social worker came back with a tray of cups and saucers and a metal pot of tea and set it carefully on the table. 'Let's talk about what you want to know, Mrs Grey. We've already chatted on the phone about what's in your file, of course, and confirmed you were at Hoodfield House from 1950 to 1962. As I believe I told you, when the home closed in 1970, all the files were destroyed, but there was always a copy of everything here at headquarters and that's what you're going to see today. Is there anything you'd like to ask before you start reading?'

Mum shook her head.

'I do have to warn you that some of the things you're going to read can appear a little . . .' the social worker paused, 'judgemental. There are times when a staff member may be trying to justify themselves. We always point out that what you read needs to be seen in the context of the time, and some of the comments can make it seem as if people were quite . . . indifferent.'

I glanced at Mum, expecting her to look anxious, but her expression was almost serene.

'I try to explain it like this,' continued the social worker. 'Imagine you're having a bad day with your child and you complain to a friend. By the end of the day you've forgotten whatever it was and it's gone, but if a member of staff at a branch home were having a bad day with a child, and they wrote something down, then that comment is here for ever.'

Mum nodded; she didn't seem alarmed by this.

'And who did write all of this?' I asked.

'Most would have been written during yearly reviews, when staff held meetings about general behaviour. In the 1950s, it was all about child guidance.'

'Mum,' I said at last. 'Are you going to read it?'

I waited while she moved her chair nearer to the table and pulled the file cautiously towards her. Then she sat there absolutely still, hardly breathing, as if waiting for permission to open it.

'The first one or two pages are your admission history,' said the social worker encouragingly, 'and family background. It tries to make the case as to why you needed care. Further in the file you'll see copies of letters and other correspondence, as well as medical records, notes and so forth. There is also a report from your foster parents.'

'Sorry?' I asked. 'What foster parents?'

'There was a very brief period with a foster family, when your mother was around six.'

Mum looked confused. 'I don't remember any foster parents.'

'You don't?' I asked. 'Why don't you remember them?'

She shrugged. 'I suppose they weren't very nice people.'

'What do you mean?' I stared at her. 'Why weren't they very nice?'

'Oh, I don't know.' Mum gave a nervous laugh. 'They were probably strict and not understanding.' Then she sighed and finally opened the file.

CHAPTER THIRTY

That day at headquarters, in that sad little meeting room, I sat on the arm of my mother's chair and looked over her shoulder at her file. I was expecting a story, a neat, touching story of how she came to be in a home and who her parents had been. I would learn their full names and where they were from. I'd be able to piece together my mother's early life, her family and her roots, because however much she always said she was complete just with me, that she didn't need to know, I thought really that she did.

What I saw was a densely typed admission report with a stark black heading – HALF-CASTE – and as my eyes went quickly down the rest of the page, phrases jumped out at me like insults. ILLEGITIMATE. MOTHER IMMORAL. VERY ASHAMED. ANY OTHER PHYSICAL DEFECTS? I sat back, slapped by the words, by the utter nastiness of it all; this was my mum, half-caste and illegitimate, and this was her mother, immoral and ashamed.

'It says my mam was in the Women's Auxiliary Air Force.' Mum looked up at me, her face full of surprise.

'Well I never. No one ever told me that. It says she met my father at a London dance hall in 1945. He was a Negro soldier stationed near Nottingham. It says she was very fond of him. Oh my . . .' Mum put out her arm and patted my hand. 'She'd been expecting they would marry. He was going to marry her.'

'And he didn't,' I said, unable to see why she seemed so entranced by this.

'It says we were very attached. She was reluctant and upset about putting me in a home. I was only meant to be there temporarily.' Mum glanced up from the file, her cheeks trembling. 'It was meant to be temporary? She was going to come back for me?'

'It would have been very difficult,' said the social worker. 'You'll see that her family wouldn't let her back home.'

'It says she regularly sent money for my upkeep.' Mum looked down at the report again.

'Most parents did,' agreed the social worker. 'They would have been required to, especially if they were working.'

'But I never knew that!' Mum clasped her hands in her lap, began to turn her wedding ring round and round. 'I never heard a word from her. No one told me a thing. I thought she'd left me and that was it.'

'Look,' I said, with a sudden urge to distract her, and I pointed at the file. 'What's that?'

'That,' said the social worker, 'is a copy of your mother's birth certificate.'

Mum picked it up and looked at it indifferently.

'Let me see,' I said, and when she handed it over, my eyes seemed to go out of focus, because I could see her name and her mother's, but where her father's name was supposed to be there was a single black line. I looked at her to see what she thought of this, and I could sense, from the way she barely examined it, that she'd seen it before. 'So,' I said carefully, 'you were born at St Mary's in Paddington.'

'That was quite unusual for the time,' said the social worker. 'Someone in your grandmother's circumstances would normally have gone to a home for unmarried mothers.'

'There's a photograph,' I said, leaning over the table. 'Is it you?' and I felt a prickling in the back of my eyes because I realised I'd never seen a picture of my mother as a child.

Mum laughed uneasily. 'Oh, I don't know, it could be anyone.'

'No, Mum, it is you. Isn't it?'

'Yes,' said the social worker. 'Children had their photo taken on admission; there was a photographer who went round all the homes.'

I picked up the photo, stared at the unrecognisable little girl dressed in heavy woollen clothes. 'And who is it who's holding you?'

'Auntie Peal,' said Mum, and she shivered.

'What's wrong?'

'Nothing. She just wasn't the kindliest of people.'

'I thought everyone was kind to you?'

The social worker gave a polite cough.

I stared at the photograph, at the woman's unfriendly face and the way she held the little girl so determinedly in her arms, and I felt angry that this stranger had had access to my mother as a child and that she was holding her like that. 'So what was she like?'

But Mum had returned to the file and was busy turning the pages. Suddenly she beamed. 'Here's Susan! Yes, that's right, I remember that. And Linda, yes, a tiny little girl. Oh, I remember the milk crates. But we never all went to Brownies. Why does it say we went to Brownies?'

The social worker murmured something about how memory has a habit of playing tricks on us.

'We never *went* to Brownies.' Mum looked at her furiously. 'How can it say that? You can't put down things that never happened.'

'Mrs Grey . . .'

But Mum had turned another page and I heard her sigh in relief, felt her body relax. 'Oh, here's Mrs McGregor. She says I'm a lovely little girl who always eats all her liver. Yes,' Mum laughed, 'I always ate everything I was given. And that tartan skirt, how I loved that tartan skirt.' Suddenly she stopped. 'How could she?'

'How could she what?'

'She says I was sulky, I was never sulky! How could she? I wasn't a sulky child. How could she say that? And she didn't need to say I wet the bed!'

As I leaned forward to read the words, to see what had upset her so much, I noticed the edge of an envelope poking out from within the file. 'What's that?'

Mum picked up the envelope and looked at it. 'It's addressed to me.'

The social worker smiled. 'That would have been from your mother.'

'My *mam*?'

'Yes.'

'She *wrote* to me?' Mum looked at me in panic.

'Yes, she wrote several times.'

I watched as carefully, reluctantly, my mother slid a nail along the back of the envelope, lifted the flap and took out the letter, a single sheet of thin faded blue paper. '"To my dear daughter Muriel" . . .' Mum stopped and licked her lips. '"I hope you enjoyed your Easter egg. Did you receive your new warm socks? Sorry not to have written for a while. I have been unwell. I love you very much and not an hour goes by when I don't think of you."' Mum held the letter up, and the thin blue paper shook in her hand. 'My mam . . . my mam wrote to me? Did I get this?'

'Yes, Mrs Grey,' said the social worker. 'You would have got the letter.'

'But I don't remember ever getting any letters.' Mum looked so distressed that I wanted to pick her up, to remove her from the room, to get her away from the file containing all these things she'd never known. 'Are you sure?' she asked. 'Who crossed out my mam's address?'

I leaned over; saw that the address on the top right-hand corner had been covered with a series of thick black lines so it was almost impossible to read.

'Was that Mr Barnet?' asked Mum. 'I bet it was him.'

'Who was Mr Barnet?'

'No one in particular.' Mum bit on the inside of her cheek and I knew she was lying, that Mr Barnet had certainly meant something to her. 'I never knew anything about this letter! I never knew she kept in touch. I thought she just walked out that day and that was it. No one told me about any letters! How *could* he have kept this from me?'

Then I saw my mother put her index finger to her mouth as she bent to study the file again, and it seemed to take an age before she began to rub it gently, absent-mindedly along her lips. As she did, I could see the veins on the back of her hand, so large it was as if they were magnified, and the intricate silvery lines of her wedding ring, and each individual crease of skin around her knuckles.

'Oh my.' She breathed in sharply and the room seemed to contract, the humming noise grew louder, the clock above the door ticked away the seconds. 'It says here Muriel Wilson's mother no longer wishes to have any contact with her daughter. She intends to marry and her fiancé doesn't want responsibility for another man's child.' Mum tipped her head back and closed her eyes. 'So that's why. That's why she never came back. That's why all that time she never came back.'

'Bastard,' I said, and I got up and walked to the window and pulled roughly at the blinds, wrenching them apart, trying desperately to see the grass and trees outside. I hated myself for saying that word; why of all the words in the world had I had to say that?

'I suppose my mam had to choose,' said Mum, still with her eyes closed.

'Not him.' I turned from the window. 'I don't mean him, he's bad enough; I mean your *dad*. He was the one who got your mum pregnant and promised to marry her in the first place!'

Mum opened her eyes. Then she bent her head, began to turn the pages again. 'Rosie,' she said, in a polite, distant voice. 'Can you leave me alone for a while?'

CHAPTER THIRTY-ONE

I left the building and hurried back to the entrance, walked quickly along a busy main street. A car beeped as I crossed the road and I saw the driver shake his fist. I hadn't even seen it coming; I could have been knocked down and killed. I walked on, past banners advertising a fireworks night celebration, and I kept on walking until I thought I might get lost.

I didn't know these people in the file, this Auntie Peal who held my mum so unhappily in her arms and whose very memory made Mum shiver. I'd never heard of Mr Barnet, the man she blamed for crossing out my grandmother's address on the letter she said she'd never seen. I knew nothing really about my mother's childhood and the people who'd looked after her and brought her up. I'd never had anything concrete, no real evidence of how her life had been, except for the occasional times she'd told me something, and now I wondered how much of that was true.

Mum had kept everything she could of my childhood: my school reports and picture books and birthday cards, party invitations and paintings, photographs and swimming certificates. She had kept them and she had stored them all, in boxes and on shelves, in cupboards and in albums. But when it came to her own life, she didn't have anything; she'd had no real proof of it until now.

That's when I decided, as I crossed the road and headed back to the building: I'm going to find her parents. I'm going to find the mother who left her daughter in a children's home because her fiancé didn't want another man's child, and the father who promised to marry her and then abandoned her. I'm going to track them down and they're going to be accountable for what they did.

When I returned to the meeting room, Mum was still reading. She didn't look up as I came in, so I went to the kitchen area, where the social worker stood at the counter filling a kettle.

'She's very upset,' I snapped.

The social worker clicked the lid of the kettle, leant her back against the counter.

'I didn't think it would be like this. I don't even know whether to go in or not!'

'We do often find,' said the social worker mildly, 'that the impetus for getting the file comes from a son or daughter, who may not have always thought things through.'

'Is that so?' I stared at her coldly. It wasn't right that she had my mother's records and who knew how many other people's records as well. This was my mother's *life* in there. Who did she think she was, to have control of all of this, all these personal letters, these intimate reports and photographs?

'It is a lot to digest,' said the social worker, turning

back to the kettle and switching it off. 'It can be very upsetting and confusing. We know that not everything is in the records; just what the adults understood at the time, and often that's not what the children remember. It's like a jigsaw; they try and piece it together as the adult they are now.' She lifted a cup from the counter and held it up. 'Would you like some tea?'

'No.'

'Perhaps you'd like to stay in here while you wait for your mother to finish? Or would you like to see our library?'

No, I wanted to say, I don't want to see your library, I just want my mother back the way she was yesterday, before all this happened, before my selfishness and my need to know brought her here.

'You might like to read some of the personal stories,' said the social worker, 'by people who were in branch homes around the same time as your mum?'

So I said a rude 'All right,' and followed her along a corridor and into a narrow room, heavy with the smell of old books.

She pointed at a large metal shelving unit. 'There are some leaflets here on tracing family members, and some general reports and stories people have written about their time in care.'

I saw a folder on the middle shelf with the outline of a cartoonish black child on the cover. I leant over and picked it up, and when I looked up, the social worker had gone.

I opened the folder; it was a report from the early 1960s, full of tables and numbers and indexes. I read the introduction. There had been very few coloured children in care until the war, but now they made up twenty per cent of children in homes when there were less than two per cent of 'coloured inhabitants' in the entire country. One of the reasons for the increase was the number of children born to white English mothers and black American servicemen. Just like my mum; hundreds of children just like my mum.

I looked down at another list of figures: children who were half West Indian, half African, half Pakistani, as if none of them were whole as they were. There were parents from Jamaica, from Bermuda, Somalia and Sudan. There were Arabs and Egyptians and Maltese, Belgians and Poles and Canadians. I skimmed a list giving the occupations of the children's mothers: factory workers and shop assistants, schoolgirls and domestics. I read a summary at the bottom of the page: *In only one case did a putative father express the intention of keeping in touch with his child.*

I put the report back on the shelf, my fingers sticky with sweat. Why did none of the fathers stay in touch? How could these men have so easily abandoned their children, and why didn't the homes find the fathers and *make* them acknowledge them?

I looked along the shelf, pulled out a thick hardback book. The pages were thin like a Bible, and I opened it at a set of photographs: a little white boy with iron-clad legs holding on to a metal walking frame; a yellow-haired baby without arms. Then I came to a photo of a young mixed-race girl, perhaps four years old, sitting on a hospital bed. The girl didn't look cold or hungry or ill or mistreated. Her clothes were new, her hair freshly brushed. She had a doll in her arms. But in her eyes there was no surprise, no worry, no happiness, no pain. They were utterly blank, as if she was sitting there waiting for someone to tell her who she was.

CHAPTER THIRTY-TWO

Name: Muriel Wilson
Age: 16
General character: quite good
Branch home report, 25 September 1962

How do you summarise the first sixteen years of a person's life? Because here it is, my leaving report. Right here as usual on my kitchen table. And all they had to say about me was this: quite good. Sixteen years in this world and just two words. Quite. Good. There is nothing about my personality. My achievements. My strengths or weaknesses. It's as if my childhood were an exam that I had barely passed.

Sometimes I wish I'd never asked to see my file. That Rosie had left well alone. Because it's not a pleasant thing to do, to attend your own funeral. That is how it was, all those progress reports, all those pages of how others had seen me and judged me. There they had been, talking about me behind my back. Watching me. Spying on me. Making notes. Filing away their prejudiced thoughts. I was a sulker. A bed-wetter. A sleepwalker. I was fostered out. And *they* didn't want me either.

Even Mrs McGregor. The lady I thought was my friend. The person I pretended was my very own adult. And she was the one who had encouraged me to see my file in the first place.

Me and Susan went to Brownies, that's what it says. I have no memory of that. I don't know if it is because I have forgotten, or if it never happened. I wish I could ask my old friend now: is it the truth in these files or did they make things up?

But still, I had to sit there and read everything. Because that was why I was there. I had to read the things I thought I already knew. And didn't. Then once I was finished, Rosie would want to know it all, because she always has.

I had been quite hopeful up until then. I had quite enjoyed looking round the old cottage. I had felt confident, walking into that place. It was like I was coming home, when the social worker let us in and I smelt the old linoleum on the floor, distinctive as powdered mustard. It was like opening something that had been closed for many years, not just the cottage, but my very own past. The polished floorboards in the dining room, the musty playroom with a grate around the fire. A hint of old air freshener in the bedroom, a heavy floral scent. And I had stood there, smelling my childhood, flooded with memory, with no idea of what was to come.

'Why did you ask me to leave?' Rosie asked as we sat side by side on the train going home, my file heavy on my lap. She had been quiet up till then. She regretted what she'd done, I could see that. I don't think she'd taken into account what it would be like for me to read that file.

So I told her. 'There was something I didn't want you to see.'

'What?' she asked.

'When I was young,' I said, 'and very upset, one day I did something terrible.'

'How terrible?'

I took a deep breath and told her. 'I stole money from my teacher's purse, to buy sweeties for the other girls.'

My daughter laughed. 'That's not so terrible, Mum. No one's going to think less of you because of that.'

I just could not make her understand the world in which I had been brought up. The strictness of that life. The terrible sense of shame when a child broke a cardinal rule. The way they had believed I had bad blood. And I had believed it too, as I walked back to Hoodfield House that day, the awful letter in my hand. 'I just didn't want you to see it,' I said. 'That's all. They said I was a thief.'

We sat in silence for a while. The carriage nearly empty but for the two of us.

'Mum?' she said.

I watched as a man got on the train, shouting into his mobile phone. 'I never went to Brownies,' I told her, rearranging the file on my lap.

'I know. It doesn't matter.'

Yes, I wanted to say, it does matter. It matters to me.

'I'm sorry,' she said at last, and she held on to my arm as if she thought at the next stop I might get off.

'What's done is done,' I told her. I just wanted to get myself home. Because I was the one who hadn't told her the truth. I was the one who had buried the past. I hadn't dwelt on those years. I had moved on. I had dismissed the bad bits. And now I had to think of them again.

'So, you didn't know your mum was in the Women's Auxiliary Air Force?'

'No.'

'What did she do, was she a pilot?'

'I don't think they ever let women fly planes.'

'Perhaps she was a code-breaker?'

'Perhaps.'

'And your dad was stationed near Nottingham?'

'So it says.'

'What do you think happened to them?'

'I have no idea.'

'Don't you want to know?'

'Oh,' I told her, 'they probably died a long time ago.'

'But what if they didn't?' she asked, still holding on to my arm. 'Wouldn't you like to know more about them, about yourself?'

'Rosie,' I said, 'I didn't spend my childhood agonising over who I was. I was too busy surviving.'

Then my daughter turned to me in that stuffy railway carriage and asked the question I knew she would, the one I both longed for and dreaded. 'Can I trace them; do you mind if I try to trace them?'

And I said it was entirely up to her.

I'm looking at the file now, its contents spread out on my table. I have made a list of everyone in that file. I don't want to forget a single person. I need to remember every place and every date. And each day I hang on to what comforts me the most. My mam had been expecting my father would marry her. For nearly four years she had kept me. She had loved me. Then she had turned to the home. There was nothing else she could have done. Her family wouldn't help her. It was temporary, and she was going to come and claim me. She paid a monthly amount for my upkeep. I had always felt she wasn't a real mother. Now I knew that she was.

She wrote to me. She actually sent me letters, telling me she loved me. She sent me an Easter egg. And nice warm socks. How my life might have been different if I had known this. It might have made me feel better about myself, about my mam. Or maybe it would have just added to the pain. Then everything had changed. She met another man and he didn't want me. The force with which this hit me cannot be described. It was like I had lost an opportunity I had never known I had.

I pick up the papers and put them in order. I hear my doorbell ring. It could be Rosie. I haven't spoken to her for a long time now. Whatever she's up to, she doesn't want to tell me. Maybe she has left her job. Maybe she is coming to see me. I get up slowly; my legs don't carry me as well as they used to. I open the door, ready to smile. But it's only the postman. I look past him, see two boys sitting playing on the lawn outside. I smell the scent of apple blossom from a nearby tree. An ice cream van comes down the road, playing its familiar tune. It seems very early in the year for an ice cream van. I watch the boys leap up, and as I do I can see Rosie as a child, the way she would beg for a 99 with the chocolate flake on top. I can see her, standing on tiptoe to pay for her ice cream and then carrying it carefully like a prize. I take the parcel from the postman and sign my name. It's been too long since I saw my child.

CHAPTER THIRTY-THREE

I'm standing at the window in the playroom of Pembleton Crescent, staring out at the darkness and thinking how naive I was when I started my search, how absolutely certain I'd been that I would find my mother's parents. The morning after we returned from getting the file, I'd arrived at school especially early and sat down at my classroom computer, eager to start before the day began. I looked up the Women's Auxiliary Air Force, the history of Whitehaven, where my grandmother had been born, websites that explained ways to trace family members. As I switched from one site to another, increasingly distracted by the shrieks of children arriving through the gates, I knew I was running out of time and this was something I should do at home. I thought about what I was supposed to be doing that day; the deputy head was leaving and I wanted to apply for the job, and when the bell rang, I was forced to hurry back to the staff room to collect my things.

That evening I rang Amina. I'd never talked much about my mum being brought up in a home – it wasn't something that often came up in conversation – but I'd told her years ago when she'd first become interested in building family trees. I told her now about our trip to get the file, explained I had a birth certificate, and asked for her help.

The next few months I spent every spare moment looking for my grandmother. I applied for records, checked her last known address, a flat in Maida Vale that she'd left in 1952, two years after she'd put Mum in the home, and which had been knocked down long ago. Amina helped me search for weeks to find a marriage certificate, until finally we wondered whether my grandmother had married her cold-hearted fiancé after all. Perhaps he'd said he would marry her if she agreed to leave my mother in the home and then he'd changed his mind. Perhaps she'd left the country then; she could even have emigrated somewhere else.

After six months I was beginning to face the fact that Dorothy Wilson had vanished off the face of the earth. 'If people don't want to be found,' said Amina, 'they usually won't be,' and I told Mum and she shrugged as if to say I told you so.

So then I turned to my grandfather. I went through the leaflets I'd taken from the headquarters library, read advice on how to find a GI father. But they made it all sound so difficult, and if I couldn't find my grandmother in England, then I didn't know how I would be able to find someone in America.

'What are the chances,' I asked Amina, one night when I was at my lowest, 'of ever finding him? I don't have an address; I don't know where his parents were from. I don't know what he was doing over here: was he a soldier, a pilot, an engineer? All I have is that he was from Louisiana and he was stationed near Nottingham and he met my grandmother at a dance hall.'

'But you do have his name,' said Amina.

And she was right; it was there on the second page of my mother's admission report, and although it was relatively common, both his first and his last name had unusual spellings, and he had a nickname as well: Jonny Rooster Murrey.

CHAPTER THIRTY-FOUR

That weekend I joined an email forum for people searching for their GI fathers, read stories of people just like my mother. Some only had the first name of the man they were looking for, or titbits of information overheard in secret or passed down over the years. They knew their father had met their mother in a German town beginning with B, at a bar in a village somewhere in northern Italy, at a flower garden in an English seaside town. I read their urgent messages, learnt how they'd spent half a lifetime searching for a part of themselves, the missing piece of the puzzle, their American father. They posted photographs of men wearing khaki hats, training in a desert, standing outside a tent; military records and discharge papers, census returns and endless links to other people's family trees. Some were successful; they found their ageing fathers and travelled to America to meet them, and I could feel their relief that their quest was over. They said they felt complete, that when they met it was like they'd known each other for ever, and I so wanted that to be my mum, I so wanted to be able to tell her that I'd found her father and he wanted her. I hadn't found her mother; I had to find her dad and give her someone in the world apart from me.

So I posted my request:

I'm trying to trace a Jonny Rooster Murrey, a black GI from Louisiana, stationed in the Nottingham area in the 1940s. He met my grandmother Dorothy Wilson in London in 1945. If anyone has any information please contact me.

I gave my email address and waited. An hour later a moderator replied, 'Welcome to Rosie Grey, she is searching for her grandfather Jonny Rooster Murrey, any of you friendly folks able to help?' By lunchtime I had three more replies: a woman searching for her half-brother in Germany said not to give up hope, an American looking for his father's children in Lancashire asked if I'd thought of taking out an advertisement, a Canadian suggested I try the American Embassy. 'It's a long, hard process,' wrote an archivist in America. 'It can take years and years, and some days you'll feel like a dog chasing its tail around a tree. I am here to assist you,' and his words were so understanding they made me want to cry.

I rang the American Embassy and was told to contact a personnel record centre; if they found any evidence of a Jonny Rooster Murrey they would send me his enlistment papers and forward him a letter by certified mail. I filled in a form, marked the envelope as instructed with 'Do Not Open in Mailroom' and sent it off. Then I waited.

During the week things went on as normal. I taught my class, marked the children's work, made displays, wrote reports, rehearsed a play for assembly. But I seemed to grow detached from myself, to be looking down on this busy primary school teacher like I didn't know her at all; because all the time in the back of my mind there was something I needed to know. I had to find my grandfather, my mother's *putative* father, and ask him how he could have abandoned his child.

School closed for the summer. The days grew hot; the trees in the parks turned emerald; the air flickered with the sound of grasshoppers. In my flat there was a constant sound of bumblebees; I found them inside when the windows had all been closed, too tired to fly. Still I waited for news about my grandfather, not able to focus on anything else.

Then one day shortly after school reopened, I came back from work to find a large brown envelope pushed halfway through my letter box. I carried it into the kitchen and put it on the table. I told myself to take things easy, not to rush to open it. But I did; I ripped the envelope apart and there they were, my grandfather's enlistment papers.

I looked them over quickly, read his name and his birth year, his race and the address he'd been living at when he'd enlisted. *Jonny Rooster Murrey.* 22. *Negro.* I couldn't wait to tell Mum that I'd found him, that finally I had good news: I had her father's enlistment papers, I knew where he'd been living and now I might be able to find him. I stood up, about to call her, when something made me turn the page, and there in the column for his marital status I saw what it said: 'married'. I put down the phone, unable to believe it, because the man who'd promised to marry my grandmother had been married all along.

Still I looked at the papers, not knowing what to do. Ever since Mum had read her file, she'd spun herself a happy tale, that her father had intended to marry her mother and that she'd been the result of some great love affair. It seemed to make her feel special, rather than unwanted, and yet now I knew that all the time her father had had a wife back home.

Perhaps I could find him. If I wrote him a letter, the personnel centre would send it on. I could confront him and ask him myself, why did you make those false promises, why did you never acknowledge your child?

Each evening after school, I sat down and I tried to write. 'Dear Mr Murrey,' I began, and then I crossed it out. 'Dear Jonny Murrey,' and again I crossed it out. I didn't know how to address him, whether to be formal or familiar, what on earth I could say. Eventually I took an old-fashioned airmail letter from a pile Mum had once given me, and I wrote as briefly as I could, 'Jonny Rooster Murrey, I believe you were a soldier who was stationed in Nottingham in World War Two. You met a woman in London called Dorothy Wilson. I am her granddaughter.'

I licked around the letter, sealed the sides, folded it up like a piece of origami, walked to the postbox at the end of the road. It was a hazy day, with sunshine left over from a warm afternoon, and the air seemed to seep into me, to coat my hair and fill my lungs. I looked down on myself, standing there by the postbox, as I slipped the letter into the hole and waited, as if expecting something to happen right away.

Every morning I thought, it will be today, today is the day I'm going to hear from him; he's going to explain himself, he's going to write and say he's regretted what he did his whole life long and is there any way to make amends? He will ask about my mum, his daughter; he will enquire as to what she looks like and if I can send a photograph. He will say, come on over to America and meet your family; he will want to know everything about us.

But he didn't; there was no reply at all, and I began to wonder if he was alive, if he'd even received the letter; had the records centre got the right person? Someone must have signed for it, somewhere in America a man had read my letter; how could he possibly not reply?

But I knew why. My grandmother was his English fling, his bit on the side, a short-lived affair in the middle of war. She had meant nothing to him, this GI who was already married, who would survive the bombings and the battles and return home to his wife, and I just wasn't going to let him get away with that.

CHAPTER THIRTY-FIVE

One morning in late October, I was sitting in the staff room when Amina rang. 'I've got a number for you,' she said. 'I didn't want to tell you before in case it was a false lead, but a friend of a friend knows a private investigator in Washington . . .'

I stood up quickly, walked to the window, away from the other teachers, and lowered my voice. 'You've got a phone number?'

'Yes, let's talk about it later. I'll text it to you. But whatever you do, don't contact him out of the blue. He's an old man, he could have a heart attack.'

I pretended to agree, waited until she'd sent me the number and then wrote it down on a scrap of paper. I took the paper home, pinned it on my kitchen noticeboard and memorised every digit. I repeated it to myself like a chant in my head, as I sat on the crowded bus going to school, as I woke early in the morning, wondering if this was the day I'd be able to do it. I thought about what I would say, prepared long speeches in my head. I could pretend I was someone else; I could pretend my grandfather had been left something in somebody's will. Perhaps Jonny Rooster Murrey was a greedy man; I could say there was a lot of money involved. I could say I was organising a reunion for American servicemen in Nottingham. I could be a family friend of someone who'd known him and befriended him in the war. But in the end I just stood by my kitchen window late at night and looked at the sleeping flats and the darkened trees outside, and I dialled his number on my mobile phone.

'Hello?' It was a woman's voice and I wasn't prepared for that. She sounded a little sleepy, and I wondered what time it was over there; it must only be the afternoon.

'Yes, hello, can I speak with Mr Murrey?'

'Who?' The woman seemed surprised.

'Mr Jonny Rooster Murrey, is he in?'

'Is this long distance?' she asked.

'Yes, I'm ringing from England, from the UK. I'm looking for Mr Murrey because—'

'Who's this?'

It's me, I wanted to say, it's me, his granddaughter! You know, the one who wrote him the letter? 'I'm a family friend,' I said, desperate to keep her on the line.

'A family friend?' the woman asked, and she seemed to sound amused.

'Yes, I'm looking for Mr Jonny Rooster Murrey. Is he there?' I heard something in the background then, the distinct sound of a man's voice, and I pressed the phone hard against my ear; was that him, what was he saying?

'He's not available right now,' said the woman, and the line went dead.

Furiously I threw down my phone, because he knew, he *knew* I was looking for him and he was refusing to speak to me. I'd given him the opportunity, I'd told him who I was and explained about my mother, and he wouldn't talk to me, just as he'd ignored my letter.

At six o'clock the next morning, I was checking my emails before getting ready for school when I saw the message.

Rosie, not sure if this is your Jonny, but it looks like your mother is the daughter of my father's cousin. Small world! She says your grandfather has a grandson in England. He's called Jonas. I believe he lives in London, does Holloway mean anything to you?

I read it over and over, wondering if it was possible that Jonny Rooster Murrey had a grandson and he was right here in London. I couldn't believe my luck after all this time, because if my grandfather wouldn't let me into his life, if he was going to refuse to answer me, to deny my mother a place in his world, then I would simply find a way to get into his.

For the first time in six years I took a day off school, pleading a migraine. I sat down at the computer, found a Jonas Murrey on a charity site doing a sponsored walk in Hyde Park. I looked at the people who'd sponsored him, found a sizeable donation and a message from his sister-in-law Shanice Lawson: 'Good luck from everyone in Holloway.' So was this him, was this the right one? And he was married, perhaps he even had children, this man who was my own half-cousin. I looked up Shanice Lawson and found her Facebook page. She hadn't made her profile private, it was there for everyone to see as she happily divulged the details of her privileged life, her holidays abroad, a new personal trainer, a recent trip to Milan from where she imported children's clothes. I looked through her photographs, saw three of her brother-in-law Jonas with his two young children, Ella and Bobby; and it took less than a minute to find his address, 68 Pembleton Crescent.

A week later I went to school to be told the news: I'd been passed over for the deputy head position; I'd been cheated out of a job that should have been mine. And if the school didn't want me, then there was no reason to stay. In a burst of fury I cleared out my classroom table and my staff room cubbyhole, took six years' worth of belongings and paperwork and headed out of the school gates. The afternoon was oddly still, and as I walked along the road I began to have the strangest feeling that someone was pulling the pavement from under me, like a moving stairway. My feet seemed to slide; I could no longer feel the firmness of the tarmac. Fearfully I tried to keep going, but I couldn't position my body, I didn't know where to put my feet, which way to go, how to move between the other people coming towards me down the road. A man came by and he seemed so tall that I found myself shrinking, almost hiding by the wall. I forced myself to walk on, but I couldn't shake off the feeling that I had finally become detached from myself. I'd found my mother's father and he wouldn't speak to me. I had lost the job I wanted. I'd just walked out on my life.

I stayed in bed for a long time that day, and all the days after. I buried myself in my room, ignoring everyone who called, refusing to answer increasingly frantic messages from the school. Sometimes at night I wandered around my flat, not knowing what to do with myself. I couldn't tell if I was hungry or tired, if I needed to eat or to sleep.

It wasn't until after Christmas that I felt able to go out again, to get a tube and travel across London to Pembleton Crescent and find the house. I saw the looming figure of Jonas Murrey coming down the steps on his way to work, the two children being taken to school. Once I thought they'd noticed me, but they were too busy for that. Every week I went there, to watch the house. I had my business cards made and still I waited. I'd been there for two hours, the day I saw him running across the Holloway Road to the doctor's surgery; I'd given up and was about to get a bus home when for once in my life I was in the right place at exactly the right time.

CHAPTER THIRTY-SIX

Dorothy Wilson appears both mentally and morally weak.
She has requested we keep her child.

Branch home report, 8 November 1950

How do you know when to interfere in your child's life,
and when to leave well alone? Rosie is keeping something
from me, I am certain of it. Ever since she failed to find
my mam, things have not been right. She kept me up to
date throughout; although there were times I'd rather
she hadn't. She told me about the house in Maida Vale.
I didn't say I already knew about that. She said she was
sorry, but she couldn't find my mam. She couldn't even
find a marriage certificate. I said it didn't matter, and it
didn't. Because I never expected to see my mam again.
Maybe once I could have found her, but not now. She
had requested that the home keep me. And that's what
they did.

But Rosie is a very determined person. She cannot accept
disappointment. She wanted to find my parents and she
didn't. And when she fails to get something she wants,

she usually cannot think of anything else. So it seems strange to me that she gave up then.

She hadn't answered the phone for two weeks when I found her. She was in an awful state. A grubby dressing gown. Hair unbrushed. Face unwashed. She didn't want to let me in at first. She didn't even seem to know who I was. And the smell inside her flat, it was as if her whole life was stale.

I cleaned her room. Changed her sheets. Made her a cup of tea. I asked her what was going on. She said she hadn't got the job she wanted. But I wondered, even then, if there was something else, what it was that had triggered her collapse. And I never thought it would come to that. That I would find my child in such a state. Because here I am at the age of sixty-five, and she is still my child.

The doctor said it was stress. He offered to make a referral. She refused. 'I'm fine,' she said. 'There's nothing wrong. I'm over it now.' And she did recover; she did get dressed and leave the house. She did eventually seem to come back to herself. She kept in touch. She came round every Tuesday and Thursday. She said she felt freer since she had left the school. And I thought she seemed excited even, the last time I saw her. As if finally she had found something that made her happy and look forward to the future.

CHAPTER THIRTY-SEVEN

It's Sunday, and Ella is in a state of nervous anticipation. 'When is he coming?' she asked when I went into the children's bedroom this morning.

Bobby had got into bed with his sister and was squashed against the wall, pretending to be asleep. 'Ssh,' he said, 'I'm really sleeping.'

'When is my great-grandpa coming?' Ella demanded.

'On the twenty-fifth; how many times do I have to tell you?'

I sat down on the edge of the bed and Bobby sat up. He smiled at me and took my cheeks with both his hands and pushed his nose up to mine. 'You *are* a lovely little girl.'

I kissed him and picked him up, removing his hands as he tried to put them in my mouth. 'You want me to get you some milk?'

'So how many days until the twenty-fifth?' Ella stood up on the bed.

'Eleven. And I've been thinking, don't tell your father the next time he rings. Let's keep it a nice surprise.'

'Okay,' she said.

Ella has been back at school since Tuesday, when I assured her there was nothing wrong with her hair and that I would make an appointment for her father to deal with everything when he gets back. Then I added that I didn't think she needed to tell her teacher about our trip to Kenwood, and just to say she'd stayed at home.

'I could tell her I was doing a school project,' Ella had said with a sly smile, as if we shared a secret, which I suppose we do.

I was anxious when I dropped her off, but the moment she ran into the playground three other children rushed up to her and I could see she was pleased by the attention as she waved at me and joined her friends. So I went to the office and made an appointment for Jonas Murrey to see her teacher first thing on 27 May, the day after he returns.

'Does Cassidy know?' Ella asked, getting off the bed.

'About your great-grandfather coming?'

'Yes, because he's mine.'

'No,' I said at last, 'Cassidy doesn't know, not unless you've told her?'

'Please don't tell her, Rosie.'

'Okay.' I smiled. 'That's fine by me.'

Ella and Bobby had got dressed and had their breakfast and were in the playroom watching TV when Mrs B arrived. Ella's been invited to play at a friend's house later today, the first such invitation she's had since I arrived, and Mrs B offered to take her there and look after Bobby, which meant I was free at last to visit Amina. She texted me last week to say she'd found Dido's baptism certificate, only I'd been too busy to respond.

I got off the tube near Columbia Road Market, and stopped at a stall to buy a bunch of deep pink roses before pushing my way through the crowds to Amina's road. Her front door is right on the street, so there's almost no barrier between inside and out; one moment you're standing on a busy pavement, the next you're right inside her living room.

'Oh,' she said when she opened the door. 'You didn't say you were coming.'

As she let me in, I felt a sudden surge of longing for my own home; it's been so long since I closed a front door and knew I was alone, that I could do what I wanted, that I didn't have to be careful about what I said or did. Amina's flat had barely changed since the last time I was there; if anything it was even more orderly, her white sofa positioned exactly opposite the door, the island table neatly separating the living room from the kitchen.

'You okay?' she asked as I handed her the roses. I watched as she took a knife from a drawer and cut off the stems, put the flowers a little roughly in a vase. 'You want some tea, or coffee?'

'Coffee would be nice.' I looked at the granite-topped table, at a pile of Sunday papers and a manila folder labelled 'Kenwood'.

'Dido's baptism certificate is in there.' Amina turned on a grinder and the air filled with the angry sound of splintering coffee beans. 'That's what I texted you about, only you didn't reply.'

'Sorry,' I mumbled, and I picked up the folder and took out a sheet, a photocopy of a page from a book with a list of children's names, their parents, and their dates of

birth, written in the same sort of cursive writing I'd seen
in the account book at Kenwood.

James Son of James & Dinah Speed
Martha Dr of Samuel & Martha Baker
Dido Elizabeth Dr of Bell & Maria his wife

I looked across at Amina, busy spooning coffee into a
percolator. 'So her dad's name *is* here? But who is this
Bell? Why doesn't it say Sir John Lindsay? It says Dido,
daughter of Bell and Maria, his wife. So was her mum
alive when Dido was baptised and sent to Kenwood?'

'I don't think so, no,' Amina sighed. 'My guess is that
the Mansfields just wanted her baptised; they would have
wanted things done properly. So they took Dido's mother's
name, Maria Belle, and implied she was the child of Bell
and Maria.'

'They wanted to pretend she was legitimate?'

'Exactly.' Amina lit the gas ring and put the percolator
on the stove.

'I read somewhere that Lindsay got married, do you
think his wife knew about Dido?'

'Possibly, if Dido was in England when they married,
then maybe she did know.'

'But the wife didn't want her?'

'Oh come *on*, Rosie, it's not that surprising. Her
husband had a child from a woman in the West Indies!
Would she really have wanted her as part of the family?'
Amina handed me my coffee and sat down. 'Maybe you
just read too much into things. Maybe you look at everything from the perspective of what happened to your
mum. Think about it. When your grandmother put your

mother in a home, didn't she think she was doing the right thing?'

'But Dido's father never even visited her.'

'You don't know that! That's just what you assume.'

'He left her money, you know, the curator told me, in his will.'

'Well there you go then.' Amina reached over the table and opened the Kenwood folder. 'I have found out more about Dido after she left Kenwood. She got married and she had three sons, twins and another boy, and she was buried in Hanover Square.'

'So there's a gravestone?' I pictured myself visiting Dido's grave, leaving flowers perhaps, or just seeing how it felt to stand there at the final resting place of a woman who'd had such a strange life.

Amina shook her head, 'No, there's no gravestone. They moved the graves in the late sixties when the land was sold for development. All the skeletons were taken away and cremated.'

'Including Dido?'

'There's no record of her remains.' Amina put down her cup. 'Sorry, but why does this mean so much to you?'

'It doesn't.' I picked up the baptism certificate, slipped it back in the folder.

'Yeah, right.' Amina laughed. 'All these questions, all this thing about how she was supposedly abandoned by her father . . . It wouldn't have seemed cruel, you know, for a child to be brought up by someone more fortunate than her own parents, and it was hundreds of years ago . . .'

'And that means it doesn't matter?'

'No,' said Amina carefully.

'The thing is . . .' I paused, aware that she was watching

me closely. 'When I went to Kenwood that day I told you about with the children, it was like . . .'

'Like what?'

'I don't know. It all seemed so familiar somehow. And when I went into the library, it was as if I'd been there before: the books, the carpet, everything. There's just something that makes me feel I'm connected to her.'

Amina looked at me oddly. 'What do you mean, connected to her?'

'This is going to sound silly, but before we went to Kenwood, Mrs B, the cleaner where I work, she had me do this thing where you close your eyes and she asks you questions and you draw on a piece of paper.'

'Like some sort of spirit writing?'

'I suppose so. She asked me where I was and to describe what I could see, and what was really weird was that I had a clear image of a room, then I went to Kenwood and there it was, the room I'd seen in my head, the library.'

Amina laughed. 'What on earth are you talking about?'

'Oh, nothing,' I said, annoyed at the implication that I was going crazy. 'All I'm saying is, I described a room I'd never seen before; how do you explain that?'

'Do you know what? I'm worried about you.'

'Really?' I tried to smile. 'Because of what I just said about Kenwood?'

'No! Because you packed in your job and disappeared. You never answered my calls . . . then suddenly you email me wanting to know about Dido, you invite me round to where you work, and you won't tell me anything about it. Now here you are. I don't know what you're doing in that house, who the children are—'

'Their names are Ella and Bobby.'

'Yes, that you told me.'

'And their father is Jonas Murrey.'

'Murrey?' Amina stood up, put her hands on the table. 'What do you mean, Murrey? Are you saying Murrey as in Rooster Murrey? As in your *grandfather*?'

I nodded, fiddled with the corner of the folder.

'I thought you'd given up on that. I thought you rang him and he wouldn't speak to you.'

'Yes, he wouldn't, but I found his grandson.'

'What, here in London?'

'Yes. I got a message, on one of those online message boards. Someone told me he had a grandson, and I looked him up and found him.'

'Well thanks for telling me! So are you saying it's *his* house?'

'Yes.'

'But how did you get a job with him? I thought you said it was advertised. What on earth are you doing there?'

'I don't know!' I cried, and suddenly I found I had my head in my hands, my fingers pressing hard against my temples. 'I really don't know any more. It's just that when I got the message, I found his address and, after a while, I went there, to Pembleton Crescent. I just wanted the chance to bump into them.'

'You *stalked* them?'

'It wasn't stalking.'

'Well what was it, then?'

'I was just waiting for them. I just wanted to know more about them, to see how they lived, what they were like, without them knowing about me.' I stopped, ashamed of myself, because I could hear how something that had felt so logical and necessary at the time now sounded so strange. 'Then one day Jonas was taking Bobby to the doctor's and Ella rushed away on her scooter and I saved her from getting run over by a cyclist. I said I was a nanny. A few days later he offered me a job. So I said yes, because I just wanted to get into that house and find out about the family.'

'And then what?'

'I hadn't planned what to do after that.'

Amina looked at me worriedly. 'This is a bit creepy, you know. They are your family.'

'Yes, but they don't know that.'

'Well obviously! Couldn't you just have approached them, written a letter or something?'

'And what if they hadn't replied either? What if they were just as bad as Rooster Murrey and wouldn't even speak to me?'

'Well that would have been their choice really.'

I looked down at the folder. Amina was supposed to be on my side; she was meant to understand.

'So you're telling me you got a job with two small children . . . on false pretences.'

'False pretences! You know all about my grandfather, you know what a liar he was. You know he was married, you know he wouldn't answer my letter.'

'Yes, but you can't blame his grandson for that.'

'Anyway, he's coming.'

'What?'

'He's coming here.'

'You've *spoken* to him?'

'Oh no.' I picked up the folder, took out the baptism certificate again. 'He won't speak to me, but he just can't wait to see his great-grandchildren.'

'What does your mum say?' Amina frowned, leant across the table. 'Oh for God's sake, you haven't told her, have you?'

'Not yet . . .'

'How can you not tell your mum?' Angrily she snatched the folder out of my hands.

'I was thinking of my mum, that's why I did all this.'

'Were you?' Amina stood up, put the folder on a shelf. 'Or were you just thinking about yourself?'

CHAPTER THIRTY-EIGHT

It's Monday, and this morning when I woke up I could sense something different about my attic room. Instead of the usual feeling that something was missing, it was as if something had been added, that the atmosphere had shifted since I'd been asleep. Then I opened my eyes and saw a figure standing in the dark next to my bed.

'Ella!' I laughed to cover my fright. 'How long have you been standing there?'

She didn't answer, but handed me a comb and a handful of hair bands. 'Can you do my hair?'

I peered at her; it was too dim to see properly, so I leant over and turned on the bedside lamp. 'Hang on,' I said. 'Let me sit up first.' I positioned a pillow behind my back, and without being asked, Ella clambered on to the bed. I heard the wooden frame creak a little as she settled herself on the duvet between my legs. Gently I began to comb her hair, to divide it into strands and then to plait it, and as I did, I had a strong memory of my mother doing something similar, in the evenings after my bath, brushing my hair and telling me how lovely it was.

Ella leant back against me, I could hear her softly breathing, and I realised that apart from the day she cried about her mother, this was the closest we'd been in all the time I'd stayed here. She's never got on to my bed before when I'm in it, she's never sought me out like this or asked me to do anything for her, and I wondered whether it was because she knows her father's coming back soon. A milk van came trundling down the road and the sun began seeping in through the curtains, bringing the room's shadowy objects to life: the table under the window, the potted palm on the floor, the frames of the landscape pictures on the wall.

'Don't you like the way your hair was before?' I asked, as I finished one section and began on the next.

'I think,' said Ella, 'it was just a phase I was going through. It's annoying me now.'

I laughed and patted her on the head. 'Well it's up to you. There now, all done.' When she didn't move, I tickled her under the arms and she giggled and leapt from the bed and ran out of the room, and as I watched her leave, I had a sudden dreadful thought: what would happen when her great-grandfather arrived, when her father came home? Would I see as much of her; would I even be allowed to see her at all?

I realised I couldn't bear not to see her; I wanted to know what would happen at her school, if she would settle down, if she would get a new teacher who liked her. I wanted to know who would bake with her now, who would buy her a new swimming costume, or give her a kiss in the morning before she ran into the playground. But more than that, I wanted to know what would happen as she grew older, as she became a teenager and then a woman; what would happen in the rest of her life.

I dropped Bobby at nursery and Ella at school, and then I caught the tube to Mum's, because I'd been putting this off for too long. I got out at Monument station and walked over London Bridge, and my heart lifted as it always does when I see the Thames, this snake of iron-coloured water in the middle of the city that seems to promise a route into the wider world. I turned on to Mum's road and saw a line of shops, half of them closed behind iron shutters, and I realised that few of the ones from my childhood remain. I pulled a leaf off a roadside hedge, remembering how as a child I would take whole handfuls of leaves that I left fluttering in the air behind me, and I split it in two and smelt the cleanness of the sap inside. I stopped at Mum's building and opened the wooden gate, looked up at a row of net curtains flapping in the breeze at partly open windows. How different this was from Pembleton Crescent.

I walked under the black brick archway with its ancient sign ordering no hawkers and no spitting, and when I pushed at the intercom, Mum buzzed me in. I found her standing in the cold grey entrance, wearing her favourite apron. I bought it for her for Mother's Day two years ago; it's white with little red cherries and two large pockets at the front, into which she never puts anything because she says she doesn't want to dirty it.

She gave me a fierce hug and then stood back, examining me from top to toe, as if she was about to tell me how tall I'd grown. 'You look tired.'

'I'm fine,' I told her. It was warm inside the flat, as it

always is, and I took off my jacket and hung it up in the hallway, its walls covered with pictures: me in the school netball team, Dad and Mum on their wedding day, Dad in his workshop, my teaching degree neatly framed.

'I saw Amina yesterday.' I followed her along the hallway to the kitchen.

Mum smiled; she's always liked Amina. 'And how is she?'

'She's fine. She's been helping me with a project I wanted to do for Ella, the girl I've been looking after.' I glanced into Mum's living room; saw the familiar jumble of things: cushions and rugs, tables and stools piled high with books, the row of antique clocks on the wall, none of them working.

'That's the girl who's been sleepwalking?' Mum went to the kitchen counter, took two cups from the cupboard.

'Yes, but she hasn't done it for a while.' I sat down at the table, looked at the fridge covered in colourful magnets left over from my childhood, big plastic alphabet letters and numbers, and postcards of places she's recently visited. In the middle was a long hand-written list, some of the items crossed out in heavy black pen. I knew this habit only started after we went to get her file, as if by constantly writing things down Mum will be more sure of herself and will never forget a single thing.

'And what project has Amina been helping you with?'

'Oh, it's just someone we saw a painting of, a woman called Dido Elizabeth Belle at Kenwood House.'

'Oh yes.' Mum put a jar of sugar on the table and an unopened packet of biscuits.

'Why, do you know it?'

'I don't know what painting you mean, but if you're

talking about Kenwood on Hampstead Heath, yes, it's very pretty.'

I looked at her in surprise. 'When have you ever been there?'

'Oh, it feels like a hundred years ago now. I haven't been back since the big drama.' Mum sat down and put a hand under each thigh, the way she does when something's troubling her.

'What big drama?'

Mum laughed. 'That was the day your elbow came out of its socket.'

I picked up my tea, got the cup halfway to my lips. 'You mean I've been there?'

'Well of course you've been there.'

'I have?' I tried to put down my cup, but it was as if my arms had hit an invisible shelf and I couldn't move them.

'Yes, you were playing with your friend . . . what was her name? She was a bit of a tearaway; was it Janet? Yes, Janet. You were both on the lawn and she leapt on top of you and the next thing I knew you were howling and you came running up to me with your arm held out all funny. We spent the whole afternoon at the hospital. You didn't want them to X-ray it and we had to hold you down. Oh, it was horrible. Then one of the doctors just grabbed hold of it and clicked it back into place.'

'But did we go *into* the house?' I could feel that I was frowning, that I had been for some time. 'Did we go into Kenwood House?'

'I would have thought so; yes, we did, that's right, we went all around it, and you made so much noise, the two of you in the library, you wanted to touch the books and you got told off. Janet's mum, what was her name? She liked

231

going around stately homes, we often used to do it in the holidays. It had all been her idea; she lived in north London then. I'd promised her we'd go, although when I think about it now, it seems like a very odd thing to have done.'

I stared at her incredulously. So I'd been there before, in that house, in that grand blue-ceilinged library, and I'd totally forgotten it. How could that be possible, if something like that had happened, if I'd dislocated my elbow playing on the lawn and ended up in hospital?

'Don't you want one?' Mum opened the biscuits and arranged them on a plate.

I pushed it away, feeling sick. 'But I thought – I thought I'd never been there.'

'Well you had.' Mum picked up a biscuit, snapped it in half.

I stood up, furious with myself. Just how gullible had I been, to allow myself to think I had some strange, mysterious link with a woman who'd lived in a stately home hundreds of years ago? How stupid I was; I'd gone along with Mrs B and her silly game, I'd given her what she wanted by describing what I thought I'd seen in my head, yet all I'd done was to be prompted. It was Mrs B who'd asked whether I was inside or out, whether the room was upstairs or down, if there were books on the shelves, and all I had done was say yes or no. But I'd actually begun to believe it, when I'd gone with the children to Kenwood; I'd really thought the library meant something to me. I'd tricked myself into thinking I had the ability to describe somewhere I'd never been before. And yet all I had done was erase an event that had happened decades ago.

I sat down again. 'How old was I?'

'At Kenwood? You were about four. The doctor said it could happen again but that soon your bones would be fully formed and it wouldn't. I remember . . .'

'What?'

'Oh, that they looked at me a bit funny at the hospital and asked a lot of questions. Maybe they thought I'd done it to you.'

'Where was Dad?'

'Where was your dad?' Mum looked startled. She put down the biscuit, stared sadly at it on the plate. 'He was in hospital. That was the weekend he was admitted. That was when the stomach pains started.'

And suddenly, for the first time I could remember, I saw him, an image so clear he could have been in front of me: his grey face in the hospital bed, the tubes and the wires, the stained green curtain, the sound of the metal hoops as the nurse rattled it along the frame.

'You look tired.' Mum leant across the table and patted my arm.

'Yes, so you said.'

'Is it the job, or is it something else?'

I stood up again, walked over to the window. Outside on the back lawn I could see a man throwing a ball to a small pigtailed girl; she missed it and laughed, then she picked it up and threw it back and the man caught it gracefully in mid-air. I turned to Mum sitting at the table. 'I've got to tell you something . . .'

'About what?' She looked at me uneasily, pushed the biscuits around on the plate.

'You know how I couldn't find your mum?' I sat down, rested a hand on her arm. 'Well, after that, I tried to find your dad.'

233

'Yes, I thought you might. It doesn't matter, I knew you wouldn't—'

'But I have. This is what I've got to tell you. I've found him.'

CHAPTER THIRTY-NINE

The whereabouts of Muriel Wilson's father are unknown. Her
mother believes there is no hope whatsoever of tracing him.
Branch home admission report, 5 July 1950

How, at the age of sixty-five, do you prepare to meet the
man who is your father? I don't know what I shall wear.
Which dress to choose. What shoes to pick. How I will
do my hair. I have written down everything I need to do.
But still, I don't know what I will say to him. Whatever
will we talk about? How do you speak to a father you
have never known? We have nothing in common, nothing
to share. I cannot say, 'Remember when this happened?'
Or, 'Wasn't it funny that day we . . .' And nor can he.
There is nothing he can say, because he knows nothing
about my life or me.

I don't know if he will like the look of me, this daughter
he has never known. Will he find me pleasant, will I please
him? Or will he glance at me in disappointment and turn
away?

It's all so easy, these modern methods of finding people.

It's no longer a matter of standing hopelessly outside the hospital where you were born. A faded birth certificate in your hands. A longing in your heart. Because all the adults you've ever known have never told you a single thing about your past. Now you can reach back through time. You can cross cities and countries and continents. You can find family members you never knew you had, all without leaving your chair. And this is what my daughter has done. She never found my mam. But my father, after all these years, after a lifetime apart, he is coming to England and I am going to meet him.

I remember the day Mr Appleyard gave me my birth certificate. How I stood there reading what it said about my mam. But when it came to my father, there was nothing. Just a dash across the page. Why my mam didn't put his name on that certificate I will never know. She told it to the people at Hoodfield House. It was there in my file. His name and the state he was from. So why didn't she put it on my birth certificate, unless that was what he wanted? He had wanted to remain anonymous. He hadn't wanted to be identified as anybody's father.

I will never know if my mam was telling the truth when she said there was no hope whatsoever of tracing him.

I remember Miss Cleary calling me into her room that same day. She said my father was a coloured soldier from Louisiana. And I looked at her brightly painted fingernails. I had felt excited then. But what could I do? I was sixteen years old. I had no inkling of how to find him. I didn't even know his name.

And what about now? I don't know what he will want. What will he look like? What will he think of me? In the mornings, as I make my breakfast, I feel my heart as it misses a beat. Sometimes it seems to stop altogether. It's not a pleasant thing, to be afraid of your own heartbeat.

When Rosie told me, I didn't understand at first. I was still trying to make sense of why she was so upset about Kenwood House. Then she explained that she had found him in America. She had got his enlistment papers, she had written to him. She'd been given a phone number. She'd found his grandson. And now he's coming to visit, to the place where she works, the job she's been so secretive about. Because it's his grandson's house. And she has known this all along.

'What did he say when you told him?' I asked.

She looked away and didn't answer.

'Rosie,' I said. 'What did he say when you told him about me?'

And that is when I realised the terrible truth: that he didn't know.

She thinks she has been doing this for my sake. That I needed to know my mam and my father. She would not listen when I told her I did not want to know, that I was fine as I was. And now I've no choice but to meet him.

'It doesn't seem right to disturb him after all this time,' I told her. 'He has his own life, his own family now.'

'Yes,' she said. 'But you *are* his own family, Mum.'

I haven't been able to sleep properly these past few days. I can't think of anything else. In the evenings, as I prepare my dinner or read my book, my heart seems to thump in my throat like a roller-coaster ride. At night I can't find any peace, any place to be still. I lie in bed and go over all manner of things. The day I arrived at Hoodfield House and Auntie Peal stood at the stone doorway, all dressed in black. The coloured bunting waving above her head. The broken cardboard crown by her feet. The hall that was cold and smelt of cough drops. The picture of Jesus on the wall and the man with thick sideburns. I didn't know what was happening then; no one told me a thing. I was a four-year-old child, a casualty of war.

'Call me Auntie,' Auntie Peal had said. 'We're like a family here.' The next morning she stitched a number into all my clothes. She took the needle from between her teeth. She looked at me with her brittle blue eyes. And she said, 'We are your parents now, Muriel.'

Only they weren't. They never were my parents. And now I'm going to meet him, at the age of sixty-five. How am I meant to feel about that? I don't know what I will wear. How I will greet him, what I will say. I cannot think how to prepare myself. But I have no choice; I can't say no, not now. I have to meet him, the man Rosie has found, my father, Jonny Rooster Murrey.

CHAPTER FORTY

Last night I woke in the early hours to hear big breaths of wind, and when I opened my curtains the sky was streaked with red. Lights were on in the house opposite; other people had been woken up as well, or perhaps they'd never gone to bed. The rain began lightly, and for a while I stood at my attic window and watched it dance around the street lamps, making wavery pools of white. But then it began slapping on the roof and I jumped as a crack of thunder split the air and reverberated around the room.

It reminded me of a morning last year when it had started to snow. At first it seemed it would just snow and stop; some would gather on the ground, the next day the pavements would be icy. But it had just carried on, until it wasn't possible to see individual flakes, snow pouring continuously from the sky like a distorted television screen. I'd had a moment of panic then, because what if it didn't stop, what if it just kept on snowing for ever? Sometimes you can't see when something will ever possibly end.

This is how the storm felt last night, it was out of control. I stood at my window, watching as power lines swung like flimsy skipping ropes and the branches of a tree on the other side of the road snapped and heaved and fell. Then the street lights went out and a sheet of lightning turned the sky bright blue, as clear as if it were morning. From somewhere above came the sound of cracking tiles, and I rushed into my bathroom and struggled with the rusty latch, pushing open the window to see what had fallen. Rain cascaded down the roof like a river that had burst its banks, but I couldn't see which tiles had fallen or from where. Then I heard a cry from downstairs and I grabbed my dressing gown and went to check on the children.

From the doorway of their bedroom I could see the outline of both of their bodies, and I went and stood over Bobby for a moment, reassured by the sound of his breathing. But when I turned to Ella's bed, I realised she wasn't there. I went quickly down the stairs to the hallway, fearful I would see her at the front door, a rucksack on her back, trying to run away again.

The hallway was deserted, so I went down to the kitchen, put on the light and looked around. The table was just as I'd left it, all neatly laid for breakfast: the bowls and cups and spoons, the cereal packets, a fresh clean bib on Bobby's high chair. I couldn't think where Ella was if she wasn't in here. I tried the door to the garden, was relieved that it was locked, ran up to the playroom and the office, but both were empty. I hurried back up the stairs, my feet pounding on the carpet, heard a rush of blood in my ears as through my open bathroom door I saw her, leaning out of the window, her chest against the top frame of glass.

'Ella,' I hissed, and I threw my arms around her, grasped

my hands together and forced her back. Then, still holding her tightly, I closed the window and picked her up and carried her to my bed.

'What were you doing?' I laid her on the duvet.

'I was looking for you,' she whispered.

'But I'm here,' I told her.

'I thought you'd gone.'

'I'd never leave you, Ella. How could I do that, not when I'm looking after you?' I remembered Bobby then. I didn't want him to wake to find his sister wasn't there, to be alone downstairs in such a storm, so I told Ella to stay where she was and went quickly down to the bedroom. Then I carried him, still sleeping, to my room and gently put him on the bed as well. I lay down between the children then and waited for the storm to pass, and as the wind and the rain raged outside, as branches fell and tiles still cracked, I felt we were the only ones safe in the world, and that whatever happened when their great-grandfather arrived and their father came home, if I could just hold on to them and keep them warm and dry and loved, then we would always be together like this.

We woke late this morning and I lay in the bed, listening to Mrs B in the kitchen, the bang of a pan being laid on the counter, the muffled sound of water in the pipes. Then Ella opened her eyes and rested an arm across my chest. 'I want Cassidy,' she said softly. 'I want to tell her my great-grandpa Rooster is coming. Sometimes I'm really horrible to her.'

'We all do things we shouldn't, Ella. I'm sure you can make it up to her.' I pulled her closer, thinking of what

241

Amina had said, that everything I'd done was because I'd been thinking of myself and not Mum. I needed to ring Amina, I needed to go round and apologise for not telling her the truth. I turned in the bed, feeling as dizzy as if the mattress were made of water; I didn't know if Rooster Murrey would really come tomorrow, or whether he would change his mind. Maybe he would suddenly email to say everything was cancelled, and for a moment I almost hoped he would. I tried to focus on the room, to feel the firmness of the bed again, the fact that Ella was beside me. 'I'm sure Cassidy won't mind,' I told her. 'Some people can be really forgiving, and we haven't seen her in a while.'

'That's because . . .' Ella pulled the duvet up so it almost covered her face.

'That's because what?'

'Her mum and dad think you're weird.'

I laughed and got out of bed, went to the window and looked down at the scene of destruction in Pembleton Crescent: the dangling power lines, the knocked-over bins that had scattered rubbish on the pavement, the broken tree branch lying in the road. I thought of Shanice and Mark, wondered what else they might have said about me and what would happen once they found out who I was and what I was really doing here. 'What was going on last night? Were you afraid of the storm?'

'It was really noisy.'

'I know it was, but why did you come up here? Was it your imaginary friend?'

'She's gone.' Ella's voice was muffled from under the covers.

'Gone where?'

'I don't know.'

'Is she coming back?'

'No,' said Ella.

There's been a strange atmosphere inside 68 Pembleton Crescent today; the house feels squeezed of air, as if it doesn't want me any more, and I seem to be endlessly walking up and down the stairs, forgetting what I'm looking for, oppressed with the waiting.

This afternoon I offered to make the children a special dinner, and asked each of them what they wanted. Ella chose sausages and mash, the meal we'd first had together, with jelly and ice cream to follow, while Bobby said he just wanted jelly. I left them with Mrs B while I went to the shop and I was longer than I meant to be; it was very quiet when I got back to Pembleton Crescent and put my key in the lock and came in.

I popped my head round the playroom door; Ella was lying on the sofa watching TV. In the kitchen Mrs B was sitting at the table, which was covered in paper and pens.

'What are you doing?' I asked, walking across the room. 'Have you been playing that game again?'

'What game is that?' She picked up a pen, twirled it in her hand.

'You know what game. I wish you'd never made me do it. I wish I'd never even heard of Kenwood.'

Mrs B smiled. 'And why's that?'

'Because I've been there before.' I pulled out a chair and sat down. 'That's the reason I remembered it.'

'If you say so.'

'I do say so. I was there as a child.'

'Oh it's only a bit of fun.' Mrs B put down the pen, began gathering the papers into a pile.

I watched her as she lined the pens up on the table, thinking of the day I'd first started work and how suspicious she'd seemed of me, as if she'd known right from the start that something was odd. 'I've been thinking. If you'd like to have tomorrow off . . .'

'Tomorrow, why's that?'

'We have a visitor.'

'Ah, yes.' Mrs B stood up and began buttoning her cardigan. 'Ella told me.'

'She did?'

'Oh yes, she's told me everything. All about the letter to her great-grandfather, and the emails . . .' Mrs B smoothed her hands down her cardigan, tucked them tightly in her pockets. 'And have you thought what Mr Murrey will say?'

'No,' I said, as if I didn't care, as if this wasn't something I'd been worrying about all day long.

CHAPTER FORTY-ONE

It's Wednesday, and all afternoon we'd been listening out for a cab, because I was pretty certain Jonny Rooster Murrey would be coming by cab. Ella made ginger biscuits and set them to cool on a wire tray, I put a fresh bunch of flowers in a vase on the kitchen table, Mrs B furiously vacuumed the house. I kept Bobby in as clean clothes as possible, and didn't even let him play outside since he came home from nursery. I didn't know why I was trying so hard; Rooster Murrey didn't deserve any of this, but I had to make the day special for Ella and for Mum.

And then, just after five o'clock, it happened.

'He's here!' Ella screamed. We were standing at the playroom window when the cab pulled up, and I watched as a tall, sturdy man got out and paid the driver. He wore a black suit jacket and a mouse-coloured hat, and as he came up the steps, I saw him take off the hat and hold it against his chest. The moment we heard the knock on the door, I expected Ella to follow me into the hall, but instead she ran out of the playroom and straight down the stairs. So it was me who opened the door to 68 Pembleton Crescent, and there on the step stood my grandfather.

He looked only vaguely like the person in the photograph in Jonas Murrey's office, the elderly gentleman sitting on a swinging chair on a porch; instead his presence seemed to fill the doorway. I took in his clothes: a burgundy jumper beneath his jacket, sharply pressed trousers and shiny shoes; this was a man who cared how he dressed. I looked at his face, his skin as smooth and dark as Jonas's, barely lined except for a pouch of skin around his neck, a little tuft of white hair beneath his bottom lip. I looked at the shape of his cheeks, the curve of his nose, the depth of his eyes; the resemblance was subtle, but there was no mistaking it: he looked like my mum.

'Hello,' I said, and I felt my heart tighten as I held out my hand. 'You must be Rooster Murrey.'

'The one and only!' He laughed, his voice slightly wheezy, and shook my hand with hot callused fingers.

'Ella!' I called. 'He's here.'

'And who are you?' asked Rooster Murrey.

'Me?' I smiled and turned away, not wanting him to look at me too closely. 'I'm the babysitter,' and I waved with one hand that he should come in.

Bobby came bursting into the hallway then and I saw Rooster Murrey flinch slightly, his confidence disturbed. 'Shall we go downstairs?' I suggested, and I picked Bobby up and put him on my hip, and waited while Rooster Murrey brushed past me and went swaggering down the stairs.

Mrs B had been working hard in the kitchen; she'd polished the vast table and set out Ella's biscuits and now she stood there, her pinafore round her waist, beaming, happy to reclaim a role she hadn't assumed for so long. 'Welcome, welcome, take a seat, sir, what an awfully long way you've come.'

Rooster Murrey nodded. He seemed like a man who was used to being called sir; he didn't seem to find anything strange about it.

'What can I get you? You must be parched. How about a nice cup of tea?'

Rooster placed his hat on the table, took off his jacket and positioned it carefully around the back of his chair. Then he sat down and I stared at him, transfixed, as he shifted slightly and then, very slowly, placed a hand under each thigh. He was aware I was looking, I could see a muscle pulsing in his jaw, but he smiled at Mrs B and said, 'If I may make a proposition . . . Is it too early for something stronger, ma'am?'

'Not at all, not at all,' cried Mrs B, delighted at the way she'd been addressed. 'A little drop of whisky, perhaps?'

Rooster Murrey gave a satisfied smile and looked around the room. 'So where the hell is my little pen pal?'

Then he saw Ella, standing outside the door to the garden, her face pressed against the glass. He laughed and waved, and when she didn't come in, he shrugged his shoulders. 'Well, I guess we all need to get used to one another. Where's Jonas?'

'He'll be here soon,' I said. 'His flight doesn't arrive until tomorrow.'

'His flight?' asked Rooster Murrey in surprise. 'Why, where's he been? I thought he'd be here.'

Ella came in then and she threw herself at her

great-grandfather, burying her face against his burgundy jumper.

'Whoa!' He laughed. 'You're a little fireball!' He hugged her close and then drew back, one hand resting on her head. 'Let me take a proper look at you, honey. I've come a long way to see you.'

Mrs B winked at me as I put Bobby in his high chair, and when I went to the cupboard to fetch the whisky and the glasses she whispered, 'He's a right charmer, isn't he?'

'He certainly is.' I gave a tight smile and poured out a generous whisky. 'Ella's been longing for you to come,' I said, handing him the glass and putting the bottle on the table. 'She was so happy when you wrote to her.'

Rooster Murrey glanced at me as if wondering who I was to speak for Ella, to include myself in this gathering, and I tried not to look at the two of them, at the easy way he had one arm around his great-granddaughter's waist. Instead I looked at the clock on the wall. Mum was supposed to be here by now.

'It must have been a very long time,' I said, sitting down opposite him, 'since you were in England.'

Rooster Murrey took his arm away from Ella and pulled at the sleeves of his jumper. 'That is correct.'

'Because you were here in the nineteen forties.'

'And how would you know that?' He looked confused, began to fiddle impatiently with a small ring on his little finger.

'And you've not been back since?' I asked, ignoring his question.

Rooster Murrey's face was uncertain as he picked up his glass and sipped his whisky. 'No, I have not,' he said, and then he began to talk about his journey, the movie on the plane, the God-awful food, the clumsy landing. He spoke rapidly, without a pause, like someone who is used to being listened to.

I was relieved when Bobby started to make a fuss and I could sit him on my lap and interrupt his great-grandfather's monologue. 'Here,' I told him. 'Have one of your sister's biscuits.'

'Isn't he cute?' said Rooster Murrey. 'It's kinda like I'm looking at a photocopy.'

'A photocopy of what?' asked Ella.

'Well, honey, this little guy here looks a whole lot like my late brother.'

'Is that right?' said Mrs B, and she came and stood by the table, her eyes shining bright. 'How strange. He does often say he wants to go home . . .'

I started to bounce Bobby up and down on my lap. Mrs B was interfering; my mother would be here any moment.

'I thought I sensed a connection,' said Mrs B. 'When Mr Murrey first walked in. Perhaps this is why he has come.'

And I wanted to say no, this is not why he's come, this is not why I got him here. Just wait and see.

CHAPTER FORTY-TWO

When the knock finally came on the front door of 68 Pembleton Crescent, I leapt out of my chair, and although Mrs B looked as if she wanted to answer it, I made it clear it would be me. I walked quickly up the stairs, and when I reached the top, I stopped. I could see myself on the day I'd first come to meet Jonas Murrey; how eager I'd been to get into his family and his house, how determined I was on revenge, and now it was almost over.

I opened the door and Mum stood there expectantly, framed between the two olive trees in their earthenware pots. She wore a purple coat I hadn't seen before and she must have come from the hairdresser's, for her hair was newly styled. 'Is he here?' she whispered, and before I had time to tell her that he didn't know, that I hadn't been able to tell him yet, she'd walked past me and into the hall. I watched her set off towards the stairs to the kitchen – she seemed to instinctively know which way to go – then place her hand on the banister and stop.

'Mum,' I urged. 'I haven't told him . . .'

'Come on,' she said. 'Let's get this over with then,' and

without looking behind her, she let go of the banister and went down the stairs.

It seemed to have grown darker in the kitchen; the flowers appeared to have wilted a little in the vase, the air smelt of coffee and whisky. Mrs B had turned on the lamps and was busy handing out the rest of the ginger biscuits. Bobby was back in his high chair, drinking from a plastic cup of juice. Mum stopped in the doorway and I expected her to shrink a little, as she usually does when faced with a group of people, as if looking for a way to make herself as inconspicuous as possible, but instead she walked straight in.

'This is my mum,' I told the people round the table. 'And Mum,' I took her hand and squeezed it, 'this is Ella, and this is Bobby, the children I've been looking after. This is Mrs B. And this is their great-grandfather, from Louisiana.'

Rooster Murrey had risen halfway from his chair in a vague show of politeness, and now he stopped and stared at me. 'How d'you know that? How would you know I'm from Louisiana?'

Pleased to have unsettled him, I didn't answer, but pulled out a chair for Mum. She looked at me for a second, as if about to speak, but then she bit her lip and obediently sat down. Rooster Murrey barely looked at her; there was no flash of recognition, no sign that she was anything but a stranger to him. How could he not see himself in her? How could he not see what I could see: the sameness in the shape of their cheeks, the curve of their noses, the depth of their eyes? Look at her, I wanted to say, forget about Bobby resembling your brother, look at the woman sitting next to you; doesn't *she* look familiar?

I sat down, poured more whisky into his glass. 'So,' I said, aware that everyone was looking at me, 'as we were saying, you were over here in the war . . .'

'Were you a soldier?' asked Ella.

'I sure was.'

'Why?'

'Really, Ella,' scolded Mrs B.

But Rooster Murrey chuckled. 'Why? Because it seemed like the right thing to do, honey. I was a young man and I was getting ready to get myself into trouble, so one morning I walked into the recruitment station and I told them, sir, I'd like to join the army—'

'And you were posted here,' I interrupted. 'Somewhere near Nottingham.'

'That's right.' He frowned. 'Nottingham. You sure seem to know a whole lot about me.' He looked down at Ella and smiled, put out an arm and wrapped it again around her waist, but I could see he was troubled, that he didn't like my questioning, that I was really unsettling him now.

'And do you remember once going to a dance hall in London? A dance hall in London in 1945, does that ring a bell?'

'Honey,' he shrugged, as if this didn't matter, 'I went to a whole lot of dance halls back then.'

Yes, I thought, I bet you did. 'But at this one you met someone, a woman called Dorothy Wilson.'

'Dorothy?'

'Yes,' I said, enjoying the look of shock on his face. 'She was in her twenties. She'd come down from Cumbria and she was in the Women's Auxiliary Air Force—'

'How do you know about Dorothy? What the hell is going on here?' Rooster Murrey removed his arm from

Ella's waist, picked up his glass and then clumsily put it down again. 'This is a hell of a welcome for an old man!'

'So you do remember her?'

'Yes, I remember her.'

I sat back, surprised that he wasn't denying it. I'd expected him to say he had no knowledge of my grandmother, to pretend she had never existed, and here he was, as casual as anything, saying that he did. 'And then you had an affair.'

'Oh it was more than that.'

'Really?' I said, and I could sense Mum looking at me, that she didn't like the tone of my voice. 'It was important to you, was it?'

'Rosie . . .' Mum said softly. 'Please . . .'

'If she meant something to you, why did you run away?'

'What is this?' Rooster Murrey snapped, pulling on the sleeves of his jumper. 'Who did you say you were? How d'you know all of this?'

'Oh I know *all* about you.'

'You do?'

'Yes, because you promised to marry her, and she believed you. But then you left her just like that—'

'Now hang on there, young lady.' Angrily he leaned across the table, as if finally he'd had enough. 'Don't you start interrogating me. I didn't leave her just like that. Let me tell you something—'

'No, let me tell *you* something. You ran away because you didn't want anything to do with marriage, did you?'

'Now listen here . . .' Rooster Murrey slammed his glass on the table. 'Dorothy and me, I met her at a dance hall like you said. How you know that, I don't know. But let me tell you how it was. I wasn't interested in chasing the

253

girls like some of the boys; I wasn't interested in any white girl. There was a novelty about them, I'll give you that, but I treated everyone as an individual. Yet there was something about Dorothy, she had this smile . . .'

I looked at Mum, saw the longing in her eyes.

'We saw each other just as much as we could,' continued Rooster Murrey. 'I came to London whenever they let me. We did everything together: we walked, we talked, it was like we'd known each other all our lives. After eighteen months I asked her to marry me, and she said yes.'

'You asked her to marry you,' Mum echoed. 'And she said yes.'

Rooster nodded without looking at her. 'Of course the army didn't like that, especially the white boys. There were riots when a black boy courted a white girl.'

'Riots?' I asked.

'Oh yes. They ran you down if they saw you with a white girl, threatened to lynch you if you so much as danced with one. What has he got that I ain't got, that's what they were asking themselves.' Rooster Murrey gave a grim smile. 'They didn't want us going into some towns, they didn't let us out when the white boys were out, there were no passes for us. If they saw you with a white girl they came after you.' He stopped and looked at Ella beside him, as if regretting what he'd been about to say.

She smiled and reached up to touch the little patch of hair under his lip. 'Are you telling a story?'

Rooster nodded. 'I certainly am, because Dorothy and me, that was something else. We made plans together. I bought her a fine engagement ring. I asked permission from the commanding officer – he was one dumb officer from South Carolina – and he said no. I was mad as hell;

I could have punched him on the nose. But what could I do? I was in the army.' Rooster Murrey stopped, licked his lips. 'You want to know what they did? They sent me straight to France. Hell, I was moved out of England in forty-eight hours.'

'What do you mean?' I hesitated, 'They moved you?'

'You think the Americans were gonna let a black boy have a relationship with a white girl? Hell, no, let alone marry her. And the British, they didn't want us here in the first place. Oh, they were friendly enough when we arrived, but they hadn't liked the idea at first. Send them someplace warm, they said, send them to North Africa, they'll be happy there. They didn't want us associating with their women.'

'*Their* women?'

'That's right.' He nodded. 'That's how they saw it. They said, send over some coloured women to keep the Negroes occupied.' He gave a bitter laugh, began fiddling with the ring on his finger again. 'And the Americans, they didn't want any more war brides, especially not for the likes of me. That was the policy, that was how it was. Oh, it wasn't written down or anything, there was nothing that said we couldn't, but they found out, they moved you on. It was either leave when I was told, or' – Rooster put out two fingers and pointed them, like a child firing an imaginary gun – 'be handcuffed and taken away.'

'Handcuffed?' I sat back in my chair, stunned.

'That's right, that's what they did.' He pursed his lips, looked down at his hands as if to say, there you go, I've told you now. 'And I knew what could happen to Dorothy. They didn't say nice things about white girls who went with boys like me . . .'

'But after you got to France, didn't you try to contact her, to stay in touch?'

'Well of course I did!' Rooster Murrey grabbed the bottle of whisky. 'You think I sound flippy?'

'Flippy?'

'Yeah, like I had the hots for Dorothy and it's no big deal? Because you're wrong. What happened over here, it blighted my life.' He took the top off the bottle, poured whisky into his glass. 'Sure I stayed in touch. I wrote her a whole lot of letters, dozens and dozens of letters, every day of every week. I told her what had happened and I asked her to wait for me. I sent her things, candy and scented soaps. Then one day they called me in and told me. She'd married an English fella. She'd changed her mind and didn't want any more to do with me. They said I should put an end to all the letters right away or there would be' – Rooster spread his fingers out on the table – 'consequences.'

Ella pushed up against her great-grandfather, looking worried. 'I'm hungry.'

'I'll fix us all some sandwiches,' offered Mrs B. 'Bobby, do you want a sandwich? Mr Murrey, can I get you something?'

Rooster didn't answer; he was still looking down at his hands.

'Well,' I told him, 'what they said wasn't true. Because Dorothy Wilson hadn't married anyone. So they were lying.'

Rooster looked confused. 'She hadn't? How do you know that?'

'Not then, she hadn't. She was waiting for you. And let's not forget,' I folded my arms, 'it was you who was already married.'

'Me?'

I glanced at Mum. I hadn't told her this; it was the one thing I hadn't told her.

'That's what it says, in your enlistment papers.'

'My enlistment papers?' Rooster Murrey pushed himself up from his chair. 'How the hell did you get your hands on my enlistment papers?'

'It says you were married.' I eyed him across the table, ignoring his question. 'Dorothy Wilson was waiting for you, and all the time you were married.'

'She was waiting for me?'

'So were you married or not?'

'Hell, I'd just turned twenty-three! I married my first wife in June of 1944, signed up in the fall, and she wrote me a Dear John letter before I'd even stepped off the boat! She'd met another fella and that was that.' Rooster Murrey grimaced and picked up his glass. 'I was divorced by the time I met Dorothy; she knew all about that.'

'So if you didn't run away from her, from my—' I stopped, forced myself to slow down. 'Then why didn't you answer me when I wrote to you? If you didn't *know* you had a child, if you weren't guilty as hell, then why didn't you answer me?'

'Child?' Rooster stopped, the glass still at his lips. 'What do you mean, child?'

CHAPTER FORTY-THREE

Rooster Murrey put down his glass, patted Ella distractedly on the head. 'What are you saying, there was a child?'

'Yes,' I said impatiently, 'of course there was a child, because you got Dorothy Wilson pregnant, and then you abandoned her—'

'That's enough!' Mum cried. 'You heard what he said, he loved her—'

'And . . .' I continued, because I couldn't stop now; I had to say what needed to be said, 'do you know what happened to that child of yours? That little girl spent her whole life in a children's home, without any parents, without any family to call her own. That's what I wrote to you about.'

'You wrote to me? Why would you be writing to me?'

'Yes, I wrote you a letter, it was sent by certified mail. I explained everything.'

'I never open letters.'

I heard myself laugh, a forced sound that seemed to be coming from someone else. 'What do you mean, you never open letters? Why not?'

'Well, who do I know that could be writing to me?' Rooster Murrey shrugged and attempted a smile. 'Look at me, I'm a widower, an old man. I've always told them at the home, don't go passing me any letters.'

'The home?'

'Where I live, honey. I've been there since my late wife passed away. They call it assisted living.'

I stared at him in disbelief, thinking of the day Ella had sent her letter, the address I'd helped her write down, Mount Royale in Tallahassee. She'd said her great-grandpa was a rich man, that he lived in a big house in Florida, and I'd believed her. 'It's not your home?'

Rooster laughed. 'Hell, no!'

'So what happened to my letter?'

'I guess it was thrown away.'

'Thrown away!' I sat back in my chair, appalled. How could my letter have been thrown away when it had taken me so long to write, when I'd been absolutely certain that he had it, when that was the reason I'd hated him, because he couldn't even be bothered to answer? 'Well you opened Ella's letter.' I shifted in my chair, aware of how petulant I sounded.

'That was because I could see it was from a child.' Rooster Murrey looked at Ella and smiled. 'I don't know what made me open it, but I did. And I'm sure glad about that. This little girl's emails, they got me thinking, maybe this old man should make the journey while he still can, maybe he should come over and see the only family he has left before—'

'But I rang you,' I told him. 'I rang you and you wouldn't speak to me.'

'You rang me? Why would you be ringing me?'

'Yes, I rang you.'

'Who answered?'

'I don't know! It was a woman—'

'High-pitched voice? Not the friendliest-sounding lady?' I nodded.

'That would be Mary-Jane; we call her the gatekeeper.'

'But I heard you in the background.'

'You can't have done.'

But I did, I wanted to say, I heard you. You knew it was me and you refused to speak to me. I stood up, feeling disorientated, I'd been so sure that he'd promised to marry my grandmother when he knew it would never happen, that he'd known she was pregnant and had abandoned her. For so long I'd wanted revenge, and now, with everything he'd told me, I didn't know what to say. I watched as Rooster Murrey took the ring off his little finger and laid it in the palm of his hand.

'What's that?' asked Ella.

'That, honey,' Rooster looked down at his hand, 'was something for me to remember someone by.'

'Are you crying?' asked Ella.

'Well, honey,' gently he wiped at his eyes, 'I guess I am.' He picked up the ring and held it to the light. 'You see this?'

I leaned over. On the inside of the ring I saw the faded outline of two letters, a D and an R.

'This was us,' said Rooster Murrey, tracing his finger along the metal. 'This was to remember her by.' Then he looked up at me, as if it had only just occurred to him. 'What happened to Dorothy?'

No one spoke; it was silent in the kitchen. Bobby yawned. The cat came in and started rubbing itself against the table leg, and I stared at it, I couldn't remember the last time I'd seen the cat; I didn't know where it had been all this time. Outside I could hear the light, erratic beginnings of rain, a gentle pattering on the roof, the sound of squirrels scrabbling down a tree.

'We don't know,' I said at last.

'We?' asked Rooster Murrey.

'I tried to find her, and we just don't know.' I looked around at the people at the table, overcome with sadness that my grandmother was never going to be here, that she was never going to know what happened to her daughter or the man she was going to marry, that she would never know about any of us.

'And what happened to . . .' Rooster Murrey looked away, as if he could barely bring himself to ask. 'What happened to the baby?'

'This is her,' I said, unable to believe he hadn't realised. 'This is your daughter.'

'Oh my good Lord,' and Jonny Rooster Murrey struggled out of his seat and staggered clumsily towards my mother.

CHAPTER FORTY-FOUR

I watched as my grandfather took my mother in his arms, saw how small she seemed, how vulnerable. I sat there in a daze until Mrs B suggested they might like to go to the playroom for some privacy, while I got the children ready for bed. I stood up, relieved to have something useful to do, to be able to get out of the kitchen, not to have to think about what a mess I'd made of everything, how wrong I'd been.

I took the children upstairs, carefully undressed Bobby and changed his nappy, made him clean and comfortable before putting him down in his cot and placing the sheet and the blanket over him.

'I want my grandad,' he muttered, holding on to the bars of the cot. 'He's funny.'

'He's not your grandad,' said Ella. 'He's your great-grandad.'

'Yes,' said Bobby, and he lay down with his bottle and contentedly closed his eyes.

From downstairs I could hear the faint sound of voices in the playroom and I tried to imagine what they were saying, what it was they were talking about. It felt so odd to think that my mother was down there with her father; it was what I'd wanted, what I'd hoped for more than anything else in the world, but the way I'd brought them together was wrong, everything I'd believed for so long had turned out to be false, and I didn't know if anyone would ever forgive me.

'What's happening?' Ella got on to her bed.

'It's complicated . . .' I began.

'Why were you angry with my great-grandpa?'

'I wasn't angry, Ella.'

'Yes you were. He was crying.'

'Okay, I was, but I'm not angry now.'

'Why is your mum here?'

'Let me try and explain. A long time ago, when my mum was born—'

'What's that?' Ella interrupted. 'It's the phone!'

'Wait!' I cried, but she leapt out of bed and ran out of the room, and I made myself stay there, listening to her bare feet rushing down the carpeted stairs, so quickly that any minute I expected her to trip and fall.

'That was my daddy,' Ella said triumphantly, when she came back into the room.

'Oh? And what did he say?'

'He said he's going to the airport soon.' She looked at me and punched the air with both fists. 'Yes! My daddy's coming back!'

'Good,' I said, as calmly as I could. I waited as she got back into bed and then I pulled up the duvet, smoothed it down with my hands. 'Off you go to sleep then, and you'll see him soon.'

'Will I?'

'Yes, of course you will. Now go to sleep.' I expected her to argue, but instead she closed her eyes and turned on to her side, and I stood there for a moment, looking at the two of them, safe in their beds. Then I turned off the light and began walking cautiously down the stairs. I stopped outside the playroom and listened. I could hear my grandfather's voice, soft-spoken and polite, and then my mother's gentle laugh. I knocked on the door, and when no one answered, I opened it a little, saw them sitting side by side on the sofa. Mum looked up, but my grandfather didn't seem to have noticed I was there. I saw him take hold of her hand and hold it in his. 'Honey,' he said, 'what do you take me for? I didn't travel this far not to be loving. You know what I believe? An honourable man will protect his children above all else.' He sighed and wiped at his eyes. 'Because a man who leaves a child behind on purpose has no honour, and a man of honour who didn't know he had a child will try and make the situation right.' My mother nodded, and feeling like an intruder, I stepped backwards and closed the door.

CHAPTER FORTY-FIVE

'So what do you think of him?' I turned to Mum, sitting next to me in the garden. I'd positioned two chairs close to each other, facing the flattened round dent on the grass where the paddling pool usually sat. I could see the lawn still scattered with debris from Monday night's storm – broken twigs, clumps of earth fallen from pots, shards of splintered tiles – and I knew someone would have to clear it up, but not me.

The garden was dark but for a faint pool of light on the patio floor, reflected down from Jonas's office; perhaps Mrs B had forgotten to turn it off before she left. Rooster had gone to bed. It was just the two of us now.

Mum picked up her cup of tea; she'd been silent since we'd come outside. 'What do I think of him?' she asked at last. 'Well, I was a bit surprised, to be honest. When I came in and saw him sitting there, I thought, is that really him? He could be anyone's father.'

'Really?'

'Well, yes, because who is he to me?'

I stared at her, unable to hide my disappointment,

because I'd seen them in the playroom, sitting together on the sofa, the loving way my grandfather had taken her hand, and I wanted to hear that whatever I'd done, she was happy now. I longed for her to tell me this, to say that she forgave me.

'I don't know a thing about him.' Mum sighed and put down her cup. 'The truth is, he doesn't really mean much to me after all this time.'

'Doesn't he?' I thought of the day we'd gone to get her file, the photograph of her being held by the woman she'd been forced to call Auntie, how unhappy she'd looked, how alone and afraid. Now she had her father and she was saying he didn't mean that much to her. But he must do, I wanted to say, he must mean something to you, he's your father.

'That's the way it is. People like me, we want a happy ending and life is not always like that, is it? You should have told me, Rosie. You shouldn't have kept it from me. How do you think it felt, walking into that room and realising he didn't even know me?'

'I'm sorry.'

'Well, so you should be.' She looked away, stared off into the darkness of the garden. 'You never should have done what you did. You do know that, don't you? You should have told me when you'd found him. You just never think of the consequences.'

'I know. I'm sorry.'

'What's done is done.' She turned back to look at me, and then finally she smiled. 'I did think he would be more handsome than that . . . I was expecting a bit of a daredevil soldier.'

'Well he probably was, a long time ago.'

'He does seem like a nice man, but I don't know anything about him. Although . . .'

'Although?'

'Well I do look a bit like him.'

'I know you do. You even sit on a chair in the same way.'

'We do?'

'Yes, it's exactly the same.'

'Well that's where I get that from then.' Mum looked pleased. 'The thing is, I've never had anyone I look like before. When I was growing up, I was always different from everyone else and the single thing that made me different was my colour, so to have someone that actually looks like me, it's a very strange feeling. It gives me a sense of wholeness, I suppose, like everything has just clicked into place. I can see him in you as well, you know.'

'You can?'

'Not so much looks, but more . . . He has a way about him, he's a passionate man. And it's good to know he loved my mam.'

'You think so?'

'Oh for goodness' sake, of course I do! Can't you see when two people love each other? If he never knew about me, well then, what was he supposed to do? And you heard what he said, what the army did. He was a victim of his time, Rosie, just like my mam, just like we all were.'

I stared at her, wondering why she was always so understanding, why she never expressed any resentment, why she was so endlessly accepting. Was this something she'd learned to do, growing up in the children's home; had it been a way of self-preservation? Or was this just how she was?

'Isn't it funny?' she said. 'Now I have relatives I never even knew about. The two sweet children, of course; maybe others in America as well.'

'You could claim an American passport.'

Mum frowned. 'And why would I want to do that?'

'Because you're half American.'

'I'm not half anything, Rosie. I'm just me. Maybe I could have belonged there once, who knows, but not now.' She looked down at her hands, began to play with her wedding ring. 'Do you know what he said to me in the playroom just now? He said he wished he'd been there for me when I needed him.'

'He did?' I put my head to one side, felt the beginning of tears seep into my eyes.

'Yes, he said he would have fetched me from the home and taken me all the way to Louisiana! But then' – Mum put out one hand and patted my arm – 'you can't rewrite the past, not after all this time. If that had happened, then I wouldn't have met your father, would I? And I wouldn't have had you.'

CHAPTER FORTY-SIX

It's Thursday, and I woke up just as dawn was breaking, my mind racing because there was something I had to remember and for a second I didn't know what it was. I heard footsteps on the landing outside my room, a whispered consultation, and then the children came in.

'Is he here?' Ella leapt on the bed and Bobby tried to follow, clutching the mattress, his legs dangling in the air.

I pulled him up and put the two of them under my duvet. 'Yes,' I said quietly. 'He's here.'

'Let's wake him up, then,' said Ella.

'No, let him sleep. He's had a very long flight, just leave him be for a while.'

But Ella got up and ran out of the room, and so I put Bobby on my hip and went after her. As we passed their father's room, she stopped and said deliberately loudly, 'I've told you, we have to let Great-Grandpa sleep, Bobby,' and then the door flung open and there was Rooster Murrey, wearing neatly pressed blue and white striped pyjamas. He gave a playful roar and made as if to grab them. Ella pretended to be afraid, and then the two of them went shrieking into the bedroom.

It felt different this morning; there were signs of life now. Rooster's open suitcase on the floor, a pair of reading glasses next to the bed, a jacket hanging on the outside of the wardrobe. I wondered what Jonas would make of this and where he would sleep if Rooster intended to stay here. I'd never thought he would stay here; I hadn't planned for this.

'How about you read me a story?' asked Rooster, settling himself back on the bed. 'See those books there, honey?' He pointed at his suitcase. 'Why don't you take the one you like?'

Ella went and rummaged in the case, brought out a book.

'Dr Seuss,' nodded Rooster. '*Come Over to My House*. Good choice.'

Ella climbed on to the bed and opened the book with a serious air, and I left them to it and went down to the kitchen.

I busied myself making a pot of tea and a pot of coffee, not sure which Rooster would prefer. I looked in the fridge for eggs and bacon, wondering if he would like a cooked breakfast, and it felt so normal, being in this kitchen, thinking about making breakfast for my grandfather, as if I did it every day. But then I looked outside. It was growing light in the garden; a veil of early morning mist hung over the apple trees, their buds glistening with dew, and I knew that I'd never be here to see them fruit. I was about to go upstairs and ask Rooster what he'd like to eat when he appeared at the doorway, with both children fully dressed. 'Would you like tea or coffee?'

'Coffee,' he said. In his hand he held the mouse-coloured

hat he'd arrived in yesterday. He placed it carefully on the table in front of him.

'How do you like it?'

'Black and sweet,' he chuckled, watching as I added a spoonful of sugar to his cup. 'Don't hold back, honey,' he said, and I smiled because he likes his coffee sweet, just like Mum does.

I handed him the cup, took in how smartly dressed he was, a fresh shirt under his black jacket and a small digital camera around his neck, as if he was getting ready for a trip.

'Has your mom rung?' He asked the question casually, but as he sat down I saw him sway slightly, placing one hand under his thigh.

'No,' I said. 'She hasn't rung.'

'Oh.' He looked disappointed. 'She was going to show me the sights.'

'She was?' I gave Bobby his bottle of milk, feeling hurt that Mum hadn't mentioned anything about this to me last night. Then we heard the doorbell ring.

'That'll be your mom.' Rooster looked nervous. He adjusted the camera strap, put his hat on his head, and we waited as Ella ran up to open the door.

Then Mum came into the kitchen wearing a light rain-coat, a folded umbrella in her hand. 'Good morning,' she said, as bright as anything.

Rooster got up. He looked as if he wanted to kiss her, but Mum seemed to be holding back, as if she wasn't ready for this.

'Here's your map,' she said, handing him a London guide. 'And your travel card. What would you like to see first?'

Rooster patted the hat on his head. 'Well now, I really don't know . . .'

'Are you wearing comfortable shoes?' Mum asked. 'Come on then, don't dawdle,' and she laughed as she led the way upstairs.

I followed them to the front door and watched as they set off down Pembleton Crescent, wondering why she hadn't told me about what she had in store for today, but then, as they disappeared around the corner, I thought, why should she, it's her father after all.

The children were excitable as I took them to nursery and to school. Ella asked, 'Will he still be here later?' three times, and then, for the first morning since I've been here, she gave me a hug before running into the playground.

I returned to Pembleton Crescent, ready to tidy away the breakfast things, but when I came into the kitchen I saw Mrs B had beaten me to it. Everything had been cleared away and she was standing in the corner, her back to me, speaking on the phone. I saw her stiffen as she sensed me come in, and I knew, by the way she straightened up before she put the receiver down, exactly who she'd been talking to. I felt a stab of panic then, because everything that had felt so normal now felt threatened; I didn't know if Jonas had landed, or if he was still on the plane. But any time now he would be back in this house.

At four o'clock Rooster Murrey came home. He'd been on an open-top bus, he said; he'd seen Big Ben. They'd had a ride on the London Eye; he'd always had a good head for heights. He had souvenirs for the children, a

272

teddy bear for Bobby, a snow globe for Ella. Your mom has gone home, he said; he was going for a nap.

I made the children an early dinner, trying to keep everything as calm as possible, telling Bobby he had to wear a bib, refusing to allow Ella more than one ice pop. But I was clumsy in the kitchen; I banged my hip on an open drawer, and I overcooked the potatoes so the oven began to steam smoke.

'Does my daddy know?' asked Ella as she sat at the table, watching as I opened the oven, swearing to myself.

'About what?'

'About my great-grandad.'

'Well,' I told her, 'I'm not sure if he does.' I took out the burning potatoes, blew on my hands, rinsed my fingers under cold water, wanting to just fling everything down, to walk out of this kitchen, this house, to run through the garden and over the wall, anything not to have to be here when Jonas came back.

At eight o'clock I put Ella to bed. Bobby was already fast asleep. 'It's too early,' she complained. 'It's still light outside.'

'I know, but it will be getting dark soon. Go to sleep without a fuss and then when you wake up your dad will be home.'

'And where will you be?' Ella sat up on the bed, eyed me suspiciously. 'Will you be here?'

I patted the duvet, got up and switched off the light.

'Rosie?' she asked. 'Where will you be?'

'I'll still be around,' I said, and however guilty I felt, I couldn't tell her the truth; I couldn't say that I didn't actually know if I would be here at all.

CHAPTER FORTY-SEVEN

I went downstairs and into the playroom, put my hands against the window and felt the coolness of the glass as I stared out at Pembleton Crescent. The pavement looked shiny and clean, the damage from the storm had been cleared away, the handsome red-brick houses glowed in the light of the street lamps, the cherry trees were still heavy with blossom. I stood there, fighting the urge to run away, to leave the children with their great-grandfather, to escape while I still could.

Then a taxi pulled up, Jonas Murrey got out and I heard the sound of the car door slam. I watched him stand at the bottom of the steps looking up at his house, and quickly I came out of the playroom and went down to the kitchen. I stood in the doorway, looking around at the room that I will miss the most, this cavernous basement with its thick medieval table and its row of brass-bottomed pans. For six weeks this has all been mine. I thought of all the meals I'd cooked in here, all the times I'd sat at this table watching Ella colouring, lifted Bobby in and out of his high chair, looked out of the doors at the children playing outside. This was where I'd closed my eyes and described a library I thought I'd never been in before, where I'd deluded myself into thinking Dido Elizabeth Belle meant something to me. This was where I had pretended that 68 Pembleton Crescent was my home, until it nearly felt like it was.

I heard the front door open and close, the sound of Jonas's footsteps coming down; saw the cat run up the stairs. Again I looked around the room, trying to think where I should sit or stand, how to position myself. I heard the footsteps stop, knew he had reached the doorway, and hurriedly I sat down at the far end of the table.

Jonas walked in, deliberately not looking at me, wearing an expensive grey suit over a pale green shirt. I saw how rigidly he held himself as he slapped his briefcase on the table and loosened his tie, pulling it roughly from his neck and throwing it over the back of a chair. He went to a cupboard, took out a bottle of brandy and banged the door shut. His hand was steady as he poured himself a drink, but I could see a pulsing at his jaw, just like Rooster Murrey.

'Jonas?' I said, because I couldn't bear the silence any longer.

'I have had a very lengthy phone call from Mrs B.' His voice was icily calm as he picked up the glass. 'Who has told me everything.'

'I thought—'

'You thought *what*?' He glared at me and put down the glass.

The kitchen seemed very dark and stifling; I longed to get up and put on a lamp, to throw open a window or a door, to let in some air.

'You thought what exactly? You came in here, you waltzed into my house and said you were a nanny, that you had experience with children—'

'I do,' I said nervously. 'I do have experience with children.'

'You gave me references—' He stopped, and I could see how dry his lips were, how hard he was trying to restrain himself. 'You wormed your way into this house and looked after my children—'

'Which I did very well.'

'I don't care if you did it well!' Furiously he banged his fist on the table. 'You had no right! Don't you get it? What do you think you're doing here, sitting in my kitchen? Do you really think you can just walk into someone's house and look after their *children*?'

'I'm sorry . . .'

'Sorry?' He looked at me incredulously. 'Sorry doesn't even begin to cover it. You have ten minutes to pack your things and get out. I don't ever want to see you anywhere near this house again.' He picked up his glass, swallowed quickly. Then he pulled his briefcase towards him, took out some papers and shuffled them in his hands, and I saw what looked like a flight itinerary.

'You're going away again?'

He gave a short angry laugh. 'What's that to you?'

'And what about your children?'

Jonas snapped his briefcase shut. 'My children are not your concern any more.'

'Yes they are. Because as Mrs B will have told you, we share the same grandfather, you and me. We're family.'

'Family? We're *family*? Then why didn't you say so in the first place?'

'Because I was distraught. I thought my mum had the right to know her own father. When your grandfather wouldn't answer my letter or speak to me, it made me desperate. I just wanted Mum to feel she had a family. And if I had told you the truth, if I had just rung the doorbell and come in and told you, then maybe you would have rejected her as well.'

'And why,' he said coldly, 'would I have done that?'

'I don't know. Perhaps because you live in a place like this!'

Jonas looked around the room, as if he had no connection with this kitchen, this wealthy house, at all. We heard a sound then, like footsteps on the floor above, and I saw his shoulders stiffen. 'Is he *here*?'

'Yes. He's in your room.'

'What?' He looked at me in disbelief. 'How dare you bring him here and put him in my room?'

'He is your grandfather.'

'Yes, and we haven't been in touch for years.'

'Why?'

'*Why?* Because families don't necessarily like each other, you know. Or perhaps' – he gave a mocking smile – 'you wouldn't know. He has never come to visit us. I have asked; I have offered to pay the fare . . .'

'Maybe he just didn't want to come to England?'

Jonas ignored me. He picked up the brandy bottle and poured himself another glass, and I knew he had no idea what had happened to his grandfather in the war. He didn't understand why this elderly man might not have wanted to come to the place where he'd met the woman he'd loved and had been forced to leave behind.

'So,' said Jonas. 'Are you still here?'

'I'm sorry. I'm sorry about what I did. But I tried the best I could.'

'The best you could?'

'Yes!' I stood up then and faced him across the table, because whatever I'd done, he was the one who'd been so eager to appoint a stranger to look after his children. When I'd come for my interview, how uninterested he'd been in Ella and Bobby. He'd hardly noticed when his daughter had run into his office with an open pair of scissors in her hands; he hadn't seemed to care at all. Instead, he had hired me, someone about whom he knew virtually nothing, to look after his children so that he could leave. 'I've been here for six weeks,' I told him. 'I've fed them and washed them, played with them, cared for them and cuddled them. I've baked with them and swum with them and I've held them when they were tired or afraid or sad. And they need that because . . .' I stopped, tried to steady my voice, 'because they have to live without a mother . . . and sometimes it's like they don't have a father either. They need you, you know, Ella and Bobby, they really need you.'

'You think I don't know that! What gives you the right to tell me how to look after my own flesh and blood?'

'Because I know what it's like when you don't know how to cope, when you think you can't go on . . .'

Jonas Murrey raised his eyebrows. 'Do you really?'

'Yes, I do. You bury yourself in your work because it gives you something to do, it keeps you occupied, it gives you a reason to get up in the morning. But what about them? You're an adult; you will find a way to cope with your grief because that's what adults do. But what about the children? Don't you think you have to put them first?'

'You're saying I don't put them first?'

'Why did it take you so long to reply to my email about Ella and her school?'

He turned and took his empty glass to the sink. 'You sorted it out, didn't you?'

'Yes, but *you* should have done that. You're her father.' I held myself very still, hardly breathing, watching his strong broad back as he stood at the sink. I imagined him in this house after his grandfather had left, going upstairs and getting ready for bed in that sterile room with its exposed brick walls. 'Jonas.' I took a deep breath. 'You don't have to do it on your own. I'm here and I love them as well.'

He swivelled round, slamming the sink with the palm of his hand. 'You *love* them? You didn't come here to look after my children! That wasn't why you came. You had your own agenda. Just pack your things before I call the police.'

We both turned then at a sound from the doorway, saw the bulky figure of my grandfather.

'I know I'm late to this party,' he chuckled, 'but what the hell is going on down here?'

'None of your business,' snapped Jonas.

'Come on, son, what's all the noise about?'

'This woman' – Jonas pointed at me – 'has lied to me. She knew who I was and she knew who you were, and she used that to get a job looking after my children.'

'I know, son, I know, I figured it out, but—'

'But what?' Jonas yelled, throwing his hands in the air. 'Are you going to stand there and defend her? She is a liar and a cheat and I want her out of my house.'

I stood up, feeling fearful. I thought I heard the creak

of footsteps on the stairs and I turned to the doorway, almost wanting Ella to be there.

'Give me your keys,' said Jonas, and he held out his hand, waited while I went through my pockets. 'Pack your things. And get out.'

CHAPTER FORTY-EIGHT

I stumbled down the steps of 68 Pembleton Crescent, pulling my suitcase behind me. I'd packed in a hurry, removing everything from the attic room as quickly as I could: my clothes and books, my toiletries from the bathroom, my picture of Dido, my diary with all the blank pages I hadn't had the energy to fill. As I moved around the room, part of me wished the children would wake, that they would hear me and come up and ask what was going on, beg me to stay. But they didn't, and so I took my suitcase and left the house, closed the door for the final time and walked reluctantly along Pembleton Crescent, dreading that I would never be allowed to go back, that I wouldn't ever see the children again.

I headed to the tube station, stood on the escalator as silently it took me underground, and as I waited on the platform for a train to come, my mind was full of images of the children. Ella sitting in her classroom with the teacher who didn't like her hair, Bobby pulling at my cheeks and saying, 'You *are* a lovely little girl.' I heard the train coming nearer like a thunderstorm, rattling and whining through the tunnel, and I thought how easy it would be to throw myself on the tracks. All I had to do was take one step, move to the edge of the platform, and fall. How simple it would be, if I could do that, if I no longer existed.

But when the doors slid open I found myself getting on, and the light was so harsh inside that I wanted to close my eyes against the lurid blue of the seats, the glowing yellow of the handrails. The words of an advert on the wall seemed to slip as I looked at them, and I gripped the rail, stared at the blackness outside, tried to find something to focus on, to get enough air to breathe.

I came out of Clapham Common station, dodged between a group of men walking unsteadily along the pavement, and turned into my road. For six long weeks I'd been away, and now I was home. I crossed the front lawn, littered with plastic bags, bottles and dog mess, passed through the high entranceway to my block of flats and along the outside corridor, its walls a familiar nubbled brown, until I came to my door.

For a second, as I put my key in the lock and stepped in, I thought someone was there. I had a sense of my flat being occupied, that someone was waiting for me. 'Hello?' I whispered, and I dropped the handle of my suitcase, looked at the open doorways to my bedroom and kitchen. There was no one there. I picked up a thick pile of junk mail from the hallway floor, saw how old and worn my carpet was, felt the smallness of my flat squeeze in on me.

I went into my kitchen. The air smelt of damp bacon. On the windowsill was a row of dead flies, in the sink an unwashed bowl. I couldn't remember leaving that; perhaps I'd been in such a state when I'd left that I hadn't noticed it, or perhaps I'd never thought I would live at Pembleton Crescent for six weeks, that in a day or so I would have been found out and would be back to do my washing-up.

I went into the living room, sat down on my sagging sofa, took off my jacket and threw it on the floor. I didn't know how I could go to bed, how I could admit the day was over. I thought of the afternoon I'd first seen the children in the garden, Bobby laughing happily in the paddling pool, and the morning Ella had climbed into bed with me and asked me to do her hair. I looked around my shabby room, at the crack that ran across the ceiling, the stain of green damp in the corner, and I realised that I had nothing to remember them by; I hadn't taken anything from that house that wasn't mine, no pictures or photographs, no drawings or paintings. After all that time I had nothing at all.

When the phone rang, it seemed to be coming from miles away and I had to struggle to wake up, to work out what it was. The room was dark; my legs ached from where I'd fallen asleep on the sofa. The phone stopped. Then it started again.

'Rosie?' It was a man's voice, and for a split second I was full of hope: it was Jonas, he'd changed his mind; he was calling me back. 'Rosie?'

'Yes?'

'It's your grandfather.'

I couldn't think who he meant for a moment; who was my grandfather, what was this man saying?

'I have someone here who wants to speak with you.'

I could hear voices in the background then, Bobby crying, Mrs B trying to soothe him. 'Hello?' I waited, but no one answered. I wondered what Mrs B was doing back at Pembleton Crescent so late at night. Still I concentrated on the voices. Rooster Murrey was speaking to Jonas, I was sure of it; his voice was low, pleading. 'You have to ask her,' I heard him say. 'You have to trust her. Well then, son, I will.' There was silence for a while, and then I heard my grandfather's voice, low and strained, so close to my ear it was as if he was in the room with me. 'Rosie?'

'What?' I asked, my heart full of panic.

'It's Ella. She's gone.'

CHAPTER FORTY-NINE

'What do you mean?' I stood up, still holding on to the phone. 'Where's she gone?'

'We're not sure, honey, but the police told Jonas to stay at home.'

'The police?' My stomach lurched and I held out one arm, pushed my hand against the wall.

'That's right. He called them when we figured she'd gone. They asked him if she'd run away before, where she might have gone, if we'd tried her friends . . .' His voice faltered and I heard the sound of water being poured into a glass. 'They asked if she'd taken any clothes or money.'

'And? Has she taken anything?'

'We don't know.'

'Is her rucksack there? Check in the hall; she always keeps it on the rack in the hall.'

'I'll do that, honey . . .' Again he stopped and I could hear Bobby sobbing in the background. 'Her father went off looking for her; he's been driving around the past hour. He asked a neighbour; he said he saw her a couple of hours ago, running off down the road.'

'A couple of *hours* ago?'

'That's right.'

'So why didn't he do something? How could he see a kid running down the road at this time of night and not *do* something?'

'He tried; he says he called out the window, but . . . She could be anywhere by now. We've no idea where she's gone.'

'I do,' I told him, grabbing my jacket, checking I had my phone and keys. 'I know where she's gone.'

I rushed out of my flat, slamming the door behind me, racing along the outside corridor and across the littered lawn, back to the tube station. I ran through the ticket hall, felt a sudden blast of cold wind as I jumped on the escalator going down. I could hear a train arriving and I threw myself in just as the doors were closing. Come on, I told the driver in my head, come on, speed up, keep going. It seemed to take an age before we arrived at Waterloo, at Leicester Square and Euston, and I stood there, my eyes glued to the map of the Northern Line, waiting for the line to split, to head towards High Barnet.

I came out of Archway station, ran round the corner of the road and flagged down a bus just about to pull away from the kerb. I leapt on, willing the driver to go as fast as he could, not to stop at any stop, not to drop any passengers off or pick any up. I stood by the doors, too impatient to sit down, wondering if Ella would be able to get here on her own; if she was heading here, then which way would she have gone? Would she have walked at night across the heath, or would she have got the bus and followed the route we'd taken when we'd come to see the account book?

I ran to the entrance we'd used before, but the white wooden gates were locked; a sign showed they'd been shut at 8 p.m. I looked towards the small lodge house; no lights were on, there was no one there. I tried to think what time Ella had left Pembleton Crescent and if she could have got in before the gates were locked. Could she be inside now, on the path with the old-fashioned street lamps, not knowing which way to go? No, I told myself, she couldn't have; she was in bed just after eight, protesting that it was too light to sleep.

I forced myself to slow down, to walk along the road and see if there were any gaps, any holes, any way she could have sneaked herself in. Again I wondered if she could have come another way, if she'd walked from the tennis courts across the heath. But if she had, if she'd found her way to the gated, holly-lined pathway, then that would be locked as well. Perhaps her imaginary friend hadn't gone at all; perhaps it was her who had made Ella do this.

I went back down the road and past the bus stop, where I saw a large open path leading on to the heath. I followed a fence marking the boundary of a house and yard; ahead was the crest of a hill and below was a dense set of trees. What was it like down there, I thought, if a child was hiding among the trees? Was it quiet and sheltered, or was it just dark and frightening? And if someone screamed from amidst the trees, would anyone be able to hear them?

I stared into the darkness, trying to make out if anyone was there, hearing the rumble of a plane in the sky and then the muffled beep of a car horn. I felt my feet splash in a puddle and looked down to see pools of milky brown, the path an obstacle course of hardened tree roots grown solid into the ground. My heart leapt as a figure slowly emerged from the darkness ahead, but it was just an elderly man having a late-night walk with his dog. I heard a suppressed laugh then from somewhere in the darkness, saw two boys sitting on a bench in the shadow of an oak tree a few metres from the path. I ran up to them. 'Have you seen a girl, about nine?' They giggled and looked at me with dancing eyes. 'How long have you been sitting here? Have you seen a little girl?' but again they giggled, and one passed the other a burning cigarette.

I ran back to the path, following the eerie whiteness of the stones, crunching a scattering of broken eggshells left over from a daytime picnic. Then in the distance I saw a building and a faint glimmer of light. 'Ella!' I yelled, cupping my hands together. 'Ella!'

I came to a set of iron railings and a gate, tried to open it but it was locked. I looked at the railings, wondering if Ella had come this way and if she would have been able to climb over. I thought of the day in the playground shortly after I'd started work at Pembleton Crescent, how I'd watched her on the climbing frame, fearlessly going higher and higher, and I put my hands on the top spikes, found them cold and covered with flakes of rust. 'Ella!' I shouted, and I hoisted myself up, put one foot on the hinge of the lock and stumbled over.

I could hear the wind hissing through the trees, the air around me swelling as I brushed my hands down my jeans and ran on along the path, and then I saw it, the grandness of Kenwood, its walls stretching out before me. I rushed up to the conservatory windows and held my hands to the glass, trying to look in, seeing nothing but my own reflection. I didn't know if she could have got into the house, if she could be in there right now, at night, all alone in that home with its gilded chandeliers, its portraits of lords and ladies, in the place she'd once said she wanted to live. That was how I'd known, the moment my grandfather had told me on the phone; I'd known instinctively that this was where she would come.

I stopped at the archway that Ella had said was spooky, remembered how she'd run through it banging a stick against its metal frame, and then I walked along the side of the house, past a row of cream benches set on paving stones. Between the benches were large potted plants, tall enough to hide a child, and I went nearer, checking to see if anyone was there. Then I hurried to the front of the house, certain now that I would see her, that she'd be waiting for me, sitting there, a smile on her face, relieved and happy that she'd been found. But there was nothing but the set of entrance pillars, the locked doors of a stately home.

'Ella!' I shouted, my voice frantic in the night air. I heard the hoarse shriek of an owl and I shouted again, knowing there was no one there to reply.

CHAPTER FIFTY

I sat down on the base of one of the entrance pillars, overwhelmed with panic because I'd wasted so much precious time. I'd been so sure that Ella would be here, that if only I got to Kenwood quickly enough I would find her, and I was wrong. I shivered, pulling my jacket around me, trying frantically to think what to do, desperate to stay calm.

Where would she be if she wasn't here? Perhaps she had gone to a friend's, as the police had suggested. But there was only one friend who'd invited Ella to play since I'd been at Pembleton Crescent. And Mrs B had taken her there that day; I didn't even know where she lived.

Could she still be at home? Had they really checked everywhere? Had they looked in the garden, the playroom, my attic bedroom and bathroom? But then I remembered: a neighbour had seen her; someone had seen Ella running away hours ago.

I looked around me in despair, at a row of small bollards strung with spiked metal, a street lamp with a darkened bulb. Ahead was the gravel path that led to Hampstead

Lane and a curve of lawn with two or three small trees, one shaped like a Christmas tree, its silvery green branches forming a wide canopy of space over the grass. I focused on the denseness of the bushes in the distance, thought I saw a figure standing there. But it didn't move; it was just a rotten tree trunk. Still I scanned the bushes. In the middle was a green pole with a camera on top; it looked old and out of use, and yet I had the sense of being watched.

I heard a sound then, a faint rustle from somewhere on the grass, and I got up and walked cautiously towards the lawn. I couldn't see if it was a bird or a squirrel, and I stood there, my whole body straining. A crescent moon appeared suddenly through a tangle of trees, and in the bushes ahead I saw a fox, standing fearlessly, its eyes glowing orange.

I heard a sniff then and saw something else on the grass, a small, solid shape under the tree canopy, the profile of a child sitting cross-legged, a rucksack on her back.

'Ella!' I cried, my whole body weak with gratitude, as if I'd woken up to find a nightmare was just a dream, that the terror wasn't real, because I'd been right, she was here, she was safe. I reached the spot where she sat, looking around to check the fox had gone. 'What's going on?' I asked.

Ella glanced up, her eyes gazing somewhere over my shoulder. She wore a navy blue raincoat and underneath I could see the pink top buttons of her nightdress.

'Ella?' I squeezed myself under the branches and sat down, felt the dampness of the lawn, soft and spongy as if it had been recently mown. I longed to put my arm around her but I was afraid that any movement might make her run off. 'How long have you been here?'

She shrugged, and I felt a sudden fury. I wanted to take her by the shoulders, to ask how she could have done this, frightening everyone so much.

'Didn't anyone see you?'

'No.' She shuffled her feet on the grass and I saw she was wearing her favourite wellington boots. 'Because I didn't go on the path, I stayed on the grass so no one would see me.'

'How did you even get here on your own?'

'I got the bus.' She looked at me, her expression proud.

'Didn't anyone ask what a nine-year-old child was doing alone at night on a bus?'

'No. And then a man in a car said he would drive me.'

'A man in a car?' I pressed down on the grass, realised my fingers were icy with cold.

'He was really nice.'

'But you didn't get in the car?'

She shook her head.

'Oh Ella, anything could have happened to you.' I put out one hand, rested it gently on her back. 'Was it your imaginary friend?'

'No,' she said flatly. 'I told you, she's gone.'

'But what did you think you were doing, coming here?'

'I wanted to see Dido.'

'Why?'

'Because she looks like you and I like her.'

I smiled then, despite myself, and as the moon disappeared behind the clouds I shifted my body a little closer to hers. 'Did you try and get into the house?'

'I went to the pillars but the door was locked. It's an ugly building, it's creepy in the dark.'

'I know, that's why you shouldn't be here.'

Suddenly she moved away from me, throwing off my arm. 'You made my daddy really angry.'

'I know, I know I did. But running away, it doesn't make it better; it just causes more problems for you, for everyone.'

'I thought everyone would be happier if I wasn't there.'

'Oh Ella,' I sighed. 'How can you say that?'

'I was angry.' She stood up and pulled her rucksack off her back, hurled it on to the grass, and I heard the thump of something inside. 'Because why don't I get a say?'

'A say about what?'

'About you!' she shouted. 'Why did you let my daddy throw you out?'

'Were you listening to us?' So she had been there, I thought; the movement I'd heard just before Jonas Murrey had told me to leave had been Ella. She'd been outside the kitchen all that time, hiding. 'Why didn't you come into the kitchen and say something?'

'Because Daddy is strict. He would have told me off. Why?' she shouted again. 'Why did you let him throw you out?'

'What could I have done?' I folded my legs, rested my hands on my knees. 'I thought it would be better if I just left. So there wouldn't be any more arguments. I was in the wrong, your father was right. I did come into your family because I wanted to get your great-grandpa here, to make him meet my mum.'

'So you didn't want us?'

I looked up at her. Is this what she'd overheard her father saying, that I'd never wanted the children, that I had just wanted a way to get to Rooster? 'Yes I did,' I said. 'I always did. I always wanted you both. I still do.'

CHAPTER FIFTY-ONE

'Come on, Ella,' I told her, standing up and holding out my hand. 'Let's go.' But she refused to move; instead she remained on the grass, hugging her rucksack. 'We need to get you home. You've just heard me ringing your dad; he's waiting for you.'

Still she wouldn't get up.

'Ella, you have to go home. You heard me saying I was bringing you straight back. Come *on*.'

'But I want to go with you.'

'You are going with me.' I looked at her, tried to think what to say that would persuade her to move. 'That's exactly why I told him I'd bring you back myself. If we don't go right now, he'll come in the car. He's waiting, Ella . . . and so is your great-grandpa.'

She did stand up then, but awkwardly, still clutching her rucksack. 'I'm cold.'

'I'm sure you are, you've only really got your nightie on.' I took off my jacket and wrapped it around her, tried to button it up.

'I'm hungry.'

'Well let's get you home and you can have something to eat.'

'No!' she yelled, and she sat down again and began to cry. 'He's going to shout at me.'

'Shush,' I said, leaning forward, taking her rucksack and putting it on my back. It was heavier than I'd expected and I smiled at her, asked, 'What have you got in here?' hoping to lighten the mood, aware that she was looking over my shoulder as if deciding which way to run. I thought of Jonas, how furious he'd been with me, how he'd shouted and slammed his fist on the table. I didn't know what he would say to Ella, how he would punish her, but she had to go home, whatever happened. I had no choice about that. I had found her and I had to take her home.

We walked back along the row of iron benches and through the archway, the stones of the pathway noisy beneath our feet, and as we passed the conservatory windows I felt Ella try to pull away. 'I want to see Dido.'

'No!' I said sharply, grabbing her by the shoulder. 'Not now.'

'But I want to see her!' She threw off my arm and dashed to the house and I came up behind, ready to stop her if she decided to run away. 'Do you think Dido liked living here?'

'Yes,' I said. 'I think she probably did.' We stood there for a moment, looking into the darkened house, as transfixed as we'd been the first day we'd seen the portrait of Dido Elizabeth Belle, when I'd found myself in the blue-ceilinged library and Ella had whispered, 'This is it, isn't it, Rosie?'

'Let's go,' I said at last. 'We can come another time and see her, okay? But right now we need to get home.'

Ella let me take her by the hand, and we walked on until we came to the gate. I climbed up first and then helped her over and we went silently along the pathway. The two smoking boys had gone; there was no one else out now. 'Are you sure my great-grandpa will be there?' she asked as I hurried her across the heath to the main road.

'I hope so. Quick! There's a bus,' and I held her hand tightly as we ran across the road.

CHAPTER FIFTY-TWO

'He's going to shout at me,' Ella whispered as we stood at the bottom of the steps leading up to 68 Pembleton Crescent.

'No he's not.' I could hear how unconvincing my voice sounded as I led her up the steps, fumbling in my pocket for my keys, until I remembered Jonas had made me hand them over. Reluctantly I knocked on the door, as if I'd never been there before, as if I hadn't lived there for six weeks all alone with the children, as if I were just any other visitor.

The door opened at once and Jonas was there, a frantic look on his face. His green shirt was rumpled; in his hand he had Ella's favourite T-shirt, pink, with a butterfly on the front. He didn't look at me, he didn't even seem to see I was there; I was no one to him, as unimportant as I'd been on the first day we met.

'Oh my God,' he gasped, and he flew forward and scooped Ella up, began to sway from side to side with her in his arms. 'Oh my God,' he whispered, his face buried in his daughter's hair. 'Oh my baby.'

I stood there not knowing what to do, whether to turn and leave, or whether I would be allowed to come in. Then I saw someone standing behind Jonas in the hallway, a policewoman wearing a bright yellow jacket.

'I take it this is Ella?' she asked, her tone officious.

Jonas nodded, his face still buried in his daughter's hair.

'And who is this?' She looked at me.

'She's my babysitter,' said Ella. 'She found me.'

'Is that right?' The policewoman looked at Jonas for confirmation. 'This is her babysitter?'

He turned his head away and didn't answer; perhaps he didn't want to say that I was no longer anyone's babysitter, that he had thrown me out of his house hours before and told me never to come back.

'Well you're very lucky that someone knew where you were—' The policewoman seemed about to say more, to caution Ella about the dangers, the foolishness of running away, but there was a burst of static from the radio clipped on her belt and she pulled it out, began to speak into it rapidly. 'I'll be in touch tomorrow,' she told Jonas.

'Thank you,' he answered curtly, and he moved to one side to allow the policewoman to pass. Then he turned round, walked back along the hallway, Ella still in his arms.

I saw her face over his shoulder; she reached out an arm as if to pull me in, and then she looked up towards the stairs. 'Rooster!' she shouted, and there he was, my grandfather moving slowly down the steps. He had Bobby in one arm and he was holding his free hand against the wall, and I felt a surge of relief that he was still there.

'This little fella was upset,' he said, sitting down on a step. 'He wouldn't sleep till his sister was here.'

Ella struggled out of her father's arms, ran back along the hall and up the stairs and threw herself at her great-grandfather.

'Hell, you gave us all a fright.' Rooster Murrey clutched her tightly and then looked over her head at me. 'Where did you find her?'

I glanced down the hallway at Jonas. He hadn't asked me this, he hadn't asked me where I'd found his daughter, how I'd known where she would be, why she'd run there in the first place; he hadn't asked me anything at all.

'Where are you going?' my grandfather asked as I turned towards the still open front door. 'Come on, son. She found Ella.' He looked down and patted her head. 'What more do you want? Invite the lady in.'

But Jonas remained where he was, refusing to look at me. 'You can go now.'

'Son . . .' said Rooster, his voice steely. 'I said, invite her in.'

'Stay out of it,' Jonas muttered. 'What's it got to do with you?'

'Hell.' Rooster shook his head. 'You sure have a funny way of thanking someone.'

'Thank her?' Jonas looked at his grandfather, enraged. 'You want me to *thank* her?'

'Well of course I do, goddam it, she found your daughter! What more do you want?'

'It's because of her, it's because of this woman—'

'Shsh,' I said. 'You're scaring her.'

The two men stopped and looked at Ella. She'd moved away from her great-grandfather and now she was standing in the shadows, her back against the wall.

'As I said,' Jonas looked at me, making an effort to control his voice, 'you can go.'

'No!' Ella screamed, and she went running down the hall after her father. 'It's not fair!' She started beating him on the back with her hands. 'I'm the one she's looking after, not you. Why don't I get a say? I want her to look after me.'

Jonas turned and grabbed her hands, held them motionless in the air, and I took a step forward, afraid of what he might do. I didn't want him to shout at her, to restrain her like this. But then he let go of his daughter and slowly he crouched down. 'Is that why?' He took Ella's face, framed her cheeks in his hands. 'Is that why you ran away? Because you knew Rosie would have to come back, that she would find you?'

I felt startled at the sound of my name, the easy way he said it, and I knew he was right, that this had been Ella's plan: they would find her missing, they would have to tell me, and she was certain I would know where she was.

'Do you know what?' Jonas sighed. 'When the police asked me where you'd gone . . . I didn't know.' He swayed slightly and I heard the sound of his knees creak as he put out one hand to steady himself. 'I had to call Mrs B and ask her. When they asked whose house you might have gone to, I had no idea. They asked if you'd taken any clothes, had you run away before . . . and I just didn't know.' He took his hand from Ella's face; I could see his lips were tight, his eyes full of tears. 'I just didn't know the answers.'

'That's okay, Daddy.' She patted him on the cheek.

He drew her towards him, sheltering her with his arms.

Then he cleared his throat and looked at me. 'Where did you find her?'

'At Kenwood.'

'Kenwood?'

'On Hampstead Heath.'

'That's miles away. How did you know she'd be there?'

'It's somewhere we've been together; I knew she liked it. There's a portrait of a woman called Dido, and Ella's been investigating her.'

'Have you really?' Jonas smiled.

'She is one smart cookie,' laughed Rooster, standing up slowly from the stairs, still with Bobby in his arms. 'You need to thank my granddaughter properly, son.'

Jonas ignored him. 'Promise me, Ella, you won't do that again?'

'You told her to get out.' Defiantly she eyed her father. 'But I want her to stay for ever.'

'Promise me you won't do that again.'

'Only if Rosie stays.'

Jonas stood up and waved dismissively in my direction. 'She can stay for the rest of tonight. That's all I can say.'

CHAPTER FIFTY-THREE

I wake suddenly, startled by sounds from downstairs: Ella and Bobby laughing, the rumble of a man's voice. I don't know how long I've been asleep, but it's morning now, the attic room is warm, and I lie on the bed listening, not sure what will happen when I go down, unable to decide if I'm still part of this house, or if I ever really was. Was it enough that I found Ella? Will that be enough to allow me to still see the children?

I hear Jonas in the hallway and I get up and lean over the banisters. His back is against the wall, his shirt is creased, his feet are bare, and the grey-eyed cat is winding its way in and out of his legs. He must have slept in the playroom, or perhaps he hasn't slept at all. On the floor is a pile of Bobby's building bricks and Ella's wellington boots; they must have been up for some time.

I lean further over the banisters. Jonas has his head down, speaking on his mobile. 'Yes, Shanice, I'm back. Mrs B rang you?' He looks up the stairs and quickly I flatten myself against the wall. 'Yes, that is the whole story, insane as it sounds. Yes, I'm sure Cassidy is very fond of her . . .'

Still I stand there. I haven't seen Shanice since the day she went to visit her sister's grave; perhaps she's been avoiding me.

I hear Jonas laugh. 'My grandfather? Oh, he's okay. I have a feeling he'll be here for a while.'

I go back to my room. It's empty now; there's no sign that I was ever here. It looks just as it did the day I moved in, a deserted attic where long ago a maid might have once slept. I think of the night of the storm when I found Ella in my bathroom because she was looking for me, and whatever she did last night, however dangerous it was, I know that at least she wanted me.

I walk down to the kitchen and stand at the doorway feeling a little hopeful. Bobby is still in his pyjamas. He isn't wearing a bib and he's balanced on an adult chair, on top of three cushions that must have been taken from the playroom. Ella is eating an ice pop for breakfast, her lips stained red. There are toys and clothes all over the place. Mrs B will be annoyed.

'Sleep well?' asks Jonas Murrey, as if he and I often enquire about each other's sleeping habits.

'Yes thank you,' I say politely. I look at Ella but she won't look back; she's busy with her ice pop. I feel awkward standing there, without a job to do; I'm itching to clear up the breakfast things, to change Bobby out of his pyjamas, to ask Ella if she has her homework in her bag, if we're all ready to go before Mrs B arrives.

'I understand,' says Jonas, 'that you have offered my house for a garden party.' For a moment I think he's going to smile, but then I see his face is tight with anger. 'Come on, kids,' he says.

'You're taking them to school?'

He looks at me coldly, like he can't believe I'm asking this. 'I have an appointment with Ella's teacher.'

I take it as a sign that I can go in, because he's taking responsibility for his daughter now, maybe he's softened towards me. I move slowly towards the table; still neither of the children has taken any notice of me. 'See you, then,' I say, and when they don't answer, I feel a crushing sense of disappointment that I'm so easily replaceable; that even after everything that happened last night I still don't mean anything to them. Jonas will hire a new babysitter; she will move into my room and inherit my place. And it's all my fault.

Then Ella does look up. I see she's wearing a necklace; her father must have given it to her this morning. It's a silver chain with a small old-fashioned pendant and I want to ask who it belongs to, if it was her mother's and if there is a portrait inside. 'That's nice,' I say, going nearer, pointing at the necklace. The moment I touch it she grabs my hand, holds on fiercely. I see her mouth is trembling, that she's trying not to cry. 'Are you okay?' I ask, but she sniffs and pulls away.

'Bye, Rosie,' she says with a faint smile, as if I'm someone she once bumped into, just an adult who temporarily came into her life and left again. I wonder if this is how her father has told her to behave, if he's warned her not to make a fuss, and if this is how it's going to be: a brief goodbye, a final unsatisfactory ending. She moves away from the table and walks towards the freezer, opens it and looks inside.

Bobby starts scribbling on a piece of paper, making wet sounds with his pen across the page. I think of how he used to say 'I want to go home' and I long to pick him up and cuddle him and tell him he's where he belongs and everything will be fine.

'Ella!' says Jonas. 'What are you looking for? Here, put on these shoes.' He picks up a pair of sandals; they're small and the straps are worn. Ella must have outgrown them a long time ago.

'No,' she mutters. 'I hate those shoes.'

'I'll see you soon,' I say again, and I look across the room at Jonas, begging him to say something.

'Come on, Ella,' he says, ignoring me. 'Just get some sneakers on.' He walks back to the table and picks Bobby up, wipes at his cereal-stained face with the edge of his shirt. Then he stands him on the floor, removes his son's pyjamas and puts him in his clothes.

'Rooster!' Ella shouts, and we all turn to see my grandfather at the doorway, a mountain of a man with stubble on his chin.

'Whoa, honey!' He laughs as Ella runs up to him. 'Take it easy now.' He looks across the room at Jonas, his eyes not quite focused. 'Morning, son.'

Jonas turns from the table, his arms hanging by his sides; he doesn't seem certain what to say.

'How's my little detective?' Rooster strides jovially towards me. 'Where's your mom?'

'My mum?' I realise I haven't thought of her since last night, and suddenly I long for her to be here, for her to know what's happened. 'I don't know.'

'I rang her an hour ago,' says Rooster. 'I want to spend some more time with her.' He smiles expectantly. 'If she'll have me?'

I open my mouth, try to speak. 'I'm sorry,' I say, and I

hang my head, aware of how badly I misjudged him, how far he's come just to see Ella and Bobby, how he wanted to make the trip while he still could, and how loving he was with my mother.

'What the hell have you got to be sorry about?' Rooster chuckles. 'You got us all together, didn't you? Hey, son, didn't she? She got us all together.'

Jonas doesn't answer. He puts on a pair of socks, pushes his feet into his shoes.

'Where are you off to?'

Jonas looks at him, tight-lipped. 'I am going to Ella's school.'

'Can I—' I begin.

'No,' he says.

I wait while Jonas picks up Ella's school bag and puts on his jacket, then I follow the three of them up the stairs, like an obedient unloved dog. I wait while Ella gets her rucksack and puts on her wellington boots. She doesn't look at me or ask for help; she doesn't say anything to me at all. Then Jonas opens the door and still I follow them because I don't know what else to do. Please, I want to beg, please, just speak to me.

I hear the call of doves; feel a blast of sunshine so unfamiliar it's as if I've stepped off a plane and into a foreign place. I go down the steps of 68 Pembleton Crescent and turn to look back, at the rakish stone face of the man with the cap on his head. He seems to be laughing at me today.

I watch as Jonas points his keys at a large shiny car; hear the beep of the alarm turning off. He opens the back door and Ella climbs in. For a moment I think she might wave, but instead she stares determinedly ahead. Jonas struggles to get Bobby into a car seat and finally fixes the belt. He gets in the driver's seat, I hear the engine start and I see the car pull away, watch as Jonas drives his children down Pembleton Crescent.

I stand there for a long time. Once or twice I think I hear Ella call my name, but it's just my mind playing tricks, because there's silence now. No one else seems to be out today in Pembleton Crescent; everyone has somewhere to go but me. Finally I start walking along the road, the pavement scattered with browning cherry blossom, thinking of the day I moved in, how I'd admired this road, how I'd enjoyed looking in through the windows, dreaming of how it would be to live in a place like this.

I feel a car pull up beside me, its wheels crunching on the tarmac, hear the swish of the electric window winding down. I speed up; I don't want to talk to anyone, to be asked for directions or whether I have the right time. I look up at the sky, see a plume of white from a passing plane, wonder where I can go now. Still the car drives slowly beside me, and I'm about to turn and snap at the driver, to tell them to leave me alone.

'Rosie . . .'

I whip around; see Jonas tapping his fingers impatiently on the steering wheel. 'They're screaming.'

I look in at the children. Bobby is straining against his car seat, Ella is trying to push him back; they both seem distraught.

'They want you,' says Jonas with a sigh, 'to come with them.'

I open the car door with trembling hands; squeeze myself in between the children. Bobby beams and pats at my face. Ella leans towards me and I smell her breath laced with strawberry ice pop. 'I think this is going to be fun,' she whispers.

Jonas is looking at me in the rear-view mirror, a faint smile on his face. 'I guess we need you,' he says. 'Plus someone's going to have to help with this damn neighbourhood party.' He puts the car in gear and I settle down on the back seat as we drive off along Pembleton Crescent, me, Jonas and the children.

ACKNOWLEDGEMENTS

I'm extremely grateful to the Authors' Foundation, run by The Society of Authors, for a grant that helped me write this book.

Hoodfield House in Kent is entirely fictitious, but Muriel's story is loosely based on the experiences of some of those who grew up in children's homes in the 1950s, particularly at Dr Barnardo's branch homes.

Thank you to Martine King, Barnardo's archive manager; Sonya Maddieson, senior archive and administration officer; and Val Clark, social worker at Making Connections, for their help, advice and access to the archive collection.

Attempting to trace a GI father is a painful and painstaking affair, but it has been made easier by the work of Shirley McGlade, who founded War Babes, and Pamela Winfield, who founded Transatlantic Children's Enterprise (TRACE).

In 1989 McGlade sued the American Defense Department after their refusal to release information about GI fathers. The resulting court settlement made it far less difficult for all those concerned.

Thank you to the members of GI Trace (www.gitrace. org), who generously shared their experiences, as well as commented on the manuscript, especially Monica Roberts for her endless support, Tina Hampton, John Munro, Marvin Walters and John Wastle. A more recent and ever-growing (private) Facebook group, GI & Family International Search, also helps people trace family members: http://giandfamilyinternationalsearch.com.

The portrait of Dido Elizabeth Belle was temporarily exhibited at Kenwood in 2007, but resides permanently at Scone Palace in Perth, the home of the present Lord and Lady Mansfield. I am grateful to Lady Mansfield for her interest in and support for the novel.

Research continues into Dido's life, and there are many gaps still to be filled, such as whether or not her father did leave her money in his will and what happened to her mother Maria.

I'm indebted to Gene Adams, author of 'Dido Elizabeth Belle, A Black Girl at Kenwood: An account of a protegée of the 1st Lord Mansfield' (*The Camden History Review*, Vol. 12, 1984), who was very generous with her help and provided careful comments on the text.

Thank you also to Sarah Minney, genealogist and record agent, who is currently researching Dido's life, and who gave up her valuable time to answer numerous questions, provide crucial documents, and generally share her knowledge.

I'm also indebted to English Heritage curators Cathy Power and Laura Houliston, as well as Catherine Stanton for access to Lady Anne's account book, and genealogist Emma Jolly for her kind help.

Thanks to my agent Clare Alexander for insisting on the best, and my editor Stephanie Sweeney for her meticulous and inspired comments.

I'm grateful to the authors of the following books: Phil

Frampton, *The Golly in the Cupboard*; Shirley McGlade, *Daddy Where Are You?*; June Rose, *For the Sake of the Children*; and Graham Smith, *When Jim Crow met John Bull*.